Natália Gomes has an MLitt in Literature & Creativ... ...ing and an MEd in Education. Inspired by her teaching experiences, Natália started writing fiction with a focus on mental health among young adults. Her debut novel *Dear Charlie* is endorsed by Amnesty International and was longlisted for the 2018 International Dublin Literary Award and *We Are Not Okay* was selected for Nottingham's Big City Reads in 2019. Natália is currently a full-time writer, PhD student and mummy to a crazy toddler.

Follow Natália on Instagram @ndgomes and on Twitter @nd_gomes

Also by Natália Gomes

Dear Charlie
Blackbird
We Are Not Okay

AFTER THE RAIN

NATÁLIA GOMES

ONE PLACE. MANY STORIES

HQ
An imprint of HarperCollins*Publishers* Ltd
1 London Bridge Street
London SE1 9GF

www.harpercollins.co.uk

HarperCollins*Publishers*
1st Floor, Watermarque Building, Ringsend Road
Dublin 4, Ireland

This edition 2021

1

First published in Great Britain by
HQ, an imprint of HarperCollins*Publishers* Ltd 2021

ISBN: 978-0-00-829181-5

MIX
Paper from
responsible sources
FSC™ C007454

This book is produced from independently certified FSC™ paper
to ensure responsible forest management.

For more information visit: www.harpercollins.co.uk/green

Printed and Bound in the UK using 100% Renewable Electricity at
CPI Group (UK) Ltd

For Scott and Eilidh xx

Note on the text

To ensure Jack and Alice's chapters are completely authentic to their voices we have matched the spelling to their backgrounds. Therefore Alice's chapters use American spelling and Jack's use British spelling.

Alice's Playlist

Smith & Thell – 'Alice'
Of Monsters and Men – 'Wild Roses'
First Aid Kit – 'It's a Shame'
Juke Ross – 'Shadows in the Dark'
Phoebe Bridgers – 'Georgia'
Birdy – 'People Help The People'
First Aid Kit – 'Emmylou'
Joy Williams – 'Ordinary World'
Gabrielle Aplin – 'Home'
London Grammar – 'Strong'

Jack's Playlist

Dermot Kennedy – 'After Rain'
Imagine Dragons – 'Birds'
Lord Huron – 'The Night We Met'
The Head and the Heart – 'Another Story'
Seth Talley – 'New Day'
The Collection – 'Beautiful Life'
Vance Joy – 'Mess is Mine'
The Head and the Heart – 'Lost in my Mind'
AHI – 'Ol' Sweet Day'
Of Monsters and Men – 'Human'

'The whole world is divided for me into two parts: one is she, and there is all happiness, hope, light; the other is where she is not, and there is dejection and darkness . . .'

Leo Tolstoy, *War and Peace*

Alice

There's nothing like the smell of a library.

A combination of dust, musk and ink.

Many of the books found in libraries, especially in the UK where they tend to be pre-nineteenth century prints, use materials like cotton, linen and groundwood pulp to make the pages. Even though it smells a bit like coffee and cigars, it's really cellulose decay we're smelling when we get to the heart of a library space. Most position their study tables here, right in the middle, to allow its most devout booklovers to bask in the smell whilst being surrounded by stacks and pillars of reading material, most of which they'll never get through in their lifetime. Because a human lifetime is too short to read all the amazing books in the world. Shakespeare, Tolstoy, Twain, Joyce, Woolf, Orwell, Fitzgerald, Faulkner, Hemingway, Austen, Dickens, the Brontë sisters.

The best libraries have all of the above.

Don't get me wrong, I'm not a book snob. I read pretty much anything, and I am a self-proclaimed sci-fi and fantasy geek. I'm not ashamed. I would just as easily pick up a Tolstoy book (if I had months to spare to get through one) as I would a novel by Wells, Bradbury, Tolkien, Brooks, Gaiman or Martin.

To me it's all the same. It's not the material, or how high it ranks in the bestseller lists or whether it's featured in Cambridge University's handbook of Faculty Recommended Texts issued by their English department each year. It's much simpler than that.

For me, it's the act of reading. The process of picking a book that you really want to jump into immediately, then the finding of the perfect space in which to do so. Now, the latter is much more difficult than the former. Finding the right book has never been a problem for me. I know what I want even when I don't know. I'll browse the shelves at the library, occasionally shifting between floors, genres, and alphabetical collections. But when I spot a title, I just know. The search is over. Most people have stacks of books by their bed; TBRs, book bloggers call them – To Be Read. But me, I've always had just one sitting on my bedside cabinet. A sole literary journey. That one book I commit to until I'm done cover to cover and need to choose another. Then I keep going. I keep a log of all the books I've read and each year try to beat my record. Stephen King reads eighty-four books a year. I've yet to beat him. But I will one day.

So the perfect reading space. It has to be quiet enough where you can really immerse yourself in the story world being presented to you by the author, but not so quiet where the world gets invaded by your own wandering thoughts – Do I feel like another latte? How many have I had today? What's worse for you – a muffin or a Danish? What did Mom say she was making for dinner tonight? What's that tapping sound, who has a laptop here?

So the perfect amount of background noise to assist you, then the perfect temperature. If the space is too hot, you get restless and pulled away from the pages of your book, and if it's too cold you get preoccupied with trying to warm yourself with additional clothing, hot drinks, and maybe a blanket if you have access to one. Then the seat you're on – not too soft where you melt into it and suddenly feel a nap coming on, and not too hard where backache strikes you at a pivotal moment in the narrative. Yes, this sounds like an impossible task – finding the right space to read in. But considering how much I've moved around in my rather short lifetime, I've always found one. In Texas, it was this little book nook in their local library, on the East Coast there were many coffee shops to choose from, usually around the Harvard or MIT campuses. Those students are also searching for the perfect space, but to write scientific essays in or jot down philosophical musings. Having only lived in London for three months, I have already narrowed it down to two spaces – the library on St James's Square and a coffee shop in Southwark.

Today, being a Saturday morning and a popular time for coffee and brunch with friends, I chose the library. My corner has a comfy weathered leather armchair underneath a large window that looks onto the square. After this, I'll take a walk towards Leicester Square and see if it's dry enough to find a bench to sit on and a tree to shelter under from the rain.

I climb up on my knees and gaze out the library window. The trees billow in the rainy breeze and stretch their branches long. Although wet from the rain, it was still fairly warm when I left the house this morning, by British standards, of course, maybe a little chilly by American, but I brought a fleece-lined raincoat today. I pull the collar of my cardigan across my throat and breathe in its warmth. This, what they call 'summer' here, is more like fall to me. I don't get it. How can people go outside in shorts and camisoles in weather like this? I lean in and spot a runner in the square. One foot in front of the other, he dodges strollers, couples, friends, dog-walkers, fellow athletes, even the rain.

Ugh.

Another thing I don't get – voluntary torture in the form of running.

Why?

Jack

There's nothing like the first step of a long run.

The moment your foot hits the ground and you're propelled to the next step. The initial shock to the muscles as the impact shoots up the ankle to the calves, knees and to the thighs. You feel it everywhere, in your belly, your chest. When people ask me to describe what running's like, I always say the same thing – 'It's freeing.' Because that's exactly how I feel when I step outside – free. When the air hits your face – free. When your muscles warm and your momentum builds – free. When you pass cars stuck in traffic and clusters of people huddled in long queues standing at bus stops, tube stations and outside quaint local cafés – free. Everyone's static, sedentary, but you, you're free.

I used to run to music. I used to need motivation to get moving, to go faster, but not now. Now I run without headphones, without playlists, without the suffocation of noise to drown out what's really important to me on a run. The freedom. You can't get that exhilarating feeling from a perfectly crafted playlist that builds from a warm-up music sequence to a series of high-paced beats aimed at synchronising your stride. That point where your muscles don't ache anymore, where your lungs don't want to burst from your chest, where that small part within you urging you to slow or begin your cool down early finally silences and accepts what you've known all along. That running is incredible.

I reach Covent Garden as the rain gets heavier, passing a bride holding a white umbrella standing next to her groom as they pose for photos by the Seven Dials clock, and continue on to Leicester Square. The crowds are overwhelming here. Tourists with extended selfie sticks posing in front of the Shakespeare statue, families feeding the pigeons, kids throwing coins into the fountain, couples huddled into each other in shop doorways sheltering from the rain. I know so many other run routes away from the hustle of central London, but sometimes I love coming here. I love cutting through the crowds, sidestepping to avoid the drones that flock here like the hungry pigeons. I love the challenge of dodging the obstacles of city life. It gives me a thrill. I only run in the city on Saturday mornings, before squash games or breakfast with the guys. The rest of the time I run near my house in Surrey taking in the quieter routes – the river trails, parks, woodland areas. Sometimes I love the silence, where it's just you and nature. Where the only sounds surrounding you as you speed up are those of the trees in the breeze, the rain on their leaves, the birds overhead, and the pounding of your feet on the ground.

It's like a drum. You're creating your own music.

Thud.

Thud.

Thud.

Free.

No burdens. No responsibilities. Just me. My runs are my own, I don't share them with anyone.

Except Strava.

I have to post my runs otherwise I won't get kudos from my 492 followers. Speaking of, what's my pace like so far?

'Hey, watch it!'

I turn and see a girl bent over, her books and a yellow polka dot umbrella scattered on the ground around her. Did I do that?

'You just ran right into me, jerk!'

Damn, I forgot to hit 'pause', my Strava post is already ruined. My pace is way down, and now I'm barely jogging on the spot. I'll still get the kudos, I always do, but now it looks like my pace is slower than yesterday's. People will think I'm getting tired.

I glance down at the phone still in my hand, raindrops on the screen, and hit 'pause'. Then I take a step towards her to help with the books.

'No, don't bother,' she yells at me. 'Clearly your phone is more important than watching where you're going.'

She's American. I know her from school, I think. A recent transfer, perhaps. I open my mouth to say hi but an empty coffee cup rolls by her feet, the milky brown contents spilled out on a couple of book covers. I close my mouth; maybe not the time. The rest of the liquid is down her coat. Her cheeks are burning red like her curly hair and she looks like she's about to go off again so I start edging backwards. She looks angrier now. She either wants my help or she doesn't.

7

I don't think she even knows. So I turn around and hit 'resume' on my run. I'd be all the way around the corner by now if it wasn't for her, probably onto the next segment of my run. That two-minute exchange cost me my PB pace. My legs are seizing up from the abrupt stop.

I feel the heat before I hear the noise. It strikes my face, my shoulders, my bare shins. It burns at first then it erupts, a dirty fog engulfing me and I don't feel pain anymore.

I don't feel anything.

Spring Awakens

PART 1

A bird's first song,
A bud's first bloom,
Raindrops on my hand,
Seedlings under my feet,
The sharpness of its birth is on my fingertips,
Nothing is as new and raw as spring,
Nothing is as temporary,
For its beauty will eventually wilt and die,
Leaving us to wonder, what will remain after?

Alice Winters

Alice

The car alarms.

They throb and vibrate against my ear drums. That's all I hear since I left the hospital an hour ago. The ringing. Everything feels different. The air around me, the mattress underneath me, the quilt on my fingertips as I drag them into a fist. My toes turn inside my new trainers and make a triangle. The white is almost too white. They're too clean, too new, too pure. I hadn't expected to have to take them out of the box so soon, but I didn't have anything else to wear. When I arrived at the hospital, I was missing one completely. Now these shoes feel tight on me. My toes are crushed against the front. I squirm, the fabric stiff around my ankle crease. I need them off. I tuck one foot behind the other and gently ease one off then I bend down to yank the other one. A sharp pain stretches across my spine. I place a hand over my mouth to stifle a cry, wondering if I just split the stitches. I'd hit something sharp on the ground when I fell backwards with the second blast. I think that's when I lost my shoe.

'Alice?'

My mom stands in the doorway, a mug of tea in one hand

and a plate of sandwiches in the other. All I see is lettuce sticking out the sides.

'I'm not hungry.' My voice sounds gravelly like I have a bad cold.

'You didn't eat anything at the hospital either.' She puts the plate and mug down on my desk then hovers in the doorway. 'Do you want a hand getting into a bath?'

'I probably shouldn't take a bath because of the stitches, so I'll just take a lukewarm shower.'

She wants to help so badly. I know that feeling, of needing to do something, anything, but also knowing that whatever I do isn't going to be enough. I didn't help people. I didn't guide the old lady onto the steps by the casino. I didn't usher the little boy and his mom to the side to let the police pass. I didn't signal to the paramedics that the vendor who saved me had glass in his face and needed medical assistance. I didn't hold the hand of the woman across the street that had blood all over her, whose purse lay about two meters from her, beside what I think was her left foot. I didn't do any of that. I just stood there and looked across the road. For him. For the runner.

'Alice?'

'I'm fine, Mom.' I slide past her, being careful not to touch her with my ripped clothes, cut shoulder, bloody knees. When I get to the bathroom, I lock the door quickly before she insists on coming in with me. I turn around to switch on the shower to let it warm slightly, and stop. Who is this person in the mirror? I look like an extra from a post-apocalyptic movie. I look like I've been knocked down by a furniture delivery truck, got back up and been run over again. I look like – I look— It even hurts to cry. The tears scald my scratched cheeks and burn my fingers when I wipe them away. I take a deep breath and let the air fill me, every inch of me. Then I unzip my skirt and tug it down my hipbones. Eventually it loosens and drops around my feet. The T-shirt and bra is much harder to get off. My whole body is on fire.

My face is blackened by ash, my hair clumps at the side and sticks to my hairline, my mascara streaks across to my temples. My bare skin tingles against the air, then the glass disappears in the steam and the face that I see, the body, the dried blood, distorts and blurs. And just like the boy I killed today, I disappear in a dense cloud too.

Jack

I hear a voice. An American voice. In my dream I look up and see a girl in front of me. She's got long wavy red hair, and it sticks to her coat in the rain. She's looking down at her shoes and all around her. Scattered books. A spilled coffee cup. And an umbrella. A yellow polka dot umbrella that's spinning on its point like someone is flicking it with their fingers, never letting it slow, never letting it stop.

It spins.

And spins.

I feel dizzy. Nauseous. I need to sit down. I am sitting down actually but I don't remember how I got down here, on the ground, amongst the books and the spinning umbrella. The girl stands above me, looking down at me. She parts her lips and says my name. But now she sounds like my mum. A sliver of bright light appears from behind her and I gaze into it. The ground beneath me fades as I slowly wake. White fabric envelops me, encasing every part of me. I'm in a room. My mum and dad both stand beside my bed. On the other side are strangers – strangers in navy and white, like uniforms. Nurses. Doctors. I'm in a hospital. Why am I in a hospital?

The girl with the spinning umbrella and red curly hair is gone.

But the pain. The pain hits me hard. My mum's hands are on me. Her touch is gentle but her fingertips sting my skin. Her mouth is open like she's speaking but I can't hear her. I can't hear anything in this room. All I hear is ringing in my ears. It's so loud. The nurse is over me shining a bright light in my eyes. Her breath is on my lips. She's talking, but again no words are coming out. I don't understand what's happening. I'm scared. I try to break free but now hands are on me. I try to push them off then one injects something through a long plastic tube that runs into me. I'm so tired. I can't keep my eyes open anymore. The darkness, it's everywhere again.

Alice

The next couple of days are a blur. I close myself off in the bedroom and try to forget. Every second I'm awake I think about it. I feel the blast upon my skin, feel the trembles of the ground beneath me. The ringing in the ears is fading now but other sounds fill my head. The doctor thinks I'm suffering from 'post-traumatic stress' like a soldier returning from war. When did the streets outside our house become a war zone? When did the world change and become – this?

So I sleep. And when I wake, when I remember, I sleep again. And that's how the days go. I'm either in a hazy fog of lucid dreams, distorted reality, flashbacks pieced together by the sounds that still vibrate inside me, or I'm huddled in the corner of my bedroom like a frightened stray animal, waiting for a storm to subside. I have no idea what time it is, what day it is. The doorbell rings, the neighbor, the mailman, a representative from a new gas and electricity company. The only people who ask about me are my nana in Boston and the neighbor who I sometimes help with her bins on collection day. I don't know anyone who goes through that much cardboard. It's like an Amazon warehouse next door. My mom checks in on me every hour or so, makes sure I'm still breathing. Sometimes she knocks, sometimes she doesn't. I thought crises were meant to bring people together but I all want is to be left alone.

I awake today face down on my bedroom floor clutching a pillow to my chest. The carpet is damp beneath me and I can't figure out if I've just woken up in a pool of sweat, or urine. That's when I decide to finally leave the room. Not because I'm ready to talk or because I crave intimacy and affection from people but simply because I'm hungry. And I definitely need a shower. My mom stares at me at the bottom of the stairs, almost like she's forgotten I'm up there, then eventually clears her throat. 'Good morning.'

'What time is it?' I croak out.

'It's um . . . oh I don't know.' She checks her watch. 'Two ten. So I guess I should say good afternoon.'

I slump down the stairs, my muscles still aching. My limbs feel tight, constricted.

'Are you hungry?'

I nod. 'I'm going to make a grilled cheese, I think.'

'I'll make it. You sit.' She scoots off into the kitchen, happy to finally feel needed. At least I helped one person this week.

I slide onto the dining-room chair. We've moved so many times in my life that after a while houses start to merge together. Living rooms look the same, and my bedroom always seems to be beside the stairs. Backyards usually consist of a tiny wooden shed in the corner and a rusty swing in the center. Kitchens occasionally differ. Some have a center island or a hanging pot rack, others have a subway backsplash and a separate fridge freezer. One kitchen had

17

yellow cabinets and Spanish tiling. That was back in Texas. I miss the food there. Tex Mex is the best. I'm so hungry.

I inhale the sandwich. It barely touches my tongue. When I'm done I resist licking the plate which still sparkles with butter and oil. My mom sits down opposite me. I wonder what she thinks about this house. We never talk about the moves. We just say 'OK', pack, and get on with it. It's never a question of whether we want to move because no one ever asks us. I'd thought maybe West Coast or Midwest as we'd jumped around the South and East Coast already, and Asia. Then Dad was offered an opportunity to contract with the British Army for a while and our move turned out to be 5,483 miles across the ocean. And once again, I moved schools. Like houses, schools are all the same, especially high schools. I'd like to say not making friends is because of constantly moving around – I don't want to get attached to one place or one person and then have to say goodbye. But even if I'd lived in one town my whole life, I'd still have difficulty making friends. It'd still just be my mom and I. Navigating friendships and social situations have always been hard for me. Textbooks, novels, science experiments, chemistry models, essays – now that makes sense. There's a clear structure for that. A mutual understanding between the learner and the material. But people and their conversation, as brief and trivial as it often is, can be unpredictable and lack structure.

'It's nice to see you out of your room. We were worried about you.'

'Did I miss Dad's call?'

'He Skyped briefly this morning. I didn't know whether to disturb you or not.'

I see Mom's handbag and keys on the table. 'Have you been out?'

'Just getting groceries. I'm going to try Dad's famous Texan pulled pork burritos tonight. Your favorite,' she smiles.

A flicker of light hits the glass cabinet behind my mom's head. I turn and see the TV muted. 'Were you watching the news?'

She stands quickly and hurries over to the set.

'No, leave it. Please,' I ask.

'The nurse thought it was best to not let you see the TV updates. She thought it might add to the – the . . . anxiety.'

'I just want to see what I've missed the past few days. I won't watch for long.'

She sighs and cradles the remote in her hand. She increases the volume, one bar at a time, until a female voice fills the kitchen and adjoining living room.

' . . . ending a four-day manhunt for the suspected terrorists. This comes only a week after two homemade pressure-cooker bombs detonated 42 seconds and 190 meters apart at 10:55 a.m. near Leicester Square, killing 22 people so far and injuring over 40 others . . . the Metropolitan Police confirm a third bomb was dismantled near Covent Garden . . . the UK is now on red alert, with major airports in London grounding most flights, especially those bound for the US . . .'

Images disperse across the screen. I hold my breath as faces of smiling victims fill the TV – I'm not ready for this,

I can't look; I close my eyes and try to block them out. Their faces. Their futures. All gone. No, please stop. I can't stop the cry that escapes my lips. When I blink my eyes open I see them, all twenty-two of the victims. Their photos side by side, like they all knew each other, like they were friends or work colleagues. My mom jumps up and grabs for the remote control.

'No, wait!'

My mom freezes, her hand so tight on the remote that her knuckles turn white.

'Wait. These are all the people who died?' I get off my chair and walk closer to the screen. A blonde-haired girl, a redheaded male, a child, an elderly man, a middle-aged businessman, a woman in her thirties with long wavy brown hair . . . but no blond-haired runner of my age. He's not there on the screen which means he's not dead. He's still alive.

I didn't kill him.

Jack

My ears are still ringing. I can't hear anything. My mum and dad walk around the bed, occasionally sitting as I drift in and out of a deep dark sleep. I can't escape images of a yellow polka dot umbrella and a girl with red curly hair. They flicker in my mind throughout waking and sleeping. Who is this girl?

I remember more now. I remember the streets, the buildings, the people. I remember the screams and the car alarms, the shattering of glass windows and blown tarmac. I was running. Fast. And then I bumped into someone. Yes, the girl with the red hair. She stepped into my path as I ran, I collided with her and she'd dropped her things. Those were her books, her spinning umbrella. She was yelling at me, cursing, telling me to watch where I was going. She had an American accent and her face was familiar. I tried to help her and then I started running again. I crossed the street and turned back to see if she was still yelling. She was standing at the edge of the pavement on the other side of the crossing, next to the traffic lights. What happened next, though?

I was hurt. I am hurt. That's why I'm in hospital. And not

just because of my ears, something else feels . . . wrong. I'm broken from whatever happened, damaged. My fingers graze my face. It stings under my touch. There's a bandage around my hairline, maybe from where I fell forward. I'm OK, though, I think. What happened exactly is still a blur, but I remember my name, my age, where I go to school, my friends, all the cities I've visited, the pace of my last five runs. I still have my memory so I'm OK. My arms are bloody and cut but they're also OK. Cuts heal, wounds close, blood is wiped clean. My abdomen feels sensitive, but probably just from the hunger. I'm still getting fluids from an IV. I can't sit up unsupported yet to eat, and my lips are swollen. My hips ache when I prod them. I wiggle my toes. Odd. I feel them wiggling but I don't feel them rub against the bed covers. I swallow hard, because I know a leg injury will take a while to heal. I may even have to rest them for the next few months before I can run again. I have events scheduled for the summer – three junior marathons, a duathlon in September and a triathlon in October. I've also got a golf weekend planned for the end of July, and my dad and I are travelling to Istanbul for some hiking in August before school starts back.

I take a deep breath and ease my shoulders off the bed. My muscles throb with the movement but I need to see how bad the injury is so I know how long it'll be before I can resume my training. My eyes narrow in on the bulging thighs. I'm so swollen, why? Beyond the thighs, there's . . . there's . . . nothing. My legs. Where are my legs?

My legs are gone. There's nothing from my thighs. It's all gone.

I can't breathe. I gasp desperately for air as it thins out around me. Hands are on me pushing me back down to the bed. I open my mouth to scream but I can't hear myself.

I can't hear my own crying.

Alice

My dad looks small through the laptop from where I sit. He's hunched over the screen, leaning in to hear me. Except I'm not speaking. I haven't said anything in about five minutes now. I'm not quite sure what to say. I've never enjoyed communicating with my dad over a long-distance Skype call. Crackling, slight distortion around the edges, the occasional echo of my own voice coming back to me, and the delays. Sometimes his WiFi connection is so bad that at least half a minute passes between us in a delay. I wish my dad was here sitting right in front of me. I wish I could reach out and touch his hand. I wish I could hug him, wrap my arms around him and pull him in like when I was a child and I'd had a bad dream at night. As an army sergeant and drill instructor he was pretty tough on me about some things, but when I had a nightmare he always let me sleep in their bed. Wedged between my mom and my dad I felt so safe, like nothing could harm me. But I see now. I see more clearly. There is no 'safe.'

'How are you doing, Alice Bear?'

My dad hasn't called me that in years, not since I was a young girl. Not since the days of bad dreams were just that – dreams not reality.

'I'm okay, Dad.' I bite my lip and look down.

'Are you really?'

'Yep. Do you want me to put Mom on now?' I just want to change the subject. I can't hear it again – How are you? How are you feeling? How are you doing? How do I answer those questions truthfully?

'I'm here for you if you need me, you know.'

My belly churns. I swallow the anger down. 'But you're not here. You're in Africa somewhere. I'm in London and you're in Africa. You're not just down the hall or a quick phone call away. We have to schedule calls with you, and only when you have internet connection. It's not like I can call you anytime I want.'

'I'm trying to get time off—'

'Try harder. Better yet, get us transferred away from here,' I snap. My chest heaves in and out wildly. I don't know where that came from. The frustration and anger courses through me. I've never gotten this angry before, and never with my dad. But I didn't want to move here, and I didn't ask for this in my life. I didn't sign up to the military – I don't want a life of warfare, of market bombs and exploding buildings.

'I'm sorry, Alice.'

Tears prick the corners of my eyes. I know he's sorry. He's sorry his job landed us here in London, that if it hadn't been for him I wouldn't have been in Leicester Square that morning. I'm sorry too. I'm sorry I'm feeling like this, I'm sorry I can't talk about it to him. And I'm sorry that deep down inside I blame him – I blame everyone.

25

Jack

Rain and wind beat against the hospital windows in my room but I can't hear it. My ears still throb, are still empty of sound. I see gusts of rain hurtling down on the glass and branches swinging wildly in the wind, but I can't hear its howls and moans. I read about a storm coming. I can't remember its name just now, but I don't how long I've been in the hospital for so I'm not sure if it's already passed through or if this is it. I don't know how many days and moments have been lost to this hospital bed. Stuck. Trapped. Everything is so foggy with the pain meds I'm on. Sometimes I'm not sure if it's day or night. Sometimes everything is dark but it can't be night-time all the time. Maybe the darkness is in my head, or maybe I'm sleeping and this is all one horrible nightmare that I just can't seem to wake up from.

Wake up.

Wake up, Jack.

I fumble around in a haze of confusion and grief, and find the pain relief drip. I push the button and wait for it to flow through my veins. I'm not in pain, but my thoughts are heavy and they hurt. My memories hurt. My past hurts. After a few moments I feel lighter like I'm floating above the pain. It must be starting to work. I close my eyes and let the drugs snake through my whole body, stretching to each fingertip. I'm still floating. I want to float as far away from this hospital bed as I can go. Somewhere no one can find me.

Ophelia.

That's it. Storm Ophelia.

Alice

It rains more over the next couple of days, coming down harder than ever before. I've never seen so much rain. Every time I look out the window and see the drops hit the pavement, I'm brought back to Leicester Square, to that morning. My chest tightens like I'm having an asthma attack but I'm not asthmatic. I can't get a deep enough breath in and out my lungs. It catches in my throat and threatens to suffocate me. When it happens I rub my chest until it relaxes and breath comes back to me. It only lasted for a few seconds when I first came home from the hospital but now it's lasting for a couple of minutes. It might just be residual debris in my lungs. It'll work its way out.

I haven't talked to my dad in days. Every time he Skypes us, I pretend to be asleep. I just feel so out of it. It's like I'm dreaming and I can't wake myself or control it. It's just happening and all I can do is observe. The only time I feel 'awake' is when I think about that boy, which is weird because I don't know him. But maybe if I found him and talked to him, he'd know exactly how I feel because he feels it too. Maybe he's struggling to talk to his mom and dad about it too. Maybe he can help me.

I don't really know where to start looking so I ask Mom to fish the latest newspapers out of the paper bin, one of them having been used to mop up my spilled coffee from the morning before. Of course that was the edition in which the media shared the names of the survivors who were out of critical care.

My laptop sits on top of a chemistry book from last term and next to a postcard of Boston, so I remember where I was born. It's easy to forget when you live your whole life between borders and state lines. My accent is so neutral someone might think I'd spent years in elocution classes when really I've just never spent long enough in one place to allow the local dialect to spread through my veins and flow from my lips. I sound like one of those news anchors on TV who want viewers to focus on the content of their stories and not on their accents, debating whether it's a Texan drawl or the rolled Rs of a New Yorker. When I was younger I thought I wanted the quintessential clipped accent of an Englishwoman. But then I realized that would mean spending more than a year in one place, and I don't think that will ever happen. Although my parents won't pull me out of university so once I enroll, I'll be there for sure until I graduate – regardless of where Mom and Dad are.

The postcard of Fenway Park drops flat as I push the laptop further away and rest my elbows on the desk. There are dozens of different reports on the bombings along with blogs, tweets, images, forums. Platforms for people to rant, to mourn. Most of the messages are filled with anger, hatred, confusion. I write down each of the people mentioned in

29

the eight reports I read voraciously. One by one, I type them into every internet search I know – Google, Yahoo, Facebook, Instagram, Twitter, even LinkedIn. But I can't find him, yet something about him is so familiar. Maybe I've seen him at school? I type the school's name into the search window and there it is. A student's posted a message on Facebook asking where to send cards and flowers to Jack.

Jack.

I scroll through 'Friends' of the school and find two Jacks – Jack Muir and Jack Addington. Jack Number 1's face is partially hidden by giant Ray-Ban sunglasses but Jack Number 2 has jet black hair with a slightly bigger build. It's Jack Addington. I know him. Not to talk to, I've never said a word to him, or more accurately he's never said a word to me, but I recognize him from school. Of course every social media account of his is set to 'Public', every aspect of his life being on display for all to see, and clearly admire. I'd probably have mine set to 'Public' too if I lived a life like his. Photos of him climbing mountains in Scotland, surfing in Costa Rica, cliff jumping in Maui. There's even one of him feeding a tiger in Peru. How do you find time for mundane things like school and studying, Jack Addington?

He's sporty, but I knew that already. He plays squash, he runs marathons, he rows, he enters triathlons, he goes on ski trips every January usually to some fancy resort in the French Alps that begins with a 'V' or a 'T', none I can pronounce. Last January he went with a big group of guys – gym-goers, blond-haired preppy guys in expensive ski gear posing on top of snowy summits. Do they even ski? Or is this all a show for their Instagram followers? He ran the Chicago junior marathon last April. There's a photo of him and his dad with their arms around each other just after the finish line. He's holding a round medal in his hand and they're both beaming at the camera. I've never run in my life, except maybe for a bus. I don't think my body would let me even I wanted to. I've never had the athletic frame; I've always been stocky with limbs like a Hobbit. Here he is at the New York City junior marathon last November. Someone caught him crossing the line mid-stride. He looks happy – not happy as in relieved to be finishing that monstrosity of an activity people actually claim to enjoy, but genuinely happy, like he would run further if he could.

He plays squash for the school team, and – damn – he even rows for Cambridge's under 18s. That boy will be for sure going to Cambridge, although I wonder if he'd turn it down to go trekking through the Sahara Desert to 'find himself.' There's a Bucket List on his Facebook page in which he lists 'Climb Annapurna.' Assuming that's a mountain of some sort, I type in 'Annapurna Mountain' into Google search and immediately face some terrifying snow-capped mountains with sharp ridges and steep partial summits. It says here that it's only been climbed by 130 people in the world and 53 people have died trying.

He's in a boat with three other guys here in this photo. They're all facing front in a narrow column clutching oars. So that's what rowing looks like. He looks like the youngest there.

A photo with a blonde girl catches my eye and I don't

pretend to hesitate before I click on it. There's four of them in this one, sitting on a wall before a beach that I know is in Brighton because of a café sign on their left that reads BETTY'S BRIGHTON BAKES. The girl is sitting close to him and he has his arm around her. She's pretty, like really pretty, as in Victoria's Secret supermodel pretty. She's thin and her long hair sparkles in the sun like she's in a perfume commercial. She's wearing a red floral sundress with spaghetti straps and a thin fabric belt around her waist that only skinny people can wear. I've never worn a dress like that. This girl seems to be in a lot of his photos. Here they are hiking. Of course she hikes too. Now they're paddle boarding, now bowling. This last one they're in a restaurant. She's wearing a leopard print top and dark jeans that fit her narrow hips perfectly as if they were sewn onto her just for that picture.

I don't wear jeans. I do actually own a pair, though. Dark and slightly bootcut at the bottom because skinny leg definitely does not suit me, but they're a size too small. Not because I've gained weight since purchasing them at a Gap in San Diego last summer but because I intentionally bought them a size too small. I'd hoped that the smaller size would encourage me to lose weight, but they're still packed in a box and will likely be auctioned off on eBay very shortly.

My finger hovers over the girl's face until her name pops up – Lauren Peterson. I wonder if they're in a relationship. I wonder if she's sitting with him right now in a hospital room somewhere, holding his hand, waiting for him to wake up. But what if he never wakes up? I need to know if he's okay. I also strangely kind of want to know who the real

32

Jack Addington is. I want the real story, not the highlight reel of a perfect life.

12:17 a.m. I'm never up this late. I'm usually in bed by 9:30 p.m. so I can rise at 6:00 to read and prep for my classes before school. I guess tomorrow isn't a school day for me, though. I've been granted a further few weeks off to 'recover.' Recover from what – from a terrorist attack?

I click on 'Sleep Mode' in the top left corner and watch the screen go dark on my laptop. Darkness surrounds me. It sits on me like a heavy blanket, pressing on my lungs until I can't breathe anymore.

Car alarms.

Voices.

Sirens.

My fingertips lunge for the lamp switch. My breathing returns to normal after a few seconds. I'll leave the lamp on tonight.

Jack

Sometimes I don't know when I'm dreaming or awake. But last night I had a dream I'd died in Leicester Square. And I awoke the next afternoon in such a state of confusion, and medication haze, that for a moment I believed it. I really thought I was dead, and just watching the people in my hospital room moving around. The nurses, the doctors, the consultants, my parents, my friends, Lauren. It got me thinking about what my funeral would have been like. Morbid, I know, but in situations like this you can't stop thinking about death and what that would have meant to the lives around me.

It would be a nice funeral – huge turnout – photos of me on poster boards balancing on easels around the casket, images of my achievements to remind people of just how well I lived my life. A string quartet, because Mum would want that, playing Barber's 'Adagio for Strings'. A bit dramatic, I know, but fitting for an Addington funeral. The quartet would be positioned at the altar like it's a concert performance, and they'd play everyone in before starting their masterpiece. Behind them would be a large projection screen with fading slides of me from baby to present. I was a cute baby. There I am in Morocco with my dad, now we're posing with our new bikes at his Snowdonia Slateman Triathlon. Here's me kayaking with my friends and Lauren. She'd be in the front pew with my parents, gripping a packet of Kleenex to occasionally blot away a tear. The church would fill with everyone from school – my year, and the years above and below. My teachers, my squash coach, my French tutor, my old rugby captain. Our household staff – Martin our care-taker for the estate, our cleaners who come on Mondays and Thursdays, the landscape designer, our caterers. My dad's work colleagues and golf buddies, my mum's friends from the charity foundation and Parents First committee. And everyone who thinks they deserve to be there – that girl I sit next to in History, the boy who takes our racquets at the end of squash games, the woman from Winter Adventures who helps us book our ski holidays, the caddy at Wentworth Golf Club, even that shop assistant at M&S who seems to always be working when I stop in for a protein shake at the end of my city runs.

The pews fill up fast. Soon people are shuffling along, having to squish together on benches to make room. My mum stands to make the opening speech. At first, she speaks so eloquently, well-paced, and with vocal clarity that shows years spent with a voice coach. But then her voice cracks and she begins to struggle. My dad will come up and take over but will be lacking the same emotion my mum brought to the pulpit. He'll instead speak of my fitness endeavours, my competitive achievements, my golf handicap, my average run pace and half marathon PB time – one hour, fifteen minutes and thirty-eight seconds at the Lille Half Marathon Under 18s last year. He'll talk only about what I did, what we did, because he's proud. But also because that's the only thing he knows about me.

My friends will make eulogies, with a brief funny anecdote like the time I tried to ski backwards to impress a girl at Val d'Isère and fell over. Then the quartet will wrap up what has now become a very long funeral service for a 17-year-old. Everyone will be invited back to the golf club for cucumber sandwiches, Victoria sponge, Earl Grey tea and elderflower spritzes. Aged single malt whisky, champagne and olives for the adults, of course. Attendees will continue to swap stories about me but then as the afternoon wears on conversations will start to digress until eventually no one will be talking about me at my own funeral. Life will go on. I know mine will too, after this. I just don't know where, or how, to start.

Alice

'Where are you going?' My mom is frozen in the kitchen, dishtowel in one hand, wet coffee mug in the other. It drips onto the floor by her feet but she doesn't notice. I recognize the mug from the last place we lived in. She bought it in a souvenir shop in La Jolla, San Diego, which is funny because only tourists buy keepsakes like that but that's what we are when we live in places – tourists, only there for a brief time. So sometimes we collect little things like keyrings, mugs, the odd postcard or pen. Only from the states or countries that we really like, never from the ones we want to forget.

'I'm going out for a walk,' I say, sliding on my green raincoat. Weather here can be so temperamental, it's best to plan for all four seasons in one day.

'I'll come with you.' She puts down the coffee mug which she never got around to drying and wipes her hands on the towel.

'No, really, it's fine. I'll be okay alone.'

There are some things I just need to do alone. But I can't tell her that. 'I mean, I might meet up with a friend from school. Walk around the river a bit.'

She smiles. She likes that answer – 'a friend.' She'd love me to make some one day, have them over for dinner, maybe even a sleepover, go shopping with them, do each other's makeup and hair, talk about boys and other things that people my age consume their time with other than homework and poetry.

'I didn't know you had a friend from school.'

'We just met. She reached out to me after, you know, what happened.'

My mom walks quickly towards me and before I can remind her of the stitches in my back she pulls me in for a deep hug.

'Mom, my back,' I grimace, squirming out.

'Oh, sorry.' She brushes a loose hair off my cheek. 'Well, don't be too late. Make sure your phone is charged, okay? So I can reach you.'

I nod and rush out the door for the bus. I can't face the train. The crowds, the noise. The bus will take twice as long but at least they don't tend to be crowded like trains here. There are fourteen hospitals in London. That's a lot of hospitals to visit in one day, and that's certainly a lot of receptionists to try and obtain confidential information from. This is going to be harder than I thought. What am I doing? A part of me wants to just give up now and send a get well card like everyone else. I don't know him, we're not friends at school. But a larger part knows that this is the right thing to do. I need to see how he is and say I'm sorry. Then I'll be free of this guilt I'm feeling lately. So, I decide to start at Royal London Hospital which is the biggest according to Google and the most likely to house the majority of survivors from last week.

'How can I help you?' The receptionist is older, Mom's age I think, and looks like she doesn't have time for what's to come.

'Good morning, nice day, isn't it?' – I don't let her answer – 'I'm here to visit a patient called Jack Addington. He was injured in the bombings last week. Is he here?'

'I can't tell you that, sorry.'

'Why not?'

'Because we're not talking to the press. If you want an official statement as to the well-being of the bombing victims then you can contact our press liaison officer or—'

'Oh, I'm not press. I'm just a . . . schoolmate.'

She finally glances up from her computer screen and meets my eyes. 'I still can't access the admission records to confirm who's being treated here and who's not. Sorry. Have you tried contacting the family?'

'No, I haven't. I was just hoping—'

'Sorry I can't be of more help. Next?'

I guess that's done.

I leave through the way I came in, and pull the scrunched-up paper to my face. Someone at these hospitals has to know where he is, and more importantly be willing to tell me. But by 4:15, I've already made my way through thirteen hospitals, a prawn and mayonnaise sandwich, a bag of cheese puffs and a Snickers bar. When I get to the last one on my list, I'm greeted by the queue that seems to have preceded me to each hospital. Why are waiting rooms always so busy? After thirteen introductions, I've finally perfected the opening greeting for the receptionist. 'Oh, good afternoon, my name is Lauren,

39

and I'm here to see my boyfriend, Jack Addington? I missed a call from his mom this morning about where to stop by and now I'm worried I'm at the wrong hospital. I hate to ask, but can you please help me?'

She pauses.

'Please, I'm really worried about him.'

Here's where the tears help me. Her face softens, and she reaches across to her computer and starts scrolling. She has a small cluster of black crows tattooed on her wrist. 'What's your boyfriend's name again?'

'Jack Addington.'

'I'm sorry. I can access all the NHS hospitals online through this general patient system and I'm not seeing a Jack Addington listed anywhere.'

'How can that be? He's surely still in care, the blast – he – he was close to it, I think. He must still be in a hospital somewhere.'

'If you're sure he's still getting medical care then he'll be checked into a private hospital if he's not listed here.'

'Private? How many private hospitals are there?'

'Try the London Bridge Hospital, over by the station. I know they admitted some patients from the bombings. Maybe your boyfriend is there.'

'London Bridge Hospital? Thank you.'

I'm still typing in the address into Maps on my phone when my mom texts, *Where are you? Dinner will be ready at 6 xx*

I quickly key in, *Home soon xx* and head for the nearest bus station.

London Bridge Hospital resembles more of a modern art gallery or a five-star New York City hotel than a hospital. Past the dark green doors is Reception Number 1, then comes Reception Number 2 and then 3. The main waiting room is a large modern space with pure white leather armchairs and crisp white walls. Reception Number 3 proves to be much harder to access than the first two.

'Who did you say you were?'

'Lauren Peterson. I'm Jack Addington's girlfriend, I'm here to visit him. He'll be expecting me.'

'Jack isn't seeing visitors at the moment. It's immediate family only.'

He's here. I found him. Now I just need to get up the stairs. 'If you could just check with a senior medical staff member because his mom specifically told me if I came here at this time I would be allowed to see him for ten minutes.' I hope the receptionist doesn't hear my heart bashing against my chest. I'm not used to lying like this.

She rises from her seat, her uniform just as clean and white as the walls and the armchairs around us. I couldn't work here. I'd have coffee or ketchup on my shirt by midday. 'Let me just make a quick phone call,' she says, and disappears down the hallway. Then I do something else equally distasteful and shameful as lying, I lean over the desk and scan the confidential patient/visitor sign-in log until I find his name and his room number. I glance down the hallway then head for the nearest stairwell. 10B is the last room on the right. I take a deep breath, and slowly push the door open, finally about to come face to face with the boy I haven't been able to get out of my mind.

A loud gasp escapes me.

My hands grip the doorframe until my fingers tingle and go numb. He's there, lying in bed, eyes closed, surrounded by get well cards, flowers, helium balloons and stuffed bears with messages of 'We Miss You' and 'Thinking of You.' But where I pictured his golden hair would be is instead a large burn mark, his athletic frame is wrapped in bandages, his face puffy from the bruises and cuts. And his legs – oh God, his legs – they're not there. Where his strong mountain-climbing, marathon-running, hill-walking, ski-adventuring, cliff-jumping legs should be are two swollen stumps that end at the thighs.

I stumble back, and edge away from the door. When I reach the exit, I run.

Jack

Lauren sits at the edge of my bed, perched on her chair that was dragged through from the waiting room. She shuffles forward and places her hands in her lap then glances at Will then Alex who seem to be leading the conversation. They all sit around my bed like I'm an exhibition in a gallery. Upright, backs straight, eyes darting around then fixing on me. I see conversation happening around me, but I can't hear it. They open their mouths, exchange glances and when they turn I turn too to see who's now the speaker. I wish I could hear what they're saying to me. I'm sure they know that my ears are damaged but yet they still seem like they're trying to talk to me. What if this is permanent? What if I'll never be able to hear again?

I desperately look at them, wishing I was a part of what's happening here but the silence in my ears just excludes me more. The sudden emptiness of sound creates a distance between us as friends, one that I fear will be difficult to mend. I glance back at Lauren, who looks painfully uncomfortable. She alternates between fidgeting with the belt on her dress and with her hair. It's up in a ponytail, then it's down around her shoulders. Up. Down. She can't decide, or

43

she's just found a very mundane task to pass her time while she's here. Don't worry, only five more minutes then you can say you've done the girlfriend duty. I flinch even though no one is touching me, and look away from her. She doesn't deserve this. I'm making her someone she's not, probably because it's easier for me that way.

Maybe we never really had a connection at all. You know, now she's sitting here, I can't remember what brought us together in the first place. When did we meet? She's always been in my friendship circle, we go to the same parties, hang out in the same group, and maybe that was it, just one day we decided to be more than friends. But were we ever really friends? I don't really remember the conversations we had together. We enjoyed the same things – travelling, running, skiing. We spent so much time together over the past couple of years but now that I'm thinking about it, what do I really know about her? What's her favourite colour? What music does she listen to? I have no clue. Probably because I never asked.

I open my mouth and try to voice something, anything to let her and the others know I'm trying. I'm trying so hard. Some kind of a sound or noise must come out because they all look up at me. I try to put together a sentence, make a weak joke about being in here. But the sounds must come out jumbled, if they come out at all because they squint their eyes and edge closer trying to decipher my words. I can't do it. I lean my head back and feel a sigh through my chest. Lauren's hand is on my shoulder now and she's gently squeezing it to either empathise or just remind me she's still there. I know she's there, because it hurts. Hurts to see her, hurts to be reminded of the life I had before. Never again will I be able to do the things that define me, that make me 'Me'. All the things I love. I'm not the kind of person that can survive something like this. This isn't me. I can't just stay home all my life. I'll never run again, or row, or climb a mountain and stand on the summit and have the wind beating against my face and feel that accomplishment rippling through my body. I did all those things with my dad, with my friends, and sometimes with Lauren. Now they'll do them with someone else.

I look at her. She's beautiful, but she looks scared. I am too. Because everything is different now. There's nothing here for her anymore. I'm not the Jack Addington she knows. Not the same one that attracted her, anyway. I don't know who I am anymore, so until I figure that out I'll just hold her back. I'll hold all these guys back.

Alice

I haven't left the house in days.

I don't know what came first – the vomiting, the fainting, or the bolt from the hospital room all the way down the hallway and out the dark green doors, back to home. Mom wants to know what happened. Of course she thinks it's something to do with this 'friend' I went to see. I just tell her that being outside is just too much for me at this moment, but that answer seems to concern her more. Doesn't help that the flashbacks are happening more often. Now I can barely breathe when it happens. My breath gets trapped in my throat and I cough and try to bring it up, but I choke on it. Then I start sweating and overheating. I can't control it. I can't stop it.

I lie in bed thinking about Jack, wondering what thoughts are going through his mind. Is he having flashbacks too? Like me, is he terrified of going to sleep in case he doesn't wake up? Or does he yearn for sleep, wanting so much to close his eyes and wake up to find this is all a nightmare? That we never collided that morning in Leicester Square, that no bomb went off, that no one died or lost limbs or lost loved ones. That we're both just tucked up in our beds at home, still blissfully unaware of the horrors that could unfold on our streets and still going about our usual routine of school, homework, friends, high school drama.

I squeeze my eyes closed, as a ringing sound fills the hallway outside my room. A quiet knock on the door forces my eyes open.

'Your dad is on the phone,' my mom whispers through the door like she's undecided whether to wake me or leave me.

I throw the covers off my bed and slowly open the door. Light from the hallway hits my face and I blink hard. I feel her hand on my face, brushing back my hair, then gently rubbing my shoulder. The phone is in my hands. I smile weakly and return to my room, closing the door behind me. I crawl back into bed, and pull the covers up over me.

'Hello?'

'How you doing, Alice?'

'I'm okay, Dad. How are you?'

'I'm okay, sweetheart. It's been really hard not talking to you these past few days.'

My heart twinges and aches at the sound of his voice breaking. I've never seen my dad cry before, but he's always taught me that it's okay to.

'Yeah,' I whisper. 'I'm really sorry, Dad. I didn't mean to lash out.'

'You never have to apologize. What you're feeling is normal.'

Is it? Then why do I feel so alone in this?

'I'm coming home, Alice. My leave request was approved. I'll wrap up here and be home soon. I promise.'

The tightness in my chest immediately loosens, and I feel my breath coming back. 'Really?'

'Not long to go. Then I'll be home, and we can do this together.'

I press the phone to my cheek, as tears fall from my eyes. I have my dad, and my mom, to help me. But who does Jack have? What if he has no one? And like me, what if he's lost?

Jack

My hearing is back. I wasn't sure at first but I know now. I was woken this morning by sounds. Sounds of muffled voices, banging desk drawers, chugging food trolleys down echoey hospital hallways. I could hear it all. It's not completely clear and the ringing is still there but it's softer today and I can hear everything around me for the first time in a while.

At first I was relieved. I'll be able to hear my mum's voice again, listen to music, engage in conversations and jokes with my friends, hear London traffic when I run down the streets. And then it hit me again. Yes, I have my hearing back but I'm still here in this hospital. And maybe having my hearing back is a curse, not a blessing. Because now I'll be able to hear the pity in people's voices when they talk to me, the verbal awkwardness when they accidentally ask when's my next race or how my squash game went or want to discuss the location for the next ski trip. I'll hear their backtracking as they splutter and stutter their way through an obvious topic change.

I'll hear it all.

I don't want to hear them. I'll just pretend for a little longer. Let me enjoy being quiet and alone for a few more days. I'm not ready to share what's left of myself with the world. Not yet. For now, I just want to close my eyes and sleep. Let my dreams carry me away from here, from this body.

My dreams are so vivid these days. I'm still dreaming about that girl from the explosion. The girl with the yellow polka dot umbrella. She consumes my dreams, good and bad. When I woke the other day, still groggy from sleep, I thought I saw her. The girl with the red hair. I thought I saw her standing here in this room, at that door, looking right at me. She had the same fiery curls, same red cheeks, big eyes. But when I closed my eyes and opened them again, she was gone.

Alice

I'm back at the dark green doors of the hospital. I just need to go inside, find a way back up to his room without anyone seeing me, introduce myself and say sorry. One uncomfortable but brief interaction to stave off years of guilt, self-hatred and regret. How hard can that be? Why do I feel like throwing up in that bush?

When I get to the white waiting room with the white armchairs and the white walls, I pretend to be a patient and tell her I have an appointment at 11:00 but I can't remember the doctor's name. She rushes off to find a nurse to help her explain why they don't seem to have my appointment written down. And while she runs around, I sneak upstairs. Back to 10B.

Jack is in the same position on the hospital bed. His eyes are wide open and he stares at the ceiling at a panoramic print of a mountain that's been taped up there. I gaze up at it too, and wonder if he's dying to reach up and tear it down like I am. The room is bigger than I remember. The window looks onto the Thames, a glass pyramid-shaped building on the other side. The walls and furniture are white like downstairs. On either side of him are tall vases filled with lilies, gerbera daisies, sunflowers and roses. At the foot of the bed by the leather ottoman are three more vases filled with lavender and baby's breath. The whole room smells like our last house in San Diego. We had a beautiful big garden there with patches of yellow buttercups, sprigs of mint, clusters of flat basil, feathery pea shoots and bulbous bluebells. I learned a lot about flowers and herbs. Now we have a square of crushed stone with a broken swing and a damp shed.

'Hi.'

He doesn't even blink.

'Hello.' He doesn't look at me. 'Jack?' I take another step closer. 'Okay. I'll just jump right in. My name's Alice. We met the other day – well, we didn't meet exactly, that's a stupid thing to say, we . . . um . . . you see, you knocked into me when you were running and spilled my coffee down me and onto my books; they weren't even mine, they belonged to the library. I'll probably be fined for them . . . um, anyway, sorry, yes, when you banged into me I started yelling at you – well we more yelled at each other, it wasn't just me you know – we had an 'exchange', shall we say and maybe I gave you a finger, then . . . um—'

Images of smoke, dust and fire fill my eyes and I squeeze them shut and try to remember what I was saying.

'—anyway, I looked everywhere for you, at fourteen hospitals, to be exact. And then I learned about the private hospitals – I mean, wow, this is a nice room. Big flatscreen TV, nice armchair in the corner too, I wonder if it comes in blue – I'm rambling, I know. I think we go to school together. I mean, we do but you probably don't know me

52

because I barely recognized you but then I just moved here. I guess what I'm trying to say, in a very inarticulate way, is that I'm sorry. I'm really sorry, for, you know' – I wave my hand towards his legs – 'this.' Now I immediately want the ground to swallow me up. But I don't know what to say in situations like this. Regular conversation with a boy is hard enough, let alone making conversation with a boy in a hospital bed who I helped put there. I fill my lungs with air and start again. 'If I hadn't yelled at you, you wouldn't have stopped and if you hadn't stopped you might have got further away from the blast and maybe have been okay.'

He's still not moving. Is he dead?

'Jack, did you hear me?'

'He can't hear.' I turn around and see a young male nurse standing behind me, clipboard cradled to his chest.

'What?'

His face softens as he looks towards Jack. 'Doctors think his ear drums were ruptured in the blast and there's permanent damage.'

'He's deaf too?!'

I stand there, mouth agape, just staring at Jack, then back at the nurse. Deaf? How can I apologize if he can't hear me? How can I help him?

I've finally found the one person who knows exactly what I'm going through, what I'm feeling, and he'll never be able to hear my words and I won't hear his. I'll never hear his voice, know what he sounded like, whether he had a low tone or a high-pitched, clipped accent. I wonder what his laugh would have been like. Teaching someone a new communication system after hearing loss could take weeks, months. I don't have that time. I'm drowning here. I need him. I need . . . I need air, I can't breathe.

I push past the nurse, mumbling a pathetic apology, and head for the exit. When I get outside, I cover my face with my hands then stagger towards the wall. My back stings when I collapse into it, but I don't flinch with the pain. I deserve it. When my heartbeat finally slows and the street outside isn't spinning, I look back at the green doors which I seem to be spending more time outside of than in.

Jack

She survived.

At first I thought I was dreaming again. Fiery red hair, flushed cheeks, large eyes that always seem to be in a state of surprise or confusion. She was wearing different clothes and she didn't have that yellow polka dot umbrella, but it was definitely her. I wasn't dreaming.

The hair, her face. Everything about her brought back that day.

The thump of two bodies colliding. The scattering of books and a coffee cup on the ground, the liquid pouring out all over the pavement. The staining of the book covers. The slow turning of the umbrella on its head. Her voice. I still remember her voice. 'Hey, watch it,' she'd said to me. What did I say to her? I don't remember. She'd been so angry with me. I wonder if the coffee had spilled on my trainers. Weird to think of that now, but I am. Where are my trainers? Are they still on my feet? Where are my feet?

A wave of nausea brings everything up. I fiddle with the call button. Dizziness is making my head spin. I lie back and wipe my mouth. The nurses are here now, cleaning me up. Why did I just think about that?

She did this.

She brought this all back. What did she say to me? 'Sorry for this'? *Sorry.* How dare she? She's up walking around without a scratch on her and I'm lying here like this, and she has the nerve to think a casual 'sorry' will make everything better. She's right, if she hadn't yelled at me I wouldn't have stopped. This is her fault. I don't want to talk to her. I've got nothing to say to her. I don't want to see her face again, that red hair, and be reminded again of that morning. I swallow hard and close my eyes, and beg sleep to take me.

Alice

I was awake again most of the night.

I can't seem to let sleep take me. I'm too scared. What if I have another nightmare? What if I relive that morning again, even if it is in my head? What if I don't wake up this time?

I also couldn't stop thinking about all the things I want to say to Jack that I thought I couldn't because of the hearing loss. Then I realized that he doesn't have to *hear* my words. He can see them. So I wrote him a letter. I debated for quite some time about how to start it. 'Dear Jack' seemed a bit formal and 'Hey, Jack' seemed too casual considering we've never really had a proper conversation. So I went for just 'Jack' followed by a comma and then a very lengthy letter that was somewhat comparable to *War and Peace*. Of course I scrapped that, and after three drafts I was left with a simple but hopefully effective note. I'm going to deliver it today. I could mail it, but what if it didn't arrive? I would never know and there would be no real resolution or closure to this – this unimaginable tragedy. So I'm going to get the bus back into London and drop it off at the front desk. I don't want to hand it to him myself.

I don't need to see him again. The last two visits haven't exactly gone well, or even as planned. And I can see from the abundance of flowers and cards and the fancy hospital suite that he's well looked after, and that he has friends to talk to about this. He doesn't need me like I first thought. Although I wish he did kind of need me, which I know is selfish.

The envelope is already sealed with his name and room number on the front, and my coat and shoes are on. I hover in the doorway, dreading those green hospital doors.

'You're going out again?'

I turn and see my mom in the hall, hands clasped around a coffee mug.

'I'm just going for a short walk. I need to drop something off at someone's house.'

'Who?'

'Just someone I go to school with.'

'Okay, but just remember your appointment with the community nurse is at 2:45 to check on your stitches.'

'I'll be back in time.'

'Phone charged?'

I nod and pull her in for a quick hug, not really feeling it like I used to. Then I release her and hurry out the door.

When I get to the hospital, there are two women working at reception today. 'Hello, can I leave a letter here for Jack Addington in room 10B? Can you make sure he gets it?'

'10B?' A blonde-haired woman in a white dress and white cardigan appears from the waiting room. Her hair is pulled back into a painfully tight ponytail, but her features are soft, kind. Minimal makeup and very beautiful. Very English-looking, if that's a term. 'Have you been visiting my son?'

Of course, the resemblance is obvious now. 'Um, yes, actually.'

'Do you go to school with Jack?'

'I do. I was just dropping off a letter to him.'

'Why don't you give it to him yourself? He's awake now,' she smiles. Jack has her eyes.

'Oh, it's fine,' I stammer. 'I don't want to intrude. Honestly, if you could just give it to him.'

'No intrusion at all. Come on up,' she says, gesturing to the stairwell.

Maybe I should have mailed it after all.

'Sure,' I mutter, following her through the stairwell doors. Her heels slap each step and it echoes through the narrow hallway. I wonder if I should say something before we reach his room. I clear my throat. 'I'm sorry for everything your family is going through,' I say slowly and clearly, like I'm reading from a teleprompter or something.

She turns and smiles, but her lips tremble. 'Thank you,' she mouths, barely any sound coming out. Then she takes a deep breath and keeps walking. When we get to the room, a tall man with broad shoulders is standing at the window looking out at the Thames. When he turns I recognize him from the photos on Jack's Facebook. 'I found this young lady downstairs at reception. She's friends with Jack.'

I reach out and offer a hand to him, like my dad taught me although I've come to realize Brits aren't really handshakers. That seems to be an American thing. 'Hi, Mr Addington. I'm Alice.'

He walks over and takes my hand. His handshake is firm and formal. 'You go to school with Jack?' he asks me.

'I'm new. I transferred in about three months ago from the US.'

He nods.

'My dad's in the military. He's working with the British Army at the moment which is why we're here.'

He nods again, then looks over to Jack, his face hardening. I'm sure he doesn't want to be engaging in small talk right now, but silence makes me uneasy, especially in a hospital. I clear my throat and take a slow, deep breath. 'I was there when it happened. I was lucky, I was further away from the blast than some.' They both look up at me, faces whitening. 'I saw your son there.'

Mrs Addington slaps a hand across her mouth but she's not quick enough and a stifled cry comes out.

'I'm sorry, I didn't mean to bring it up. I . . . I . . . I should just leave.' I back up and hit my hip off a table filled with vases. It wobbles behind me. I try to steady it but a vase falls and a loud smash fills the room.

Jack startles in the bed.

Did he just jump with the noise? I'm still staring at him, when his parents come over. 'Careful with the glass,' his mom says holding out her hand. I slide my palm into hers and step over the broken glass and puddle of water.

'I am so sorry. I am so clumsy. I can't believe I did that.'

'Don't be sorry, it's an accident. Besides, I hated those

flowers. Who buys baby's breath? It's a weed not a flower,' she mutters picking up the bigger pieces of glass. 'I'm going to get the nurse to help me with this.' Jack's dad follows after her. The hallway is silent again, bar the muffled voice of Mrs Addington at the other end.

I walk around the bed and pretend to organize the vase of water lilies on the bedside table, pushing the stems deeper into the pool of water at the bottom of the glass. Then I lean in. 'Jack Addington, you're busted. I saw that. I know you can hear just fine.'

He grimaces slightly but doesn't look at me.

'If you don't want to talk right now, it's fine. I won't tell anyone.' When I stand back, I push my hands into my coat pocket, my fingers tickling the top of the letter that still sits inside.

Jack

That girl – Alice, she said her name was. She knows I'm pretending. Now what? Will she tell my parents? Will people find out and immediately bombard me with their words? Words of sympathy, words of pity, words of guilt. Everyone wants to talk about how they feel, how this is impacting them. I've seen my mum hug my dad, Lauren hug my friends, even Nana hugging a nurse. Everyone in my life is seeking comfort and solace from others to get through this, to get through my pain. Yes, that's right. I'm going through this, not them. It's my pain, my loss, my grief, my burden. I feel like half these get well cards are for my parents, not for me. People feel sorry for them.

Why did Alice have to come here and ruin this?

I just needed a few more days or weeks of the silence. Preferably until I'm out of this bed and in a wheelchair, able to remove myself from a conversation if it's dripping in sorrow and pity. Not when I'm bedridden and stuck here, forced to acknowledge people's emotions and uncertainty over the future. I'm still figuring that out myself. Of course I wouldn't have let it go on forever, I'd never do that to my parents, especially my mum. It's horrible not being able to have a conversation with her, knowing she's desperate to hear my voice again. But no one could possibly understand how I'm feeling right now. And speaking about it with those around me will just make things worse. Who else will Alice tell other than my parents? People at school?

I hope she never comes back.

Alice

He's faking being deaf.

I couldn't believe it when I saw him flinch at the sound of the glass shattering. He heard it. He can probably hear everything. Maybe he even heard me the other day. I didn't even need to write the letter that I spent hours agonising over. The first draft alone took me over an hour and a half. The hand cramps after weren't fun either. And all this time he's been pretending!

At first I was a little annoyed even though I don't really have a right to be. He doesn't owe me anything and we don't really know each other. He's free to pretend to be anything he wants. But still, I couldn't help but be slightly annoyed at the situation. Then I felt a little jealous. The thought of temporarily shutting the world out, just taking a few moments to process what happened without other people's words of sympathy coming at you. I kinda wish I'd thought of that. And finally, after the annoyance and envy subsided, I started to wonder what must be going through Jack's head if he actually put up that façade and maintained it for this long? Who or what is he avoiding? It sounds strange, but I just can't shake the urge to go back there. Regardless of all those get well cards, flowers, balloons, social media messages, maybe he doesn't have anyone to talk to about this.

'Out again? I made marmalade muffins,' my mom says, leaning against the kitchen doorway with a silver cup of icing sugar in her hand. Her hair is dyed pink again at the ends. She's had it blue, green and even gray before. She's a little more adventurous than me when it comes to her appearance. I don't even experiment with product in my frizzy hair.

When I follow her into the kitchen, orange zest, honey and cinnamon hits me at the doorway. She hasn't baked since we left San Diego. She said she couldn't understand the measurement conversions here so her cookbooks were meaningless. I did point out that there's such a thing called Google now for things like that. 'Can I take two away with me?'

'For you and your friend? What's her name, by the way?'

'Um . . . Jack.'

My mom stops, the oven door wide open and turns to me. 'He's a boy.'

'Yes, Jack is a boy's name.'

She's still staring at me, the oven light flickering behind her. I walk over and take the mitt from her. Sliding the muffin tray out, I do my best to avoid her open-mouthed stare that's now turning into a 'I'm so excited' smile.

'Is he your boyfriend?'

'No. Definitely not my boyfriend. Just a boy from school. That's it. We're not even exactly friends.'

'But you've been meeting up with him a lot lately?'

Oh right. That's what happens when you lie, you have to continue to lie to protect the original untruth.

65

'Is there a container or something for this?' I hold two steaming hot muffins in my hand and wince with the heat. My mom takes them from my hands and folds them in a paper towel. 'Are these for Jack?'

'I don't know if he can even eat them.'

'Why not?'

'He's not exactly . . . himself at the moment.'

'How so?'

'You're asking a lot of questions. Can I go now?'

'One last one.'

I roll my eyes. 'Yes?'

'How's your back?'

'Still hurts in the shower but it's getting better.'

'Now you can go,' she smiles.

The muffins have cooled by the time I get from Twickenham to the hospital. The Thames is a little busier today with it being a Friday afternoon. There's always something in the air on Fridays anywhere you go. That sense of excitement for the weekend, for what's to come now that school or work is out of the way. That deep breath you take when you look at your watch and it's officially Friday afternoon, and you know you have two whole days of switching off. New York had it, that feeling. London definitely has it.

The sun is out today. It's a little warmer than it has been the past couple of weeks, and more people are eating their lunch outside beside the river. They're laughing, smiling, sharing plans for their weekends, digesting a busy week of work. The air even smells different. It's like restaurants start their dinner service earlier on Fridays, start sautéing vegetables, braising beef tenderloins and barbecuing chicken even before opening the doors to their first diner. I used to love Fridays. Mostly because it meant I had two days away from the mean girls at school and the idiot jocks, but also because weekends were a time for me to hang out with my mom. Skype with my dad wherever he was in the world, read, write poetry, get ahead in my studies.

I've only been out of school for three weeks but it feels much longer. So much has happened since I was last there. I feel so detached from that place now, from the trivialities of high school. The past few weeks have been a blur of overlapping days, messed-up routines and erratic eating patterns. The only consistent thing in my schedule the past week has been going to the hospital, even though I'm pretty sure I'm not wanted there. I still have that letter I wrote and even knowing he can hear me if I wanted to talk, I still want to give it to him. Because maybe I just need to, or maybe this is my life raft. Maybe I'm drowning, and nothing in my life can pull me out of the water that threatens to swallow me whole. Except this, whatever this is. Maybe I need this, this distraction, this purpose, to survive. Or maybe I'm just selfish and I need to hear him say it wasn't my fault so I can leave and never come back again and get on with my life, while he rots in a hospital bed rotating between surgeries and unwanted visits.

I stop dead in the hospital hallway. The door to 10B is closed and a piece of paper is taped onto it, just above the handle: PATIENT IN 10B IS NOT RECEIVING VISITORS TODAY.

Jack

I've been refusing food for the past couple of days. People think I'm sick. They take my temperature almost every hour and occasionally check my bloods, probably for infection or abnormality. Whatever they think, it's working. I heard my mum request no more visits from friends for this week, at least until I'm accepting food again. It's bought me a few days from Alice, assuming she is coming back which I'm sure she is planning to. I'm still hoping she hasn't told anyone about my secret. I don't know why she comes here. We have nothing to say to each other. We were both in the wrong place at the wrong time. Being involved in a terrorist bombing doesn't give us a 'common interest'. We're strangers to each other.

The door clicks open and I don't turn. I've got quite good at predicting sounds around here and not responding to them – the click of my room door, the ting of the incoming elevator, the whirling of the food trolley wheels, the footsteps of nurses sharing the halls, the faint telephone ring from the hallway receiver. I turn at shadows, movement in my peripheral vision, but not sounds, not anymore. It's quite easy pretending to be deaf actually.

'Hi, Jack.'

My mum comes every day. She's here from the start of visiting hours to the end and sometimes after too. No one says anything to her. Everyone is very respectful to my family. They sometimes let her sleep here too. She curls up in the armchair in the corner. 'We got more flowers today. These are from your friends and this bouquet is from your PE teacher.'

Great, more flowers. It's a good thing I'm not allergic otherwise I'd have been in serious trouble.

'Your cuts are healing well,' my mum says, edging closer to me. She gently strokes my hair and I visibly flinch to pretend I've just noticed her presence. 'The doctors don't think you'll have much scarring at all.' She takes a deep breath and stops talking. The ticking of the clock on the wall interrupts the silence in the room. 'I don't know what to do.' Her voice cracks. 'I can't imagine not having a conversation with you again, never hearing your voice again.'

My jaw aches and I know I must be clenching hard. I hate hearing her like this. I hate what I'm doing to her.

Another click. Strong footsteps enter the room, a slight shuffle as they get closer to the bed and an overwhelming smell of coffee and cologne. My dad. He stands at the other side of the bed. 'How's he doing today?'

'The same. Temperature is normal which is good. Hopefully he'll feel like eating again otherwise I don't know. He may have to receive nutrition through the gastrointestinal tract.'

Wait, what? OK, I'll stop pretending now. I don't want any more needles and intervention.

'OK,' he says, shuffling away.

'You could say something to him,' my mum calls.

'What do you mean?'

'I mean, you can say something to your son.'

'He's deaf, Agatha.'

'He's not deaf. The otolaryngologist couldn't find any permanent damage to his ears. He thinks it's just residual ringing or neurological shock which will fade over time. We don't know how much he can hear. It would be nice if you spoke to him.'

My dad sighs. 'What do you want me to say?'

'Say whatever you want. I just want you to say something.' My mum's voice is short and clipped. She's getting frustrated.

'This is ridiculous,' my dad snaps. The door clicks open.

'Is it so difficult for you to speak to your son?' she demands.

'That's not my son—'

My belly churns and recoils like I've just been punched. I'm not sure how well I'm pretending at being deaf. Maybe they saw me flinch. Silence fills the space between us all.

'I didn't mean that. *Of course* he's my son, I just mean that I don't recognise anything about Jack anymore. He's a shell of who he was.'

'Don't say that, don't—'

'Agatha, look at him.'

'Then leave. If you don't have anything to say to your son, then just leave. Go home.'

Don't leave, Dad. Say something, anything. If you say something to me, then I'll speak. I'll be honest about being able to hear again. We'll talk. We'll have a conversation.

But the door closes and I know he's gone.

My dad's right. I'm not the same Jack. Our relationship will never be the same again. We see the world together, we climb mountains, we pitch tents in forests and on wild land, we run races, soar on road bikes, swim in open lochs, glide down snowy summits. That's who we are. Who are we without that?

Alice

I know he doesn't want to see me right now, but I came back anyway. I'm still carrying around this stupid letter, wondering when would be the right time to give it to him. It doesn't weigh much but I feel it heavy in my coat pocket every day. Sometimes I slide my hand into my pocket just so I can touch it with my fingers and know it's still there, that there's words still to be said to him.

I sit here, gazing out his hospital-room window. My spine pushes into the armchair as I try to straighten up. Mom says I have bad posture. I remember watching a modeling show in America where girls practiced their runway walks while balancing a book on their head. Apparently it's a technique for improving posture. So I tried it, placed a hardcover copy of *Pride and Prejudice* on my head and took a step around my bedroom. It immediately fell off, falling forwards, of course, hitting my little toe and carving out a small triangle shape. So I tried again, practicing all day in my room until I could walk in a full circle without it dropping. By that time I had several small 'corner punctures' plus a very painful paper cut on my big toe. And it was only then I questioned why I was even doing all that to begin with. It worried me how easily I was duped into conforming, and worrying about my appearance. I wish I could say I stopped wasting my time with these silly trivial things after that, but I didn't. That year in particular was a collection of silly trivial things to try and better my place at high school. From balancing a book on my head to putting dye in my hair to worrying about my outfit in the mornings. And after Brittany Wilson told me I was 'paler than death', I tortured my skin in a sunbed. All I did was surface from that box the brightest red my mom says she's ever seen on a human being. And I blistered a day later too and had to lather myself head to toe with aloe vera balm. I wasn't any cooler for my efforts, or the slightest bit more popular at school; in fact, people like Brittany made fun of me even more. The weird bookish, overweight, pale-skinned girl that never stayed more than a year in one place. Starting fresh didn't help. It just made me relive being the new girl over and over again. Once, I hid in the toilet cubicles for a whole afternoon until my mom came to get me. No, starting fresh didn't help me at all. I didn't accumulate friends when I moved, only a bigger school file and a bigger roster of people who didn't *get* Alice Winters.

I'm not sure I even understand myself in this moment. Here I am again, having snuck in through the green doors, past the receptionist who made the foolish error of leaving her desk unmanned to refill her tea mug. I'm completely surrounded by flowers of all shapes and sizes and colours and smells. I wonder if he even likes flowers. Maybe he's allergic. Many people are. I'm not. There was a girl back in

73

Upstate New York that was highly allergic to flowers, plants, herbs. Animal fur too. And dust and household cleaning liquids, if I remember correctly. Pretty much everything then. But I remember one day our Math teacher got a bouquet of flowers and how a stifled cough quickly turned into a full-blown allergic reaction that needed the school nurse to administer an epi-pen in the class in front of everyone.

There's still a ridiculous amount of balloons and Get Well Soon cards in here. Photos that friends have left for him, some in frames, others just scattered on table surfaces like the pages of a scrapbook. And then there's me – the only thing here in this room that doesn't fit. We weren't friends before this. I never knew the boy in the Facebook photos who climbed mountains, dived from cliffs into water, and ran marathon distances all over the world, probably while maintaining an A average in his studies. Although I doubt his sixth-year syllabus consists of Math and Sciences like mine. His is probably made up of PE, languages and English Lit. My eyes wander over to a copy of *On the Road* on his table beside the lilies.

Yeah, definitely English Lit.

Maybe I'd have faced him in a literary debate about Kerouac or Faulkner if we'd taken the same English class. But I was in the US last year when I got my A+ in Advanced English. I helped out on set props on *A Midsummer Night's Dream* at the end of it. I painted a tree. It was no Monet, that's for sure, but it was a tree and for a play about the forest at night, it was central to the overall set design. Integral to the entire production, if you ask me.

He's still not said a word to me and it's been twenty minutes since I arrived and said hi. I clear my throat and try again, 'Jack? I'm still here.'

Of course he knows that. And he doesn't look at me.

'I don't think anyone can hear us if you want to talk?'

Nothing. He just stares up at the poster. Silence encompasses us, presses us into an even tighter space. I hear no noises in the hallway. No footsteps, no groans of pain, no sounds of sleep or cries for loved ones. I hear no sounds from him. I just see the trembling of his temples, the twitching of his muscles underneath the covers which I read was normal after an amputation. The lavender from the tall vase by the window is strong and there's also the scent of peonies from the corner table, my mom's favorite. I wonder if he thinks any of it is me, my perfume. I don't wear perfume, never have. I don't wear makeup either unless I have a breakout on my chin which happens occasionally. I see his fingers on his left hand flicker and notice his breaths turning to deep sighs.

Go on, Jack. Say something to me. Please just speak.

I give up.

Jack

I take a deep breath and glance at my mum who came in shortly after Alice finally left. I don't know how much longer I could have kept that up for. Twenty minutes felt like hours. My mum has her back to me and is trimming stems of calla lilies to fit the new vase she bought. Each snip reverberates around the room and through the empty hospital hallway. I haven't heard any other patients in this wing, just me – visitors for me, medical staff fussing around my dressings and wounds, my mum sorting through the bouquets of flowers that still stream in every day. Everyone coming and going in this hallway appears to be here for me only. They think I can't hear them but I do. I hear their whispers, footsteps and frustrated tears clearer than I ever have. The ringing in my ears is just a dull sound now in the background of the chaos of my thoughts.

I was up again most of last night, thinking of how I would do this. But every scenario felt false, faked. I don't want Mum to know I was pretending all this time and I don't want my dad to know that I heard him the other night when he admitted that I was no longer the son he knew. But I also don't want Alice to be the one who tells them.

It's been a long time since I've heard my own voice. What if, after all this time, I have damage to my vocal chords and I can't speak? Wouldn't that be ironic. I pretend to be deaf, only to discover I actually can't say anything.

The clipping stops and I see my mum holding the vase up to the window light. The soft rays from the afternoon sun reflect off the lavender-hued vase and cast streaks of violet onto the white floor.

'Mum?' I croak out.

She turns slowly to me, like she's just heard a ghost.

I clear my throat and say it again. 'Mum.'

She quickly places the vase on the windowsill and rushes to my side. 'Jack, can you hear me? Can you – *hear*?' Her hand sits on my shoulder, gently squeezing.

'I can hear you. I can hear everything,' I whisper. My voice, it's so loud in my ears after all this time.

'Oh, thank God,' she gasps. She reaches for the nurse call button and presses down. 'I just want to get your ears checked, make sure there's no fluid or blood or anything like that.'

'I'm OK.'

'When did this happen? When did you start hearing things again?'

I take another deep breath and remember my mum and dad standing over me the other night, my dad's words. 'Just this morning,' I lie.

Alice

I slide a bag of magazines, chocolate buttons and sea-salt crisps onto the reception counter and smile at the women behind it. I don't know what Jack likes to read other than Kerouac so I got magazines on pretty much every subject I could find at the WH Smith downstairs. Helicopters, boats/sailing, DIY/carpentry, travel and leisure, *Runners Monthly*, *Cycling Addicts*, *Wellbeing Weekly*. I even got him a copy of *Yoga Journal*, in case he's into the 'ohm'-ing. Truth is, even after hours of what I'm hesitant to label as 'social media stalking,' I really don't know him at all. I know the online character he's created but I don't know the real Jack Addington.

'Can I leave this here for room 10B? It's just magazines, chocolate and so on. In case, he's . . . I don't know, bored or hungry or something. Will you give it to him for me?'

'Would you like to go up and give it to him yourself? Visiting hours have just started.'

'Oh, I don't know.'

She slides the sign-in log to me. I look up at the ceiling, as if I can see through the concrete and copper and steel beams, right to his room, where he's probably staring at the ceiling too. 'Okay, I'll take it up.'

When I get to 10B the door is open, propped wide by what strangely seems to be a weighted toy bunny. 'Nice rabbit.'

He doesn't turn his face to me, but I know he knows it's me. He's looking up at that poster again.

'Nice view?'

He turns to me, his eyes burning into me. 'Is that supposed to be a joke?'

His accent is just as I imagined, clipped English with an unnecessary hint of formality for his age, but his voice is deeper. 'No, sorry. I just meant . . . Never mind.' I rub my forehead and try again. 'I think there's more flowers this week, if that's possible. Looks like a garden in here.'

'I hate flowers.'

'Oh, um, want me to get rid of them?'

'Forget it. Just sit down if you're going to.'

I scoot over to the leather armchair by the window and plop down. 'Nice room.'

'Thanks,' he mutters staring out the window.

'How's the food here?'

He turns to me, forehead creased.

I shrug. 'Sorry, I just don't know what to say.'

'You've been coming here all this time and you haven't thought about what to say?'

'I guess.'

He turns his head away from me again. Was that my cue to leave?

I get up and move for the door. What if he refuses to see me again? If this is our only and last meeting, I should say something. 'Look, I know what you're going through so if you ever want to talk, I'm here.'

'You know what I'm going through?'

'Yeah, I do.'

'Did you also have your legs blown off? Because from what I can see, you don't even have a scratch on you. Were you even there?'

'You bumped into me!' My cheeks burn and I'm breathing loudly. How dare he, of course I was there.

'I bumped into you? I think you mean you bumped into me.'

'What?'

'You stepped onto my path while I was running—'

'You weren't looking where you were going and you—'

'You almost knocked me over—'

'I dropped all my stuff—'

'I stopped to help you with your things. Then you started yelling at me on the street—'

'My coffee, my books, my umbrella—'

He takes a sharp inhale like someone's just punched him. 'I don't know why you're here. But please don't pretend like you have any idea how I feel.'

'I do. I was there. I know exactly how you feel,' I argue, the heat building inside me.

'I have no legs, Alice!' he screams. His voice reverberates and thumps against the walls that hold us.

There's nothing I can say to make him feel better. But what words will make him hate me less?

'Please just leave,' he whispers.

'I'm sorry. I'm so sorry,' I stammer.

'Just leave.'

This isn't why I came. I wanted to make him feel better. I wanted to comfort him, to be comforted myself. And now I feel worse. I slowly slide the letter out my pocket and leave it on the bedside table.

Jack

'Will Alice be visiting again today?'

My mum is sitting in the armchair in the corner, by the window. A heavy hardcover book with a frayed brown binding sits on her lap.

'She won't be coming back again,' I mutter, prodding the bag Alice brought. It still sits on the table. I place a hand on the top and push down. It crinkles and crunches, like crisps. I tug at the handle until it spills open. Is that a Curly Wurly poking out of the top?

'Why won't she be coming back?' She places her book on the windowsill behind her.

'Because I don't know her.'

'I thought she goes to your school?'

'Maybe.'

'Maybe?'

'It's a big school.'

'It's a *small* school, Jack. Too small to not know every face.'

It is fairly small compared to most London schools, especially the state ones. But it's not the kind of school where everyone is friends and we all sit round one big communal table at lunch and share stories. The school is divided up into three simple yet defined groups. My group consists of mostly athletes, albeit some with a passing or feigned interest in a particular sport their dads have roped them into, like rowing or golf. We love to compete – contact sports, races, duathlons, triathlons, junior marathons, basically all competitive events. Our grades aren't the best but they're good enough to advance to a university of our parents' choosing. Then there's the serious students, those with Oxford or Cambridge or MIT in their futures. Their social skills are lacking, I'd say, but to them socialising is a distraction from their studies. Then there's the third group, the 'transfers' like Alice. Children of foreign diplomats or military officers, those from big financial or oil families who get transferred to London for specific projects or to cater to high-end clients. They don't tend to stay long. They float in, some with very limited English, then they disappear before the school year ends. They're relocated to some other part of the world. We don't tend to get to know them. They won't be here for very long so what's the point?

'She seemed very upset when she left yesterday.'

I remember her standing there, in the doorway, flushed red cheeks, eyes watering. I don't like seeing that. But I don't want pity from one more person. 'And?'

'And I was just wondering why she was so upset.'

'Mum,' I sigh. I know she means well, but I'm tired of this conversation.

'Jack, you have an opportunity to talk to someone else who was there that day, someone else who was a victim of terrorism—'

'She's not a victim. She seems to be just fine,' I mutter.

'We don't really know what happened to her.'

'Well, she fared better than me. I think we can both see that.'

'Just because she doesn't have any *physical* injuries doesn't mean she wasn't injured.'

'It's not the same thing.'

My mum takes a deep, loud breath and sits back in the armchair. 'OK,' she finally says. Then goes back to her novel.

I gaze past her, out the big picture windows. The rain beats hard again against the glass, giving me that fluttery feeling in my belly again. I wonder if Alice gets the same feeling every time it rains. I wonder if loud noises scare her, if she can go back into the centre of London without looking over her shoulder and wondering if the building behind is about to explode. I wonder what she remembers about that day. I'm wondering about a lot. I could just ask her. But that would mean letting her in, opening up to her. I don't know this girl. I don't know what she wants from me. All I know is that no one could possibly understand what I'm going through. Not even her.

Alice

'I don't know, Mom. This just seems too soon.'

I'm standing in front of the mirror in my bedroom, wearing my navy floral skirt that sits below the knee, gray ribbed tights, and my school jumper with the insignia on the chest. My mom stands behind me finishing the French braid she insisted would look good on me. She lied.

'It'll be good to return to a predictable routine, and be back with your peers.' She sounds like she's rehearsed that. She turns my body toward her and starts hairspraying loose strands. She pats them down against my head until I hear a crinkling sound like a crisp packet being scrunched up. I think the crisp packet is my hair.

We take the bus together, swaying silently beside each other. Outside the rain hits my face, and I flinch, remembering. I look to the school gates, a group of students rushing by me. I freeze at the entrance. 'I'll be fine from here,' I lie.

'Really?'

'Yeah, I should do this myself.'

'If you're sure.'

I nod and resist glancing a second time at the man who just passed us with a long, dark coat and a black backpack.

Mom hugs me tight. 'Be careful. Text me if you want me to come get you.'

'Will do. Thanks.'

I watch her leave and rub my chest as if I can physically calm my heart rate. But I can't. I stand for a moment longer, a stillness among the chaos of students, teachers and parents. Then when I can't take the stillness any longer, I start moving again, closer to the front door. I recognize a couple of girls ahead but they don't turn around, and even if they did they wouldn't notice me. If they don't notice me in a small IT lab, they're not going to notice me out here.

The school is smaller than I remember, the gates weaker. If a bomb went off the building would crumble and we would all die inside. A slight tremble on the ground around my feet unbalances me and I stagger back a few steps. It's just the Underground, it runs right below here.

Screams inside the building force my head to snap upwards. It's just people excited to see each other or telling a story, or the first years playing stupid childish games like tag or something. It's not . . .

It's not—

The bell blasts and I scream. I cover my ears, pushing so hard against my head that it hurts. I can't block it out, it's getting louder. Is it the school bell? It sounds different today. It's slightly higher-pitched, a burst of separate sounds then one long, endless stream. A little too loud. Perhaps too deep in tone. Maybe it's not an alarm at all, but a warning bell. No one else seems to be panicking apart from me, though. Everyone else seems to be going about their day, not noticing it. But they weren't there. They didn't see the chaos I did, the crowds, the blood. They didn't hear the screams I heard. They don't know. Or maybe they do know. Maybe they're a part of it. No one can be trusted, no street is safe.

Someone bumps my arm running into school and I fall to the ground imagining the crowds fleeing from the blast, knocking others over. Many stopped to pick each other up, while others ran faster, stepping over the fallen ones. I read somewhere once that people have three natural instinctive responses to an emergency – fight, flee, or freeze. I froze that day. I didn't run to safety or battle to save others. I just sat there, like I am now.

There's a car alarm going off too. I hear it above the school bell.

It's happening again.

I rush over to the black bin by the gates and cower behind it. I pull my knees into my chest and hold myself tight into a ball. Maybe the bombers won't see me if I'm small. I cover my ears to block out the alarms. It's not working, I still hear them. They're coming for me. I won't survive this time. Maybe I'll lose a leg too, or an arm, or my head.

The alarms get louder, pounding and pounding against my eardrums. It hurts. My brain is going to swell and explode, blood will seep out of my ears and nose.

I don't realize I'm screaming until the alarms stop. By then people within the gates have stopped and are now staring at me. A man in a burgundy blazer and tie starts walking over to me but I don't recognize him. What if he's not a teacher? He could be a terrorist. Anyone could be a terrorist.

I stagger to my feet and stumble against the bin. Then I turn and start running. My thighs throb, my body begs me to stop. I run and run and run until I can't run anymore. Air. I can't breathe.

I walk aimlessly through the streets, still in a fog of confusion and fear. I hear my heartbeat through my clothes. It's all I can hear at first, then it gets quieter and I start to hear the world. I hear footsteps, mumbled conversations, phones ringing, birds, raindrops on restaurant canopies opening for breakfast specials. I hear a boat. I open my eyes and glance over the bridge, seeing a Thames tour boat sailing down the river; tourists gripping their cameras. Some look up at me and wave, like I'm part of the sights, a static point of interest. I slowly wave back. A little boy in a red cap and a raincoat keeps waving, as the boat moves further away down the river, away from me, finally blurring out of sight. I cross the bridge and continue wandering the streets. Everyone moves so fast, passing each other but not really looking, living in the world but not really experiencing it. That's what I did. It was all about my books, my schoolwork, my future. I wish it was still about that. I wish that's all that occupies my thoughts. But it isn't. Now I've experienced life. And I don't like it. I don't like one moment of it. I can see now that books exist purely to transport us from this reality to another, a better one.

My legs are tired now so I sit down on a bench. It's stopped raining and patches of blue sky push through the gray clouds. I look down and notice an empty coffee cup under my bench. I bend down to pick it up, to throw it away. I hate litter on city streets. But as I do my jaw suddenly tightens and my fingers tremble as I remember my coffee from that morning, and how it spilled when Jack knocked into me. I remember how it trickled out the cup and spread over the pavement, seeping into the cracks. I stifle a cry. When I finally look up I realize I'm sitting outside London Bridge Hospital. I don't remember coming here, looking for this. But I found it, or it found me.

I fling my backpack over my shoulder and stagger exhausted inside. I sign in and head up to 10B. The door is open, a breeze flowing in through the window. When I enter I see a tray on the bedside table still full with breakfast. Jack is propped up, one of my magazines in his hand but he drops it to the floor when he sees me.

'I thought I told you—'

'I know. I just want to sit here for a while and not talk. Not think.'

I let my bag fall to the floor. Sweat spills down my face. I shimmy out of my school blazer and drop into the chair.

He continues to stare at me, but I ignore him and just stare at the tiled floor by my feet while my chest pounds and my mind keeps going back to the spilled coffee on the ground. I sit there for almost two hours in total silence, except for the short gasps of breath struggling to escape. I sit there until the screams fade from my ears and the dust clears from my eyes. And then I cry.

And he lets me.

Jack

Volunteers in yellow vests scattered about like buttercups in a field. Brightly coloured tents pitched at the finish line – some giving analytics of your run, pace breakdown, endurance zones, advanced performance metrics. Others boast a marketing campaign to rival any competitor, selling big-brand running and active wear or multi-sport watches with GPS tracking-technology. Then there's the sponsor tents where you can sit down at the end of a race, grab a sports drink or sneak a beer if you're lucky, and meet other athletes. A chance to connect with people who think like you, who have dreams and ambitions like you. People who remind you that there's more races to run, more athletes to bond with, more adventures to seek. I love those tents, those interactions, those moments.

Energising upbeat music blasts from every speaker around the marathon event village which takes months to plan and days to assemble, but usually only hours to take apart. Music that hopes to propel you through the finish line, past the other runners who hesitate or lag for a second too long allowing you to take the lead.

Food trucks tend to park in one area, all with potassium-filled and protein-packed hot meals, most you get for free with your race entry. I always refuel with a steak burger and chocolate milk. My dad always makes a beeline for the fish-and-chips van, and always regrets it. Oil, batter and salt: bad choice for a post-marathon meal, although sometimes it's worth it. The marathon village in Lille housed a crêperie on wheels. We tucked into about half a dozen sweet crêpes and savoury galettes, most flavours I'd never heard of or imagined being put together – champagne and cinnamon, beer and chocolate, filet mignon and Roquefort, orange ricotta with sweet fennel. That was a fantastic day.

All the perks that come with an upgraded race entry ticket pale in comparison to the best part of competing in a national marathon event – the crowds. Those who come to cheer on loved ones, and those who are there purely for the same adrenaline rush we athletes seek. A mix of people who just love to gather and socialise, or those who come for the food and atmosphere, and a small group who share the same goal – to one day be entrants themselves. To one day run alongside those who already can. I know how that feels. When I watch my dad compete in the adult runs I feel the same overwhelming desire to be on that start line with him. I can't compete in the major city marathons until my eighteenth birthday. London was supposed to be my first. I had my place for next April. That was when my dad and I were going to run our first race together, side by side on the start line, pounding the pavements of London in unison. Supporting each other, encouraging each other.

I can still hear it now. The crowd at my last race. I can hear them yelling, clanging cow bells and whistling with both hands. They're cheering me on, edging me closer to the finish line. I'm almost there—

'Jack?'

I glance up and see my mum standing over my bedside table. The sounds of whistling and bells fade from my ears.

'Hmm?'

My mum moves closer to me, clutching an envelope in her hand. 'You haven't opened this. It's addressed to you.'

'It's just a letter from Alice.'

'Aren't you going to read it?'

I shrug and look away. I don't feel like talking about Alice today.

My mum gently rubs my shoulder. The only part of my body that doesn't ache with pain. 'You know, Jack. You're very lucky in the sense that you have a lot of friends who care about you. You've had a lot of visitors, a lot of flowers and cards come every day. People ask after you constantly. You have a lot of people who are here for you. Perhaps, she doesn't. Maybe you're the only person she has.'

'But we're not friends.'

'I'm not asking you to be best friends with her. I'm just asking you to not turn her away. Let her in. Maybe talking to you is all she has right now.'

'Mum—'

'Please, Jack. If not for her, then do it for me.'

My mum has a big heart, she always has done. Helping people with her charities and fundraising galas and volunteering efforts is her passion. I can't fault her for wanting to help one more, even if that one is the last person I want to see.

I sigh deeply, and nod.

I can almost hear those crowds again. They stay at the back of my mind, playing with my memories, playing with my sadness.

Alice

'Do you want a takeaway tray?'

I blink at the five coffee varieties sitting on the counter, wondering how I envisioned carrying them down the street to the hospital. 'Um, yeah, that'd be great, thanks.'

'That'll be 15p. Sorry, we have to charge for disposable cups and trays now. You know, the environment and all.'

'Right, the environment,' I mutter, my eyes skimming across the tower of plastic water bottles stacked on the counter along with the plastic straws and minuscule glass jars of Dorset honey.

When I get outside, a group of tourists on city bikes whizz by and I remember the photo on Jack's Facebook of him and his friends biking the coastal trail on the west of Scotland. Jack, dressed in tight black cycling shorts and a fitted blue T-shirt. Blue like the color of an ocean on the brightest day possible with a sky so vivid and clear that the sea sparkles an effervescent cobalt blue. A sky so beautifully calm and inviting that even I would want to get my feet wet.

On the steps close to the river sit a couple. He says something funny and the girl giggles and throws her head back, her blonde hair lifting slightly in the breeze. They look a little like Jack and that girl Lauren from his photos. I watch them for a second longer, wondering what it would be like to be them, then turn towards the green hospital doors.

It's always so quiet in here. I feel like the only one who truly comes and goes, the rest confined here either for medical shifts or patients themselves. I never see anyone being discharged, or other visitors signing in at the front desk or wandering the hallways looking for the rooms of their family members or friends. Why am I the only one here all the time?

Although I don't exactly have a busy schedule. My days have been unexpectedly freed up since—

'Back so soon?'

This receptionist must hate me. I don't even know her name, yet I talk to her almost every day now.

'Visiting doesn't start for another ten minutes.'

Perhaps today isn't the day I'll ask her for her name. Maybe tomorrow.

'I'll wait,' I say. I perch on the closest armchair and balance the tray of cups on my lap.

She leans out of her seat to call to me. 'I don't know if Jack will be up for visitors today.'

'Can you ask, please?'

She nods and lifts the phone receiver to her ear. She turns away from me, her whispers muffled by the buzzing of the humidifier on her desk. I lean towards her but still can't hear anything. She cradles the phone between her cheek and shoulder and gets back to her computer screen. The tapping of long acrylic nails on plastic keys filter out the humidifier sounds. Is it a yes or no from upstairs? Probably a no. I gently slosh the warm liquid and wonder what would happen if I dropped the tray on these white chairs and all over this whitewashed flooring. Watch as spilled coffee stains this place, like the memory of it stains my thoughts. Would she yell, or just roll her eyes, not expecting anything less from me?

'You can go up,' she says, still cradling the receiver.

'Really?' I stifle a smile as I push open the stairway door, the tap-tap-tapping of nails and whirling of a moisture fan at my back. I'm worried about the temperature of the drinks by the time I reach Jack's room but perhaps lukewarm coffee is still an upgrade from what he's been getting here. A nurse walks by balancing a porcelain teapot and a large plate of muffins on a tray. Perhaps my lukewarm coffee in a paper cup won't be so appealing now.

The door's open again today. Jack sits propped up by half a dozen pillows, his lower body covered by a thick gray blanket. The blanket flattens out after his thighs and I suddenly feel breakfast churn in my belly. I wonder how he feels when he looks down.

He looks at me but doesn't say anything when I enter, so neither do I. I slide the tray onto the bedside table between two vases of fresh flowers. I shimmy out my coat. 'Coffee? I didn't know what you'd like so there's a latte – that's the one in front – a flat white, the one in the red lid is an Americano, this one here is a cappuccino, and the one at the back is the seasonal special. I think she said a lavender chai latte. I don't know what that will taste like though. It sounds . . . um . . . floral.'

His eyes flicker to me then the tray then back to the TV on the wall. An old episode of *The Simpsons* is playing. The one at the theme park where Bart and Lisa get stuck on the 'It's a Small World' ride. I like this one. Reminds me of the time I went to Disneyworld with my mom and dad. It was the only time we were ever in Florida. We drove there from Georgia. Took around five hours, I think. I'm not sure exactly, I just remember it felt like days being stuck on the backseat of a rental car with a broken A/C unit and a window sealed tight with child locks that my dad couldn't figure out. We'd parked in lot F, which I still recall because my dad told me, 'F for Fun.' I thought it was funny at the time. We waited for the little pull train that picks you up and brings you to the park entrance. We showed our ticket and got yellow wrist bands. Then we went through the metal turnstiles. Staff at the ticket office had greeted my dad by his military rank. He must have got a discount and had to show ID. Even Goofy addressed him correctly.

My favorite ride had been 'It's a Small World' which is probably odd because it's usually the one most people skip. The queue is always tiny, one of the reasons why I liked it so much, but it's predictable, repetitive. I know the song, I know the way the dolls move, I know the pace and rhythm of the boat as it sails gently through the water that I know is only two feet deep. I can see the metal tracks beneath the water, the direction of the plates, the slow, steady churns of the boat wheels as it sails past knee-high mountains of card-

97

board houses and plastic figures dressed in hats and satin clothes. My least favorite had been Splash Mountain. I hate rollercoasters, and I certainly hated being plunged 53 feet into cold water. And each time I plummeted down – yes, my dad insisted I went on at least twice to 'face my fear' – the water hit me in a different way, depending on where staff seated me in the single-row boat. The first time it hit me right in the face, filling my nostrils and stinging my eyes. The second time I turned away and it hit me on my cheek and at the back of my neck. I cried. Seems silly now, being terrified of a Disney ride, of being wet, being cold. I didn't know how safe I really was. I'll probably never feel that safe again. 'I miss my dad.'

Jack turns to me. I didn't mean to say that out loud. I feel silly again. I wiggle the lavender chai latte out the tray and plop down into the armchair. He's still looking at me. I take a sip of the coffee and immediately cough. When I look up, he's smiling.

'Definitely floral,' I splutter, sliding the cup back onto the table. 'Mind if I take the Americano?'

He shrugs and I feel slightly happy at receiving a response at least. I tip two sugar packets into the black coffee and sink back into the chair, cradling the lip of the cup between my hands and my chin. We watch the rest of *The Simpsons* episode in silence, bar the slurping of my coffee. It ends, the credits flashing on the screen in rhythm to the tune that I remember fondly from my childhood evenings, then Jack flicks to the next channel.

A BBC broadcast shows a group of heavily armed police

officers filing into a house in a residential area followed by images of five men. *'Following the tragic bombing of Leicester Square, members of the Met Police and MI5 have made several further arrests this morning in East London. At least five members of a known terrorist group have been taken into custody following one of the worst terrorist attacks in the UK where twenty-two people lost their lives and . . .'*

Jack quickly turns off the TV and throws the remote control on the floor. The crack echoes against the walls. Batteries spill out on the white tiles and roll towards me. We sit there in silence, images of the men responsible for what happened to us burning painfully in our minds.

Jack

I didn't ask her to leave yesterday and I didn't push the call button to have her removed by hospital security. I let her stay, sit, watch TV and drink her ridiculous-sounding coffees. I even engaged in a brief exchange over the drinks. Sort of. I don't dislike her because there's nothing to dislike. She seems like a nice person, albeit a little overly 'American'. We don't appear to have much in common, other than the obvious. She doesn't seem into athletics, or hiking or skiing, or travelling, or getting outside really. I just don't know how much longer to let this go on for. Do I let her visit me indefinitely? Do I try to forge a friendship from this? What is Alice – and my mum – expecting from me? I've been polite, isn't that enough?

Her letter still sits sealed on my bedside table beside another delivery of fresh flowers – gerbera daisies this time, my mum tells me. I slowly pick at the paper edges of the envelope and pull out the folded-up note. The first thing I notice is the neatness and precision of her handwriting. It's quite impressive. She's dated it. She wrote it the day before she caught me pretending to not hear. I wonder why she didn't give it to me then? I skim her words with my finger.

Jack,

I didn't know how else to communicate with you upon learning of your hearing loss.

You don't know me. We go to school together but I haven't been a student there for long and we have very different social circles. See, I move around a lot, never sticking to one place for much time. And because of it, I don't make friends easily – or at all. You probably think it's strange that I've been coming to the hospital since we don't know each other. Truth is, I'm not exactly sure why I do. I think that this is the first time in my life that I've needed a friend, and I realize I have none. I'm not asking you to be my friend, I know you have many. I'm just asking to keep visiting for a little longer, until you get discharged, maybe, then I'll leave you alone. We don't have to talk about that day, or what happened. I'm happy to not talk at all. I think I just need to be around someone who was there, who understands.

I will say one thing, though, since I have this opportunity, since I have your attention – I am so very sorry for that day. I'm sorry we collided and I'm sorry our exchange cost you those precious few minutes that you'll never get back.

If after reading this letter, you still want me to not visit then I'll respect that, and I wish you well.

Thank you for reading.
Regards,
Alice J. Winters

I fold the note slowly and loudly exhale. I think I've been holding my breath for that whole time. I stare at the torn envelope in my lap, the folded letter with the words still visible, and feel a hot sting at my eyes. The faces of the men on the news yesterday still flicker in my mind. I don't know Alice Winters but after this letter, maybe I should try to know her. Even for a short while, like she said, until my discharge. I can do that.

Alice

I stand at the door to his hospital room, peering inside. It's a little later than I usually come, close to dinnertime, and I can see my letter sitting on the bed in front of him. He's read it, now what? I can't figure out what he's thinking. His face is expressionless and his shoulders are stiff. Is he angry? Did I say too much, or not enough? In my first draft I wrote that I thought he might need me, then I realized how patronizing that sounded, like I'm doing him a favor when really it's the other way around. He'd be helping me, if he lets me in. I stand here for what feels like forever, awkwardly holding my takeaway coffee until he finally waves me in. I take a deep sigh of relief, and step through. I shuffle in and lean against the window ledge, my back to the river and to the rain. Why does it always rain in this country?

His eyes glance back at the envelope on his lap, and then to me. He slides it back onto the bedside table where I'd left it.

'Can I get you anything?' I ask. 'Water? Coffee?'

'No thanks,' he says slowly. His eyes briefly meet mine then he looks away. It feels so awkward around him now, like we're meeting properly for the first time. My cheeks feel warm like I'm blushing. I keep my eyes focused on the ground around my feet.

A gust of rain blasts the glass and I jump, a short scream escaping. When I look behind me, my reflection stares back in the window. Wide eyes, full of fear, mouth open, and my hands are trembling. It's just rain. When I turn back, Jack's looking at me with a pained expression on his face. Does the rain trigger any flashbacks for him? He glances away, and breathes heavily. Then he turns the TV on again. It looks like a new remote control. I wonder if he broke the last one. He avoids the news channels and instead we watch the end of a show called *Tipping Point* which reminds me of the penny-drop machine at an old arcade. Then the screen quickly changes to a chat show, showing a family of five arguing on the sofas, then onto an old episode of Family Fortunes which we call Family Feud in the US.

'*We asked a poll of people what is the most common kitchen appliance used in Britain . . .*'

'An oven,' I blurt out.

He looks at me, then back to the TV. 'A kettle,' he counters.

'*And our survey says, a kettle.*'

I glance at him. I think he's smirking.

'*Name a place you visit where you aren't allowed to touch anything . . .*'

'An art gallery.'

'A zoo,' Jack says.

'*Our survey says, a museum.*'

'Close enough,' I say.

'Best of three?' he asks. Now he's definitely smirking.

'I think we have time for best of nine.'

Jack

Yesterday was OK. She stayed for the whole of *Family Fortunes* – lost – and for the first part of *Tenable* – won, of course. Her knowledge of bird species and political leaders was impressive. And I didn't completely hate her company. It was nice, actually. When my friends visit, there's an unspoken pressure to keep the conversation up, to be positive and not act all negative and 'wounded' all the time. There's a lot of history between us, a lot of shared adventures, and now that just seems to add to the divide I feel when I see them. I feel different. I am different. And whether it's all in my head or they're feeling it too, something's changed when we all get together.

But with Alice, it was different yesterday. It was a little weird, of course, as we're still pretty much strangers to each other. But it wasn't forced. There was no pressure, and the majority of the time was spent just watching TV or sitting in silence. I don't feel pitied when she's here. In fact, I find myself sometimes worrying about her, like when she jumped at the rain. Rain brings me back to that day too, but not to the extent to which it seemed to unnerve Alice yesterday.

She's back again today. This time we've got through

another episode of *Tenable* and a repeat of *Only Connect*, both of which she is scarily good at. We've sat mostly in silence, bar a few quick awkward glances at each other to see if the other one is looking.

'Words that can be preceded by "under," she calls to the TV. She seems particularly skilled at *Only Connect* which makes me wonder if she has a social life at all.

'Seven years in Ireland . . .'

'Next clue,' she shouts.

'They can't hear you,' I mutter quietly.

'Six years in Russia . . .'

'Hmm,' she mumbles.

'Five years in France . . .'

'Length of Presidential terms!' she says, pointing to the TV screen.

I'm also wondering whether this will be the extent of her visits over the next few weeks. Me lying in bed watching her shout at a TV screen and managing to beat the contestants. I scoot onto my side. My back has been aching for days now. I'm not used to all this sitting and lying. I'm used to being up and moving my body. I reach back and try to grab a pillow to stuff lower down my back, hoping for some temporary relief.

Alice suddenly jumps up. 'Here, let me.' She slowly leans in at first then starts ferociously fluffing the pillows behind me, punching and slamming them.

'It's fine,' I stammer, but she keeps going.

'No, I want to help. Almost done.'

'Alice, I think that's—' No, she's not done. Now she's got

me upright, leaning over my tray table that still houses my leftover lunch. She's shaking the pillows now, one by one. Now she's slamming them on the wall.

'Watch out for the—'

Too late.

A corner of the pillow hits the emergency call button and suddenly the room is flooded with a silent red siren. It illuminates the space, even blocking out the sunlight streaming in from the window. She drops the pillow and starts backing away. Three medical staff rush in, one pulling on gloves already. The nurse at the back pushes an equipment trolley. Is that a defibrillator?

Alice stands at the window, still clutching a white pillow to her chest, mouth agape. Her cheeks burn red like her hair. 'I . . . I . . .'

'Sorry, false alarm. We hit the button by accident trying to sort the bed,' I quickly say.

The first nurse leans over and switches the alarm off. 'No problem. Just be careful where you fluff those pillows next time,' she smiles at me. She briefly glances at Alice, the smile fading from her face. Then she walks calmly out of the room, the other two following.

Silence fills the empty space, except for the low whirling of the air-conditioning vent in the corner and a faint flow of traffic from outside the window. Alice is still standing by the window, still not moving. I clear my throat and look her way. 'So, can I have my pillow back?'

Her eyes dart at me, her face still rigid and flushed. Then she softens around her jaw and forehead, and starts smiling.

Then she starts laughing, hysterically. It's the worst laugh I've ever heard. Small bursts of deep belly laughs, with the occasional high pitched cackle, and . . . was that a snort too?

I don't know what to do, except watch her keel over and get herself more worked up.

So I laugh with her.

Alice

'What are your favorite subjects at school?' I ask, leaning back in the chair by the window. We've been engaging in tentative conversation now for almost an hour, which for us is huge progress. The TV is off, which helps, I suppose, although I am very aware that a new episode of *Tenable* started five minutes ago. I resist the urge to reach for the remote.

'PE—'

'Of course,' I nod, smiling. 'My least favorite subject.'

'Languages. And English.'

'You enjoy reading?'

'I do. My family has a huge library at the house, and I love just looking at the books wondering what to read next. What about you?'

'All of the Sciences, Math, and also Modern Studies here because I like learning about your political system.'

'Hmm,' he says. He probably expected me to say that. I am a stereotype through and through: military transfer, no friends, academic pursuits, a ten-year life plan. 'What do you do for fun?'

'Fun? What's that?' I tease, raising an eyebrow. 'Just

kidding. I like reading too. I love the libraries and little bookshops in your city.'

'You should take a walk down Cecil Court sometime. It's a little alleyway near Covent Garden filled with antiquarian booksellers and rare finds.'

'Good to know, thanks.'

'What else do you do in your spare time?'

'I write poetry and I listen to music.'

'Will you read me some of your poetry sometime?'

'Definitely not,' I scoff. 'No way. But I'll play you some of the music I listen to, if you want?'

He smiles, 'Yeah, I'd like that.'

He's not what I thought he'd be, based on his social media profile. He's more than that. I knew he'd be articulate, well-read, funny and yes, a bit charming. But he's also kind, and a good listener. And oddly has a calming way about him. I thought he'd be bursting with impulsivity and adventure, but he seems quite grounded. I assumed we'd be polar opposites, and I guess we are in many ways but not in every aspect like I first thought. Sitting here and talking to him is strangely natural in a familiar kind of way, and not forced like you get with two people who have no apparent shared interests.

'When are you going back to school again?' he asks.

'I've actually been thinking about home-schooling. I bet the school has amazing tutors, and my grades are near perfect anyway so it's not like home-schooling is a risk to my academic future. In fact, some might say that I am an ideal candidate for independent study.'

Jack raises his head off the pillow and stares at me. 'Home-schooling?'

'Yeah.'

He shrugs and rests his head back on the propped pillow again.

'What? It's not completely uncommon,' I say.

'No, but it's completely weird.'

'How so?'

'Home-schooled kids are . . . odd. When they finally break out and make it to university, they're like unsocialized rabid animals.'

'Wow,' I laugh.

'Sorry.'

'I was home-schooled for a few years and I turned out okay,' I argue.

He looks at me strangely, then nods. He's probably still deciding that. I roll my eyes and swirl my latte to mix the espresso and milk again. It sloshes up the side and a drop splashes out the lip onto my hand. I lick it off and suddenly become aware that Jack is still looking at me. 'What?'

'So why home-schooling? Why not go back?'

I shrug. 'It's just a lot right now. And since I won't take the train, it takes forever to get into the city for school in the mornings.'

'Why won't you take the train?'

'They're too busy and . . . I don't know, *exposed*. Something might happen again,' I say quietly. Jack drops his gaze to the bed. 'No one in London seems to take the bus. Not if they can get to where they need to on the tube. It's much faster that way, so buses are pretty quiet usually.'

He nods. I think he understands why I'm avoiding crowds and tight, cramped spaces with few exits. 'Why did you home-school before?'

'I didn't have an easy time like you when I first started high school. Freshmen have a tough time anyway, but mine was even more difficult. People called me names and it got to me. So Mom decided to take me out for a bit. I had a tutor come to the house and studied online until it was time to move again. I guess that's the one good thing about moving around a lot. If I hate the school and the people, I know I won't be there for long anyway.'

'Sounds lonely,' he mutters.

'Sorry, visiting hours are up,' says a nurse from the hallway. She pulls a trolley into the room, filled with new bandages and dressing treatments.

I nod and gather up my hoodie and coat. 'See you.'

'Don't home-school,' he calls back.

'Why?'

'Because then they've won.'

The nurse slowly closes the door, leaving me standing in the dark hallway alone. Who did he mean by 'they' – the bullies, or the terrorists?

Jack

She fiddles with the speakers, turning them up so the music fills the whole room.

'What is this? From the 70s?'

'Seriously? It's First Aid Kit. They're the greatest modern folk band of our time. Listen, what about this one? You must like this one.' She cradles her phone in her hands and leans back in the armchair. 'This song reminds me of my dad. Listen to the lyrics. They're singing about Emmylou Harris and Gram Parsons, and June Carter and Johnny Cash. The great country singers. It's sort of like a tribute to the couples – to love, I guess.'

'They've got OK voices.'

'They're not just OK. They're amazing.'

'Skip forward. Let me hear the rest.' I reach for the Bose speaker on the bedside table but she playfully snatches it away.

'Only if you appreciate the sounds filling your uneducated ears.'

'Next time it's my turn. I'll show you what real music is. Not this American stuff.'

'They're Swedish.'

The nurse sticks her head in. 'Visiting hours are almost done, guys.'

'Please, just another few minutes,' Alice pleads, turning the volume down low.

The nurse sighs and looks behind, down the hallway. 'Clare's on shift in twenty minutes. If you're still here by then you'll definitely be in trouble, OK?'

'OK. Thanks, Sara.'

She leaves and Alice turns the volume back up.

'Do you know everyone's names?' I ask her.

'Yeah, don't you?'

'No.'

'That's because you're a snob.' She pulls a face and takes another swig of her ridiculously large coffee. 'And possibly because I've spent more time bargaining and pleading with staff to let me in so I've come to know them all quite well, except Mrs Clarence. She's a hard one to crack. She won't tell me her first name.'

'Who?'

'The receptionist downstairs.'

'I guess I don't make it downstairs very often,' I mumble, fidgeting with the covers on the bed. I don't know why. I'm not a fidgeter. That's for people who have nothing to do. I suppose, that's me now. My jaw suddenly aches.

She crosses and uncrosses her legs, then crosses them again. 'I've been thinking about what you said and I've decided to try school again.' She plays with a stray thread hanging from her skirt, tugging at it then winding it around her middle finger. She seems to pull on it until it goes white and numb, then releases it and watches the blood flow back in. Then she does it all over again.

'When?'

'It's all arranged for me to go back tomorrow.'

'Don't worry, it'll be fine. It'll suck because it's school, but it'll be fine.'

She's tugging on that thread again, this time scrunching her face as she wraps it around her finger tighter like she's trying to hurt herself. She pulls on it, so hard her cheeks burn red with effort. Then her body relaxes and she eases it off her finger. When she's done she places her hand in her lap and waits patiently for whatever feeling that was to pass.

I look away so she doesn't know I saw her.

Alice

The headteacher is waiting for me outside the side gate when I arrive with my mom. I muster up a weak morning greeting and stand awkwardly around them as they talk about me like I'm not there. They quietly discuss the schedule for the day, my classes, what I've missed, and finally 'protocol' if I have another panic attack. In front of us, students flood in through the main gate and hurry up the stone steps. The chatter around me intensifies as a large group of girls hover by the building doors, excitedly exchanging stories from the weekend. Sounds like there was a party at someone's house on Saturday. I wouldn't have got an invite even if things had been running as normal. Jack, on the other hand, would have been there no doubt. He would have arrived with that cute, skinny blonde Lauren from the Facebook photos, strolled in like it was just the first of many parties he had to attend that evening, and immediately been engaged in a group conversation where people laughed at all his jokes and hung onto his every word. He should be here right now. Not me.

'Ready, Alice?'

I glance at my mom who repeats Ms Perrie's question like I didn't hear it. 'Ready, sweetheart?'

Is there an option to say 'no' at this point? Probably not. I can't lie to my mom, so rather than reply 'yes' I just walk around them and begin the slow ascent into school. One foot in front of the other. Just keep going.

'Want me to stay a while?' Mom calls out.

I turn back and shake my head. I could try to fake a reassuring smile, but again, I can't lie to her. She'd see right through me. I stand there at the top of the steps and watch her walk away, her bag swinging against her hip. I want to scream, 'Don't go! Please don't leave me here!' I want to run down the steps and into her arms – where it's safe, where the bombs don't fall and the blood doesn't flow. I want to press my cheek against her shoulder so hard it blocks out the sounds.

Where it's safe.

Where it's safe . . .

But nowhere's safe.

Not here and not in my mother's arms. Not anymore.

So I don't scream after her and beg her to turn back. Instead I move deeper into the school, the walls tightening around me as the headteacher closes the doors behind us. We pick up my new schedule from the main office and she walks me to first period, Physics. I shuffle to the back and take a seat. I usually like to sit up front, it's easier to answer the teacher's questions and I get a better view of the SmartBoard for taking notes. But not today. I didn't even bring my notepad today. Today is just about being here. If I can get through today then tomorrow I'll concentrate on the content. I finally glance up and meet the eyes of the guy next to me. He's staring, and now so is the girl beside him, and soon the girl next to her. No one's noticed me since I first transferred here. I was a nobody, an insignificant, and now everyone sees me. It's funny, I thought I always wanted that. I don't.

I shift my chair to an angle that faces away from them, towards the window. If I can't see them, then maybe they can't see me, even though I know it doesn't work that way. The teacher is rabbiting on about astrophysics but I block out his voice until all I hear is the gentle hum of the air-conditioning unit in the back corner of the room and the odd student's pencil-tapping around me. The voices begin to overpower the humming, tapping, and occasional heeled footsteps of teachers passing by outside. Then whispers trickle from behind, creeping up over my shoulder and spilling out onto my desk, seeping into the wood and staining where I sit. I can't make out everything they're saying but I know they're talking about me. Now I want to know, so I lean back in my chair and lift my ear towards them.

'She looks fine to me.'

'Not a scratch on her.'

'Why did they give her so much time off?'

'I heard she doesn't need to sit exams.'

'What? Why?'

'Stress or something.'

'I wish I can skip exams. I'm stressed.'

'I heard she was nowhere near the blast when it went off.'

'I heard she wasn't even there.'

'That's Americans for you, exaggerate everything.'

119

'And here's Jack Addington lying in a coma; now, he's a real victim.'

'I heard he's on life support and might not make it.'

'Such a shame.'

There are so many voices now. I don't know who's who. I open my eyes and glance up at the teacher but he's looking at me too. Why is everyone focused on me? What do they want from me? I close my eyes again and rest my forehead down on my hand. Sliding my palm down over my eyes, darkness takes me for a moment.

Darkness. That's all I saw after the first blast. Then came fragments of light, spots of sunshine that seemed to sparkle off the pavement under me. And the cloud. The thick dense smoke. I can still smell it. It fills my nostrils and burns the tiny hairs in my nose. It circles me like a fog, but it doesn't block out those around me. I see them still. Watching me, whispering about me. I cover my eyes again—

A loud alarm fills the room, jolting me up from the desk. Students stand up and start shuffling towards the classroom door. Bags, pencil cases, notepads, they sit scattered across the empty tables. The siren gets louder. The teacher lightly touches my arm to get my attention. He's saying something but I can't make out what the words are at first. *Fire drill?* I look back and see my bag beside the desk. I gesture to it and try to tell him my phone is in there. I need to call my mom. I need to go home. I can't be here but he signals towards the door. Out in the hallway, bodies pack together and move towards the emergency exit. Footsteps flood the hallway, shoulders bumping into me. I no longer see my

120

teacher, he's gone. I edge towards the wall and let the stream of bodies trickle by.

It's happening again. It must be.

Sliding down the wall, I bump down on the floor and hug my knees to my chest.

Not again.

Not again.

I cup my hands over my face and let the world outside disappear. Hands are on me again, pulling at me, clawing at me. I push them away without looking up. I won't go out there. It's safer in here. It's a trick. They want us to leave the safety of this building, to go outside. They'll get us there. *They* – the bombs, the terrorists. They're winning. Because all I feel right now, all that's coursing through my veins, is terror. Absolute, infinite terror. Soon my screams are louder than the alarm.

Summer Blooms

PART 2

Meadows of yellow buttercups,
Sprigs of mint,
Clusters of flat basil,
Feathery pea shoots,
Bulbous bluebells,
Patches of snowdrops,
Broken glass,
Shards of metal,
Cracked tarmac,
Spatters of blood,
Open briefcases,
Papers spilling out,
Abandoned shoes,
Fields of daffodils and rows of poppies,
I see chaos,
And I see death.

Alice Winters

Jack

Slumped shoulders, slightly gaunt face that's lost the golden hue of time spent outdoors. Hair that now sits at the top of my shoulders and curls around my ears. A neck where a collarbone now juts out. A jawline that's sharp, and clenched. My hands are clean, too clean. Hospital clean. Usually they have dirt under the nails from rock scrambling while hiking or the palms are riddled with callouses from cycling long distances. They don't look or feel like my hands. These are the hands of a stranger, of someone who sits in a wheelchair staring at a mirror in a hospital room.

This is the first time I've looked at myself, since everything happened. I don't know who I see anymore. Yes, those are my eyes; 'bluer than the open water we just swam in,' Lauren said once. That's my nose, although it looks a little out of place now that I'm thinner than I used to be. My old clothes are too big on me, having lost a lot of muscle mass. Mum's tried her best to tailor my jeans at the knees, but it's still obvious. The cuts around my face have healed well, with minimal scarring. Not that anyone will be looking at my face these days. The absence of legs on a person really captures the attention. It's the main attraction. It's now, and forever will be, my one defining trait. I'm no longer mountain-climbing Jack, the Jack who has an unbeaten record on any junior squash court in London, the Jack who can finish a 150km cycle and then go for a run, Jack who will say yes to anything because everything is an adventure. Well, almost everything. Who is this new person? This isn't me. Please, don't let this reflection be me. I still think this is all one horrific nightmare. That I'm still unconscious from the explosion, that I'll wake in a hospital but be injury-free. This can't be my life now. My jaw throbs. I'm clenching it so tightly. A hard knock on the door startles me.

'Jack, you ready? Van's outside,' says my dad.

I close my eyes and take a sharp inhale. My friends are waiting downstairs for me. They're so excited for my discharge. I thought I was too. So why do I have this churning sensation in my belly that feels more like fear, than excite-ment? In here I have a goal, to get out. But out there, I have this overwhelming journey ahead. And I have no idea where to start. I raise my chin, swallow hard, and practise that smile that everyone downstairs will be looking for.

Alice

A large black van sits outside the hospital when I arrive. It's parked close to the curb, with a silver rubber-matted ramp spilling out onto the pavement edge. The windows look tinted like a celebrity escort vehicle. I wonder who's checking in today. A hospital this private and this nice must attract the wealthier patients, unlike the old clinic Mom and I went to once in the San Diego valley after she tripped down the stairs and landed on her ankle. We'd thought she'd fractured it, the way it swelled up and turned purple, but it ended up just being a bad sprain. She was on crutches for two weeks, rehab and physiotherapy for two months after that, until she could get back to her morning jogs and occasional weekend hikes with Dad when he was home.

I'm walking to the visitor log book when the sound of the elevator turns my head. The high-pitched beep fills the reception area and when the doors slide open I see Jack sitting in a wheelchair. His dad appears from behind and pushes him out into the lobby.

'Where are you going?' I ask.

His dad stops the chair at my feet and maneuvers around me to get to the desk.

'I'm being discharged early,' Jack says.

'Oh.' The room feels cold suddenly, as if someone's just opened a window and let a gush of cold air in. But it's summer outside. 'To where?'

'I'm going home.'

'Oh, of course. Is that your van outside?'

'Yeah, must be. Dad said they got a new one that can accommodate wheelchairs. How does it look?'

'Fancy,' I smile, feeling the forced pressure of it burrowing into my cheeks. Do I look as shocked as I feel?

'Looks like you get your days back to yourself.'

'What?'

'No more visiting me in hospital.'

'Right, yeah . . .' I don't know what to say. Everything I think of gives away how I'm really feeling inside, and I don't want him to know. It's silly because we barely know each other. 'Shame, I'd just gotten on first-name terms with Mrs Clarence. I was quite enjoying calling her Bridget.'

'You should visit her every now and then,' he laughs.

'Nah, I'm sure she's glad to see the back of me.'

'So you're at school again?'

'No, there's only a couple of weeks left before summer break. No point now,' I mutter. I won't burden him with my recollection of the fire-drill incident. This is his day.

'Any big summer plans?' he asks.

'No I guess not, not now you're being discharged.'

There it is again, that word, discharged.

'You?' Suddenly I feel like we're strangers, having bumped into each other on the street and making small talk about our summer plans. Next we'll be talking about the weather.

'Hopefully the weather will be nice this summer for you. First British summer, eh?'

There it is.

'You must be so happy to finally get out of here,' I mutter.

He smiles and nods.

'Discharged, finally. I'm so happy for you.' But why don't I feel happy for him? If I was a true friend, I'd want to see him out here, back to his old life and with the people who love him. Why do I suddenly feel left out, and left behind?

'Hey, look at you, Jack!' I turn round and see two guys from school. One of them looks a bit like Jack. The other is taller, bigger, with dark hair. They sport an attempt at facial hair and wear T-shirts that look two sizes too small.

'Guys, you know Alice from school.' He gestures towards me but I already know they won't recognize me. They've probably never glanced my way for a split second. 'Alice, this is Euan and Will.'

I smile and awkwardly hold out my hand, as if I'm being interviewed for a job. The bigger one laughs and cautiously takes it, practically dislocating all five fingers whilst shaking it.

'Ready, Jack?' asks the other one.

Mrs Addington appears from behind them. 'Ready?'

Jack nods, his shoulders stiffening. Is he okay?

'Thanks, boys, for your help today,' his mom continues.

'Not at all, Mrs Addington. We've missed our boy J here.'

Mrs Addington touches my arm gently, as I watch Jack being wheeled out. 'Alice, thank you for coming here so often to visit him. I hope you both stay in touch.'

'Of course,' is all I can manage just now.

'Take care of yourself. I hope to see you at the house.' She smiles then leaves out the same green doors I've been walking through for weeks.

Discharged.

I knew it was going to happen sometime, obviously. Patients in hospitals don't stay patients forever, they either get better and are discharged to go back to their old lives, or they – well, you know. Maybe that's why it's so confusing for me right now – Jack is neither 'better' in the 'whole' sense of the word, nor is he returning to his old life. He can't. Can he? And what happens to me now? After all these weeks of visiting him, all those conversations, all that effort in the beginning to find him, to know him. I thought we were becoming friends, like real friends. But that's what we agreed. I visit, we hang out – until he's discharged. And now he is. So that's it then. No more Jack Addington. Now what?

Jack

The first thing I notice when the van pulls up to my house is the new ramp that's been installed at the entryway. It changes the whole look of the front. It looks like the entrance to the hospital I just left, not to my home. I'm unloaded out of the van like a suitcase from the boot of a car. I'm still getting used to the chair, but I try for the ramp. The wheels catch on the crushed stone in the driveway.

'Sorry, I should have thought of that,' my mum mutters, a look of disappointment quickly spreading across her face.

'It's fine. I'll get used to it.' I slide the heel of my hand down on the wheels like they taught me at the hospital and start to edge myself up the ramp. It's harder in reality, and I can feel exactly where I've lost the muscle and strength in my arms and shoulders. My mum takes a step towards me. 'I'll get it,' I splutter, sweat already dripping. When I finally get to the top and into the house, I lean back in my chair and pant heavily. Then I continue pushing myself further inside the house, through the entryway, past the stairs that have been fitted with a mobile stairlift, up the next ramp into the kitchen. Dishes and containers of meals and homebakes from neighbours and family friends flood the countertops, vying for space.

'Here, I'll show you your new room.'

'I'm not in my bedroom upstairs anymore?'

'We thought – for the first couple of months – you'd be more comfortable down here in the guest suite?'

'Oh.' I'd actually been looking forward to sleeping in my own bed.

'Here, just take a look and see what you think,' my mum says, leading the way through the kitchen.

I follow after her, already struggling to keep up. But I pause at the back door.

'What's wrong?' she asks.

The shoe rack. It's empty. The white wooden rack that once held my run trainers, my trail runners, my hiking boots, my cleats for the bike, my squash shoes. I even leaned my hiking poles against the stand, and sometimes a squash racquet. But now it sits empty. The whole thing. This was the door I left from. I'd sit on the back step, lacing my trainers while staring out at the gardens my mum spent most of her days tending to. I'd breathe in the country air, stretch, then go down the garden path, out the back gate to the lane to start running. Down the farm road until the dead end then up through Epsom Downs, through the woods for about five miles, passing the fields where they hold the Derby every June then around and back home. I'd come through the back, slide out the shoes, spray them and place them on the rack for the next day's run.

'Sorry, Jack.' My mum gently places a hand on my shoulder.

'Your father and I thought it would be best to move your shoes to the cupboard for now.'

I nod slowly, and continue pushing myself down the hall. The guest room is tucked away at the back of the house with views of the garden I once played football in with my dad. It's a big space with an en-suite bathroom, and right next to the social room where I held parties for my friends and the gym where I trained for my events when the weather was bad. The indoor pool is back here too, not that I'll manage many swims now. My mum's replicated my bedroom upstairs as best she could. The walls are filled with photos and posters. The cupboard has all my clothes already hung up. A pile of schoolbooks sit on the desk by my laptop. Looks just like my bedroom. But it's not.

'Can I get you anything?'

'No, I'm fine. Thanks, Mum.'

'I'll leave you to it then. Let you settle in. Let me know if you want to take a nap, I can help you into bed.' She closes the door behind her, silence suddenly pouring in and trapping me. I glance around. For the first time in almost three months, I'm finally alone.

And I already hate it.

Alice

Heathrow Airport is packed with bodies. People leaving, people arriving, people just standing still while they wait on their loved ones. I couldn't get two feet through the doors without hyperventilating. So instead we're standing outside, near the drop-off zone. The cars make me nervous but at least we're away from the crowds and chaos. We stand facing the sliding doors, cardboard signs in our hands that we made with old Amazon packaging, a few multi-colored Sharpies and some silver star stickers. The corners are still a little damp from the drizzle of rain that greeted us when we left the house. One of the stars is stuck to my coat collar and I'm sure I have some pink Sharpie on my chin some-where. We don't get to do this very often for him because sometimes he flies direct to the military base but today he's flying commercial to get home to us faster.

'He should be coming through any moment now,' Mom says eagerly, checking her phone. And as if he heard her words, the doors open and there he is. His boots are polished meticulously so I can see my reflection from here. Camouflage print from neckline to boot edge, an array of medals pinned to his chest, and a crest of stripes encasing a star on his arm.

Even after twenty hours of sitting on a plane or walking between transfers, there's not a crease to be found. When I was young, he'd iron my clothes for hours. Straight edges, flat surfaces, absolutely no wrinkles. Now he doesn't even try to iron my clothes, mostly because I don't let him. I like looking a little 'imperfect', it matches the rest of my appearance, I guess.

My mom is in his arms, her sign on the floor by his feet. I'm still clutching mine, the sweat from my fingertips staining the edges. He releases her slowly and walks over to me. 'Alice Bear,' he says, his arms stretched out.

I close my eyes and hear him call me that over and over again, feeling like a child again, warm, safe. I rest my cheek against his chest as he hugs me tight, gently rocking side to side. He grips me tighter, and whispers in my ear, 'Sorry I couldn't get home sooner.' He finally releases me and I sink back down, suddenly aware of the people and sounds around us. Faces turn towards us but their eyes aren't on me this time, not like school. They're on my dad – the returning soldier. The war hero. As my dad picks up his camouflage duffel by his feet and hoists it over his shoulder, a man approaches us from the side. My whole body tenses. Sweat tickles the skin around my forehead and under my arms as the air around me heats up. I grab my dad's hand and squeeze tight. He doesn't flinch. His body manner doesn't change in the slightest. He stands strong, unnerved by this stranger in dark clothing with black eyes and creases in his forehead, who now stands in front of us. The man holds his hand out. My dad takes it and they shake.

'Thank you, for all you guys are doing over there,' he says.

My dad nods and squeezes my hand back to let me know that I'm okay. The man walks away, back to his family who wait for him with their suitcases. They all smile at us. My dad puts his hand around my shoulders and we slowly walk back to the car.

At home he shifts through each room, surveying the change, the distance that's suddenly formed between him and this place we now call home. I lean against the doorframe watching him, still dressed in his uniform. 'How are you doing?' I ask.

He stops pacing and turns to me. 'I should be asking you that.'

I shrug my shoulders and kick gently at the rug beneath my feet. 'You back for long?'

'For as long as I can.'

He sits finally, pulling up the knees of his trousers first. He doesn't lean back in the sofa Mom's covered in an array of colored plaid cushions, but perches on the edge like he's waiting for something. He stands suddenly as Mom enters the room with a tray. She balances glasses filled with juice and a plate of chocolate chip cookies from Marks & Spencer that she's about to tell Dad she freshly baked this morning. She pauses, the tray in her hand shaking slightly, then laughs nervously at the unusual formality between us. It's Dad, just Dad. He laughs with her and takes the tray from her hands, placing it down on the coffee table.

'I'll go change,' he says. He leans in and gives her a soft kiss on her forehead. Then he walks over to me and does the same. 'We'll go for a walk when I come back down? You can show me the neighborhood.'

We walk with the warm breeze at our backs and the sun on our faces. It's a gentle sun here that tickles our cheeks and caresses the tops of our noses, not like the sun we have back in the US. I lead my dad down towards the river, passing through Kneller Park where dogs run free from their lead and do a quick circular of Mereway Nature Park which takes about fifteen minutes. It's pretty congested here with residential streets, large chain grocery stores like Tesco and gas stations on every corner, but the few grassy areas are lovely and quiet. The ground crunches under the soles of my trainers, as low-hanging branches skim the crown of my head.

'It's been a long time since we've walked just the two of us,' he says finally, breaking the silence.

'It's been a long time since you've been home,' I mumble, looking away.

'It's been hard for me too, Alice.'

'Sorry, I'm not trying to make you feel guilty. What you do is really important.'

He leans over and rubs my back, like when I was a child and full of the flu.

'Your mom told me about your friend Jack.'

'He's not really a friend. I didn't know him at school before – before . . .' Before It.

'Your mom says you've been visiting him quite a bit since.'

'Yeah, but I don't really see him anymore.' I kick at some stones on the path. My mind wanders back to the hospital, to the van that took him away after he was discharged.

'Why not?'

'He was discharged.'

'And?'

'And we said at the time that I'd come hang out at the hospital until he got discharged, and well, he did.'

'And you're sticking to it? Who set that rule?'

I screw up my face. 'I think I did?' It sounds silly now. Did I even ask him if he still wants to hang out after he was discharged? 'I don't know. But anyway, he probably doesn't need me now that he's home.'

'He needs you more than ever now.' My dad sighs and looks to the stream on his right, partially shielded by a large willow tree that hangs low. 'Do you remember in Malaysia when your mother and I went through that rough patch?'

I nod, my body recoiling at the memory. I used to hear them fight from my bedroom. I'd lie on my bed, headphones on, music blasting trying to drown out the voices. It didn't always work. Sometimes the sounds from the hallway would snake in under the door, past the hum of the air-conditioning unit and creep up to my bed where I lay. Sometimes I heard exactly what was said, other times it was muffled voices and the occasional door slam. I'd never seen my parents argue like that before. My dad had just returned early from a two-year stint and was recovering from a shrapnel injury to his left shoulder.

'I'd spent a week in the hospital getting stitches then fighting that infection, but that was the easy part. It was coming home that was harder. Coming home to normality, knowing I'd just seen my friends shot at in a raid, knowing

I was one of the few that survived. I saw men, close friends, die that day. I had nightmares about it for months. Still do.'

I stop walking. 'I didn't know that.'

'I didn't know how to talk about it. I felt like I couldn't talk about it to you or your mom because you hadn't been there. It's hard to talk about things like that to someone that wasn't there. So I kept it in, until I couldn't anymore. Going home was harder than I'd ever expected. Especially when I knew there were families out there who'd never see their dads again. I just felt . . .'

'Guilty,' I say. I reach up and skim my cheek with my fingertips. They're wet. I hadn't even noticed.

'Jack needs you more than ever. He's going to be struggling getting back to what everyone else thinks is normal for him. Because it's not. Especially with the injuries he sustained. Everything will be different for him. Do you know where he lives?'

'Yeah, his mom gave me their address. I have his number too.'

'Well, call him.'

'What if he doesn't want to speak to me?'

'He will.'

When we get back to the house I write out a message to him. My fingers hover above the 'send' button. Uneasiness washes over as I imagine his face when he receives a text from me. He won't want to hear from me. He already has friends. A lot. So I delete the text and drop my phone on the bed.

Jack

Lauren sits opposite me, too far back in the sofa so she looks tiny and uncomfortable. She wriggles but only seems to wedge herself between the stiff pillows more. There are a lot of pillows on the sofa. My mum likes decorative, lacy, frilly, boxy pillows. The stiffer and more nonfunctional, the better. She finally unwedges herself and scoots to the front of the sofa. She clasps her hands on her lap and continues looking around the room, anywhere but at me.

'So, how's school?' I finally ask. It's been twenty minutes of silence. I can't take any more. I wish I was still pretending to have my hearing blown out.

'It's summer.'

'Oh right. Sorry, my days are all mixed up.'

She smiles, sympathetically, like keeping track of days is understandably a very challenging task for me now. 'You look . . . good.'

And there's the first polite lie of the conversation. I most certainly do not look 'good' by any standards. I'm skinny, having spent over three months in a hospital bed, I have chin stubble, and I'm in joggers that have a stain on the thigh. She,

140

however, does look good. She always does. We used to look good together. But now if someone were to take a photo, it would be laughable. Her and me together. It just doesn't work anymore. And this awkwardness and distance that's grown between us confirms that.

'I've sent you a few messages.'

'Yeah, sorry, been busy,' I mutter. And there's the second polite lie. Busy is the opposite of what I've been.

She scoots further down the sofa, closer to me. 'You know, if you ever want to talk, Jack, I'm here.'

My belly flips and I clench my jaw to make it stop. I know she's trying but there's nothing she can help me with. I don't know how to talk to her. She couldn't handle some of the things that I want to say, want to vent, want to scream. She couldn't understand the rage inside me. So I simply nod, and ignore her offer.

'I don't know what's going on here, Jack. You don't answer my calls. You don't text me back, and now you can barely say two words to me.' Her cheeks flush and her eyes water at the corners. I hate seeing her like this. Even if there's nothing between us anymore, she's still a friend and I still care about her.

But I don't tell her that.

She stands and loops her handbag over her shoulder. She stands, waiting for me to tell her to sit back down. But I don't. I don't say anything, and she leaves. When the living-room door slams, I hear polite murmurings in the kitchen between her and my mum and then she's gone.

'Is everything OK?' my mum asks after.

I shake my head. 'If Lauren comes back, can you tell her I'm not seeing visitors or I'm sleeping or something?'

There's a long pause before my mum clears her throat. 'OK,' she says quietly, then shuts the door, leaving me here in this cold, stiff, formal living room that we don't even use on special occasions like birthdays or Christmas.

I slam my hand on the armrest and feel a shooting pain up my arm. Feels good to feel something again. I need to get out of here. I need space, I need air, I need . . . something to change. I take a deep inhale and pull out my phone; I still have a photo of Lauren and me at a party last term as my wallpaper. I immediately jump to my settings and open up my recent albums to choose from. Travel images, nature shots and photos of me skiing, hiking and cycling come up. None of which I want to see daily, and be reminded of. So I select one of the default images, of what looks like the inside of a bubble. I'm not sure but at least it doesn't remind me of anything from my past life. Now that Lauren's gone from my homescreen, I scroll down to my WhatsApp group with Will, Euan and Alex. I want to tell them about my conversation with Lauren, about how I'm feeling, how I want to throw this chair against the wall and then myself. But when I start typing, I suddenly don't know what to say. I've never needed advice before or an opportunity to vent. I've never had any issues or stress in my life, therefore I've never needed anyone to talk to. How do I voice what's going on inside my head right now? And if I do, what if they don't know what to say, what if I make them feel awkward. Or worse, what if they just don't care? It's silly, I've known those guys for years. I went to primary school with them. I should feel comfortable enough to say absolutely anything to them. But 'this' is something they know nothing about. They can't help me, even if they wanted to. Everything they say, all the advice they have, will be meaningless because they don't know what I'm truly feeling. They don't know what I've been through, what I'm going through. Like with Lauren, there's this huge gap between me and the guys right now, and I don't know how to close it. This isn't something I can simply 'get over' with a cold beer and a game of golf or a 100km cycle with them.

I delete my message to the group and instead scroll through my phonebook, looking for Alice. Then I type and press 'send' before I change my mind. She responds right away.

Alice

My dad drops me off by the road, the engine still running just in case I change my mind. Jack's house is easy to identify, it sticks out amongst the fields and country lanes. It's huge with whitewashed stone walls blanketed in Virginia creeper and a long, gated entrance up to the front door. I count at least four chimneys dotted along the roof and a crushed-stone path leading from the drive and disappearing around the back of the house. I wonder what's housed in the back, perhaps tennis courts or a pool, maybe even a second home? In the driveway are three black cars and an array of potted flowers in full bloom. I've seen houses like this back in the US, especially in Texas where everything is bigger. Properties like this are owned by NBA stars or privileged politicians, and feature on TV shows such as Million Dollar Properties and Live Rich: Real Estate Special. My hands are shaking as I approach the front door. I was buzzed in at the front gate after a ten-minute explanation of who I am and why I'm here. I had to disclose my name, address and date of birth. I'm surprised they didn't ask for my CV and social security number. Then I stared into a small round camera lens, like I was having passport photos done. Getting in here is harder than getting through Heathrow Airport.

I press a finger on the bell and wait for a deep gong to vibrate through the ground I stand on and all through the house. Or maybe a tinkle of bells like in Downton Abbey. But nothing. Is it broken? I push it again, and again, and well, I guess just for fun, one more time. The door swings open and a tall man stands in the doorway, wearing a black shirt tucked into gray trousers that look like they've been ironed by my dad and his regiment for a training drill. 'Alice Winters?'

I nod, and wonder if this is the butler, a distant relative, or a bodyguard about to take me down.

'Come in. Jack has been expecting you.'

I stumble through the door into a large entryway with tiled flooring and fleur-de-lis motifs. A side table sits by the wall, stacked high with unopened cards and letters. All for Jack, I'm sure. Framed photos line the opposite wall, mostly of Jack but there's the occasional one of his parents – wedding day, possibly honeymoon, and then them standing beside . . . wait, is that—

'Prince Charles.' Jack sits in his wheelchair under an archway that seems to lead into another branch of the house. He looks different out of the hospital. He looks . . . smaller.

I point at the photo, framed in antique bronze. 'Your parents know the royal family? What, are they close friends? Do they have a WhatsApp group?'

He laughs, 'Not exactly. My mum does a lot of charity work for the Prince's Trust. This was taken at a fundraising gala a few years ago.'

Mrs Addington looks beautiful, as usual. Her slender frame is silhouetted in a long, fitted emerald green dress with matching jewelry. Her hair is tied back neatly in a bun to show off the earrings which seem to sparkle even in this photo. I wonder if she could ever be friends with my mom – would they find common interests, shared passions? Or would their only connection be us – be the bombing that brought Jack and I together?

I know my mom's been finding it hard to meet people, to socialize since moving here. Unlike me, she seems to care about that. I've always been a bit of a loner. I prefer my own company. No one really understands what it's like to move around so much, to never really feel at home or settle anywhere, to always feel detached from everything. But my mom struggles with the military family life. She's always had a lot of friends. She was really popular at school. High school prom queen – that's her. She had a crown and everything. But then she met my dad and he joined the army, and his first relocation came faster than either of them expected. She's been active as a 'military wife' as much as she could be. When we lived in Texas she hosted book club evenings, wine and cheese nights, and dinners with the other military wives. When we moved to the East Coast, she organized fundraisers like bake sales and Fourth of July BBQs for the military community. But since coming here, she's not found her place. She didn't really connect with the other military families. She feels like an outsider, much like me. But whereas I'm used to that feeling, I'm familiar and honestly quite content with that, she's struggling. Some days I find her going through old photo albums of her high school days, of the days before moving vans, cardboard boxes, shipping containers and airline tickets. Facebook doesn't help. While she busies herself with profile posts of yoga outside and of the odd solo robin that flutters into the garden, there's always someone from her old friendship circle that boasts pictures from a recent girls' trip or reunion dinner. She used to 'like' all those posts, occasionally comment with a 'Have fun!' or wine glass emoji, now she just scrolls through the photos then pretends she never saw them, that they don't bother her. I told her to reach out to her old friends, but she just shrugged and said, 'They've probably forgotten about me now.' This move was the hardest. In the past, when bake sales and book clubs didn't cut it with the stationed military wives, she could turn to work colleagues for friendships. But she couldn't get a visa here to work. Other parents at my school aren't that friendly. It doesn't help that I'm one of the few low-income 'scholarship kids' there. And our neighbors kind of keep to themselves. We're different here. We stand out. People look at my mom's tie-dye leggings, occasional pink-tinted hair, and judge her loud American laugh and yoga-hippie lifestyle. They don't know how lucky they'd be to have her as a friend.

'Do you want to come out the back?'

I turn and start wandering towards him. 'I don't know, what's 'out the back' in a house like this?'

His wheel gets stuck in the doorway as he tries to turn around. He curses under his breath, his cheeks turning a light coral.

I discreetly nudge the wheel past the wooden doorframe

with my trainer as I gesture up to the wall behind him. 'You play squash too?'

'Captain of the school team,' he says looking up.

'Of course you are,' I scoff. 'Anything else I don't know about you?'

He pushes the heel of his palm against the wheels and thrusts forward. We move through a large kitchen with a center island made of gray swirled marble or granite of some kind, and enter a thin hallway with three doors on each side. He opens the first door, and wheels in. 'I sail too, and I speak three different languages. I meet with language tutors in my free time.'

'Free time? Do you even know what that is? Don't you ever just want to veg out on the sofa with a pizza and a good book or some trash reality TV?'

'Sitting bores me.'

'Not me. I quite enjoy it.'

Jack points to a blue journal sticking out my open bag. 'Is that your poetry?'

I immediately move my bag away. 'Maybe.' I'm not ready for people to read my poems. They were never meant to be reviewed by others. They're mine, just for me. A way to write down words or sentences that float in my mind with nowhere to go. I don't always use the journal, sometimes I just scribble on napkins, backs of envelopes, stray paper, whatever I can find. Sometimes I keep them, glue them into the journal, and sometimes I throw them away.

Jack pushes the door open to a large games room. 'Where are we?' I ask. White leather stools circle the wooden bar table that houses most of the beverages we're not supposed to know about at this age, let alone be left unsupervised with. Brown leather armchairs and a sofa line the walls and are angled towards a large pool table in the center. Hunting rifles are mounted in glass on the wall in front of me.

'My social room.'

'A social room? What is that?'

'A room where my friends and I can hang out without anyone bothering us.'

'And the booze?'

'We only house the fifteen-year-old scotch here and mildly matured wines. The good stuff is down in the cellar.'

'The "good stuff",' I smirk. 'I wouldn't even know what that is.'

'Take a guess.'

'Tequila.'

'Tequila? This isn't spring break in Mexico. We're in London. I'm talking about a 1982 Bordeaux Pauillac.'

'Wow. Your life and my life couldn't be further apart,' I laugh, settling into one of the armchairs. My body melts into it and I suddenly feel a nap coming on. These really are comfortable.

'Maybe we're not as different as you think,' he mutters, rolling a black ball under his palm on the pool table.

'No, I'm not a marathon runner, if that's what you're thinking, although I know my athletic physique can be deceiving,' I smirk.

He launches the ball against the edge of the table, it bounces off and steers directly into an empty pocket.

'Oh right, yeah, we've both been almost blown up. Forgot about that. Is that what you mean by "not so different"?' I say.

He rolls his eyes and wheels himself away from the table over to the large window.

'Whoa, is that your garden?' I ask, coming up behind him. The back of his chair is covered with stickers, inked markings of messages from friends at school. WE MISS YOU JACK to SORRY to COME BACK SOON!

'Nice shrine.'

He doesn't turn around. 'They're stupid. What do they know?'

I nod, lightly tracing each message with my fingertips. How do you convey sympathy or empathy for something you could never understand unless you were there? I was there and I can barely understand it.

'At least people care about you. I didn't get any Get Well or Thinking of You cards. Not even from distant relatives.'

'You can take mine, I don't know what to do with them. Line them up? Frame them? They come by the dozen almost every day. I'm not dead, so is it even appropriate to send a sympathy card? Mum's started donating the flowers to the local hospice. They were beginning to swamp the shelves and tables.'

'Have you had many visitors since you got home?'

'Not so much. Do you know the papers contact my parents all the time asking for an interview?'

'Yeah, I had a couple of calls too. My mom just pretended they had the wrong number and they stopped calling.'

'Smart. My mum made the mistake of talking to one. Now they ring all the time.'

A dull creaking seeps in from under the door, followed by some muffled footsteps.

'That's just my mum. She's always just outside the door, waiting to see if I need anything.'

'That's nice of her.'

'Everyone just wants to feel useful.' He rolls his eyes.

'Is that so wrong?'

He pushes himself away from the window and slams his chair into the armchair. Then he edges back and drives into it again.

'Careful, I don't think the expensive leather can handle the impact,' I smile, dropping down into it again.

He scoffs and shakes his head.

I lean forward and rest my hands on my lap. They're only inches from his knees. We're physically closer than we've ever been before, pulled into this little bubble we've created around us. Him in his wheelchair, me in my fog of anxiety. My loud breathing stifles his, and I can feel my chest pounding. Suddenly, I feel like we're the only two people in the whole world. And that doesn't scare me. In fact, it calms me. I close my eyes for a moment and continue feeling the breath building in my body, from my toes to my fingertips. He doesn't pull back or turn his head away. 'I feel . . . I don't know how to describe it,' he says, finally breaking the silence between us.

'I know. I feel it too,' I whisper.

'Sometimes I wonder if it would have been better if we'd died too.'

A warm tear escapes my eye and before I can catch it, it spills down my cheek and onto my collar. 'But we didn't die. We're alive,' I say. His hands quiver in front of me. I place mine on top of his and his trembling stops. I swallow my next tear and it burns my throat. 'So let's start living.'

'I don't know how,' he mutters.

'Well, what do you want to do?'

'What kind of question is that?' He slides his hands out from under mine.

'A simple one. What do you want?'

He throws his hands in the air. 'Look at me! I want out of this chair! I want to get back to all the normal things I used to do! I want to run! I want to play tennis, ski, climb a mountain, hang out with my friends without them all looking at me with that pitying expression they all have.'

'So, let's do it?'

'What?'

'You want to go outside?'

'Yeah, I want to go outside! I hate being cooped up like this, with my mum hovering outside every door I close!'

The creaking intensifies then the footsteps move away.

'I think she heard that.'

'Good!' he yells at the door.

'Well, I want to learn how to be outside without freaking out every time, without thinking another bomb is going to go off. Because unlike you, I actually would prefer to stay cooped up, to never have to leave the house again.'

He shrugs.

'So let's do it.'

'You want to go for a run?' he laughs. 'I might find it hard to keep up.'

'Actually, I think you'd still be faster than me. But no, that's not exactly what I had in mind. We can find other things to do that gets us both out the house and away from all this.'

He rolls his eyes and starts backing up, away from me.

'Fine,' I say, sliding off the chair. I start for the door. 'Stay here – all summer, all cooped up.' I turn the knob and yank it towards me.

'What do you have in mind?'

I try not to smile, but I can feel the corners of my mouth creeping upwards. 'Not sure yet but I can come hang out tomorrow?'

'See you tomorrow then.'

Jack

Instagram.
Facebook.
Snapchat.
TikTok.
Strava.
I have profiles on all of them. Before this, I uploaded group cycles with friends, travel adventures, race times, event images. I used social media to document my achievements and engage with similarly minded people. I didn't post photos of what I had for dinner or filtered selfies where I have dog ears or twinkling stars around my head, but retweets, reposts, tagging, likes, loves, comments, hashtags, Insta-stories, all competing for engagements feeds – I did all that. And I did it well. Every time I posted a new photo or a personal update from a holiday, the likes poured in. I got a new Facebook friend request almost every day. Followers flooded my Instagram account and many of my photos were featured on athletic and travel group feeds. I never understood people who didn't have a profile on at least one social media platform. Until now. I realise now, having not posted anything since the day before the bombing,

that if you're not doing something then you have nothing to post. I don't know if I'll ever post again. Anything I do upload will just be met with messages of condolence, sympathetic comments and that annoying emoji that holds a heart.

A light knock on the door startles me. I log out of my Facebook app and slide the phone in my pocket.

'Jack? Alice is here,' says my mum.

'I'm coming out.'

I wheel myself down the hall and bump across the threshold into the kitchen. Alice stands at the centre island, hands clasped in front. A plate of pastries and croissants sits on the counter beside her with a teapot and small ceramic pots of sugar cubes and honey. My mum is over by the kettle filling the cafétière. The smell of coffee floods the kitchen, spilling aromas of chocolate and oak around us.

'Hey,' Alice says.

'Hey.'

My mum potters around, placing the French press next to the platter of breakfast treats, then sorting napkins. Alice smiles at me awkwardly, hands still clasped. She gazes around the kitchen and starts to whistle.

'What is that?' I ask.

'The tune? *Star Wars.*'

I nod and we continue standing in the kitchen while my mum circles around us. She's now watering the plant pots on the windowsill. The sun shines sharply through the windows, striking us in the face. 'Want to go sit outside in the garden?' Alice nods, then slowly slips a custard pastry off the plate onto a napkin. She licks her fingers and turns for the back door. I ease myself down the ramp behind her, and out into the sunshine. It hits my face, warms my cheeks, my hair, my hands.

The garden stretches over fifteen acres, some of it lost to the woods by the farm. Most of it is trimmed, watered, and flooded with vibrant flowers, many I can't name. My mum loves being out in the garden. We have a landscaper and gardener who are here regularly, but in between my mum does the maintenance work. I often find her reading a gardening book on rainy mornings – the best mornings for longer runs in the country.

'Wow. This is all yours?' asks Alice, gesturing to the garden. 'And here I thought an eight by ten shed and a rusty swing was a big garden by British standards.'

We head down the stone path towards the rose patch, by the apple and peach trees. There are blackberry bushes over to the right that my mum makes great jam from. The strawberries by the bird baths are often picked at by the rabbits and birds. We follow the path to the left and head further away from the house, until it starts to fade at our backs. The bench by the duck pond is my favourite place to come to. There's a patch of grass that seems to always get the sun, even in the winter months. You can see the pond and the ducks from here, and you're close enough to smell the gardenias and roses. And if you're lucky, you can pluck a ripe fruit from one of the trees.

'I can't believe you live here. I'd never leave this place if I lived here. Why do you travel so much?'

'I won't be travelling so much anymore.'

'You can get a wheelchair on an airplane, you know.'

I shrug and gaze around. It really is beautiful here. There are so many places in this garden to explore, to hide in. There's even a small cairn at the bottom by the brook that runs through our property and onto the next. London feels like thousands of miles away. I pull the brake lever on my chair and lean back. The sun beats down on my face. It's probably around 25 degrees and it's not even midday. Alice tiptoes carefully between the flowers. She weakly lifts herself up onto a low wall that separates the roses from the fruit trees, and sits on the top, legs dangling over. She starts picking at the pastry in her hands, flakes falling around her. My phone vibrates so I slide it out. A Facebook notification tells me I have four friends with birthdays today and there's a new message on the Messenger group labelled 'Ski Trip Plans'. I won't look at that one. They know I can't go, but my mates would never take me off the group. My thumb hovers above the 'Leave Chat' option.

'What are you doing?' she asks.

'Nothing. Just scrolling through Facebook,' I mumble, stuffing my phone back into my pocket. I can't do it. Not now anyway. I'll just mute the notifications from the ski group until I can find the courage to leave the group discussion completely. I don't want to know their plans, everything I'll be missing out on.

'Why?' she asks. She kicks her legs off the wall wildly, like she's on a rollercoaster or something. 'Social media messes with your mind.'

'You sound like my mum,' I scoff.

157

'I'm serious. No one actually puts their real life on social media. What you see is just the highlights reel.'

I think of my travelling, my events, my races, my ski trips – that was my real life. Not this. 'Are you on social media?'

'Nope.'

'Nothing at all?'

'I'm off the grid,' she says, sliding on her sunglasses. Frames as red as the hair that curls down her back.

'I don't think I've ever met anyone not on social media, even if it's just to keep in touch with friends.'

'See, that's where we differ, Addington. I've never been in one place for a long enough time to make friends to warrant a social media account to stay in touch.'

'You don't talk to anyone from your old schools?'

She shrugs and rests her hands on her knees. 'Do you think if I moved tomorrow you and I would stay in touch?'

I shrug and look up at her on the wall, high above, floating over the yellow roses and white gardenias. Honestly, I don't know if we'd stay in touch. Do I really know Alice Winters at all? She hops down off the wall, stumbling over a rock at the bottom.

'So where to tomorrow?' she asks.

'You want to hang out again tomorrow?'

'Unless you don't?'

'Sounds good. It's not like I have any other plans,' I shrug, backing the chair up onto the stone path again.

She walks slowly beside me. 'Let's go somewhere away from here.'

'I don't know if my mum will let me leave the house grounds.'

'Well, she's going to have to at some point. You can't stay here all summer. I'll talk to her.'

'Good luck with that!' I laugh. 'Where are you thinking of anyway?'

She looks around, glancing back at the roses and gardenias. 'I have an idea.'

Alice

'What are you wearing?'

I stand at his door the next morning, 9:55 a.m., wearing beige chinos, a sun visor and a large oversized pair of sunglasses.

'Are we going on an expedition to an animal safari?' he laughs.

I slide the glasses off. 'I thought for the summer it might be fun if we adopted a herb patch in a community garden in the city.'

'Adopted a herb patch?' he says slowly.

'Yes, you're saying it right, don't worry.'

'That's the concern.'

'It'll be fun! We'll go down there once a week and tend to it. It'll give us something concrete to physically take care of and watch all summer.'

'You're serious?'

'Of course! Now, do you have a hat to keep the sun off your face so you don't burn?'

'I tan really well.'

'Of course you do,' I mumble, reaching for his chair handles.

'How do you propose we get to this 'community garden' once a week? You going to wheel me there by hand?'

'We drive. Your parents put me on the insurance last night so I'm going to drive us.'

'Can you even drive?'

'Sure,' I shrug.

'Can you legally drive over here in the UK?'

'It's the same thing as driving in the US.'

'Actually, it's not. We drive on the opposite side.'

'Really? You do?'

He grabs his wheel, immediately stopping himself as I try to push him up the ramp of the van.

'Kidding!' He exhales loudly as I laugh.

The guy from yesterday appears from beside the van. He gently takes the chair from me. 'Here, let me help.'

I stand aside and watch as he wheels Jack up and into the van with complete ease, anchoring his wheels down to the metal flooring. I lean in, watching him. 'See this here? Back the chair up into the Q-Lock until you hear it click. Don't forget the wheel brakes.'

'Into the what?' I ask.

Jack shrugs. 'I can show her. I do still have function in my brain . . . for now.'

I roll my eyes at him and nod my head towards the guy like I understood everything I just heard and observed. Hopefully, I won't send Jack ice-skating around the van floor on the return journey. After he leaves, I slide into the driver's seat. It still has that brand-new-car smell even though I don't exactly know what that is as we've never owned one before. A star-shaped car deodorizer hangs down from the mirror, apparently filling the vehicle with a scent of 'newborn baby' which both confuses me and freaks me out. I yank the belt across my chest and adjust the mirrors. Then I readjust them, and then shift them once more.

'What's happening up there?' he calls to me.

'Just going through all the safety protocols before I start the engine.'

'Oh God, you swear you can drive, right?'

'Like I've driven all my life.' The engine roars to life, the van pitches forward, immediately shutting down again. 'Oh, what happened there?'

'You stalled.'

'How can I . . . oh of course, it's not an automatic. Gears, yes, right. It's all coming back to me.'

'You can't drive a manual?'

'You mean can I drive stick?'

'What's stick?'

'Stick is stick.'

'I think we're having a major language barrier issue here. Have you only driven automatic transmissions before?'

I readjust the mirror, seeing Jack bury his face in his hands from behind. 'I learned using stick, I mean, on a manual car, so I just need to . . .' I wrestle the gear back into place and push my foot down onto the clutch. '. . . jog . . .' Then I gently release the clutch, catching it in first gear. '. . . my . . .' The engine builds and starts to move forward. '. . . memory. There, perfect.' We start edging forward down the driveway, but the van feels like it's dragging a crate of bricks behind us; is that the weight of Jack's chair? I've never driven a vehicle this large before. 'See? Easy. How awesome am I?'

'Hey, Captain Awesome, your handbrake is still on.'

When we pull up to Godolphin Garden, the car park is bustling with retirees, volunteers and families. Some carry large ceramic pots in their hands, others heave bags of soil over their shoulders, or pull empty watering cans, shovels and hand rakes from their car boots. I ease the van into a space at the back, far away from other cars I can potentially hit, and turn off the engine.

'That wasn't so bad, was it?'

'You do realize you can drive over 30mph here?'

I open the side door and catch Jack's face as he turns to me. 'I promised your mom I wouldn't take it above forty.' I draw myself up and onto the van floor. My head disappears under his chair as I scramble for the lock. 'Now, how do I unlock this thing?'

'Press the release hatch.'

'And then?'

'Unlock the brakes.'

I smack my head on his armrest when I eventually resurface. 'Ouch.' I rub the back of my hair. 'Okay, now what?'

'Now press that button right there to let the ramp down.'

A soft whirring accompanies a flat metal platform gliding out from under the van flooring. It extends about one meter outside the van then lowers gently down.

'Oh cool, it's automatic. Finally something in this van is.'

'I would hope so, we paid enough for it.'

I raise an eyebrow – 'We?'

'Okay, Captain America, get me out of here.'

'Yes, Boss,' I smile. I push the same button and up the ramp goes.

'Wow, you figured that one out all on your own,' mutters Jack.

I smile, quite pleased with myself. I got him here, I got him out, and when I return him back to his palace, I'd have proven that I can handle this, that I can handle something.

The weather is perfect. Warm enough to remove my cardigan but not too warm as to make me regret the long-sleeved shirt underneath. My visor is slightly itchy on the forehead so I throw it onto the passenger seat before I lock up.

'Excuse me?'

I turn and see one of the volunteers beside us. She's wearing almost exactly the same outfit as me, except hers comes with a pretty impressive clipboard and bright purple pen with a flower on the end. 'Hi, welcome to Godolphin Garden. Are you here to support an existing group or just wander around? We have some beautiful flowers to the left of the entrance.'

'We actually have adopted our own little patch. I spoke to someone called Linda about it yesterday?'

'Oh, okay, Linda, yes. Well, it's probably one of the empty patches beside the fountain so once you're through the gates, just head to your right and you'll see it. There should be a little sign with your name on it in the soil. Do you need tools?'

'Tools?'

'Shovels, shears, trowel, loppers, forks—'

'Yes to everything.'

'I'll bring it over. So you know, the lot closes at five o'clock.'

'We won't be here that long,' Jack says, not meeting her in the eye.

'Five p.m., good to know,' I say.

'You know, next time you come, there are reserved spaces up front and they have a little stone path leading into the garden just in case it rains and the ground is soft.'

'Spaces up front?' I ask.

'Disabled spaces. It's indicated by yellow marking on the ground. You have a mobility sticker on your windscreen.'

I turn to where her finger is pointing and see a small square sticker with a wheelchair symbol on it.

Disabled.

I can't help glancing over at Jack when the volunteer leaves. His eyes are cast down on the ground and his cheeks are slightly flushed. I want to tell him not to be embarrassed, that it's a stupid word that means nothing. But I don't. Because I don't want to draw more attention to it, and because it does mean something. That one word – **disabled** – means everything. It means a person who's physically unable to do everything a regular person can do. And if he's not regular, if he's not 'normal' – whatever that means – then he's irregular, he's 'abnormal.' Nothing I can say here will make him feel better. Maybe I shouldn't have brought him here, this was a stupid idea. 'Planting a garden to have something concrete to watch grow' or whatever I said to him.

165

He slides a pair of Ray-Bans out his shirt pocket and hides his eyes. 'Alright, let's do this.'

The wheels occasionally get stuck in clumps of mud and grass but we make it eventually to the gate, then to our little patch.

My name is written on a small chalkboard shaped like a flower, piercing the top layer of soil of a very messy, very overgrown area. I'd requested a tall planter box based on the fact neither of us were in any physical state to be kneeling on the ground, bent over a patch of earth. I stand beside him, miniature rake in one hand and shovel in the other. 'Right, I'm thinking we just start pulling the weeds out then raking the soil?'

'What's the shovel for?'

'Um, I don't know. Digging out rocks?'

'Rocks?'

'Okay, look, I've never done this before. I'm not much of a gardener myself. Or an outdoorsy kinda person.'

'No, really? I'd never have guessed.' He stares at the patch of earth, looking understandably perplexed. Then he shakes his head. 'Can't believe I'm doing this,' he mumbles as he starts yanking weeds.

The sun beats warm on our backs as we pull weeds for at least an hour or so, unwinding roots from larger clumps of soil. I don't let on but I'm exhausted after twenty minutes and ready for an ice-cold drink and a nap. Our patch looks a little tidier, a little more worthy of the herbs I'd bought from a ridiculously expensive garden center just outside the city. We're the only ones in this section, but voices carry towards us across the flower heads and grass tips, reminding us this is a shared space; a space to enjoy as a community. And that's what I'm trying to do here, create a community for Jack.

'Right, I'm just about ready for a break. You?'

'Oh, thank God, I thought it was just me. I'm exhausted already. My hands are on fire. This rake is not comfortable, these gloves itch like crazy and I'm starving.'

'Anything else?' Jack laughs and puts his hands down on his wheels.

'Wait, stay right there.' I slide out my old Polaroid from my tenth birthday and position it at eye-level. I don't wait for him to say 'no' before I press the button.

'What was that?'

'I'm documenting our summer.'

He raises his eyebrows.

'Assuming you'll want to keep hanging out,' I mutter, feeling my cheeks warm and redden.

'Are you going to make a scrapbook for me?' he teases. He tries to back himself away from the planter box, but his wheels stick in the grass. He mumbles something, then starts moving the wheel back and forth, but that just seems to be digging him into the earth deeper. 'It's fine,' he quickly says, laughing nervously. 'I'll just be a minute.' He continues wiggling the wheels, then using the planter box as leverage tries to push himself off. 'I think I've almost got it.'

It doesn't look that way at all, but I don't say anything. I don't want to take over. He can do this. Now he's starting to sweat, the smile fading from his face. I don't want him to get annoyed and have his day ruined by this so I move in. 'Here, let me.' But I can't shift him, one wheel seems to be wedged between a small incline in the ground and a divot in the grass. I try lifting his chair over it, but it's so heavy it barely moves a quarter inch up. Maybe if I bend my knees, put more back into it. Nope, that doesn't work and only prompts a twinge in my spine. Finally, I resort to just shaking him back and forth, hoping to break away more ground beneath the wheels.

'Alice!'

'What?'

'You're going to knock me out the chair.'

'Oh sorry.' I release the handles and he tips back into the wedge. 'We're stuck.'

'I'm stuck,' he says quietly.

'No, we're stuck. I'm not exactly going to leave you . . . actually, I am. I'll ask someone for help—'

'No, don't—'

I start walking away from him. 'I'm sure there's someone just down here.'

'Alice, wait, I don't want any help. I can do this myself.' He leans to the side and frantically slams his hand into the wheel. It's not going anywhere.

'I'll be back in a minute.' I head back to the main gates as he shouts my name again. I don't turn around. I know he doesn't want help, but the longer he stays stuck in a patch of earth, the more he's going to hate it here, and hate his new life.

Mud sticks to the toe of my boots and sweat still drips

down my face after battling that chair. When I get to the gate, I don't see the volunteer who greeted us in the beginning. All I see are people. Everywhere. They pile out of a long bus, out of cars, vans, and start filing through the entrance. One large group looks like an outing from some kind of a summer camp, there's at least twenty to thirty people here. Another group look like retirees from a nursing home as some use walking sticks and are supported by nurses wearing lilac smocks and name tags. Whoever they are, there's a lot of them. Too many of them. I can't see their faces, I can't see their eyes. They're strangers, all of them. A fallen shovel against a car door startles me and as I turn to find the noise, more banging and clanging sound off. Then a car alarm, only for a few moments, but enough for me to find myself back there, back in Leicester Square.

The sounds of the bombing erupts in my ears. The car alarms, the screams, the shattering of glass. I drop to the ground but the grass beneath me starts to dissolve, disappearing in front of me. Now I see glass, dust, debris, and blood. It's happening again—

'Alice?'

Suddenly, everything around me is silent. Then voices of excited school children, families and elderly people filter back in. There's grass all around me. I'm not on the street in the city. I'm in a garden.

I'm safe.

'Alice?'

I slowly look up and see Jack. A tall volunteer stands behind him. 'Are you okay?' he asks.

169

I quickly scramble to my feet. 'I was just looking for . . .
um . . .'

'It's okay, I found help,' Jack says.

My whole body is drenched in sweat, and I'm shaking.
'I'm fine,' I splutter.

'Let's go home.'

I nod. 'Yeah, let's go home.' I walk back to the van, still
trembling.

'That was fun,' Jack says. It's definitely a lie but I appreciate
his effort. 'Where to tomorrow?'

Jack

'Um, are you sure about this?' I glance up at Alice who stands at the entrance to the train station, her toes not yet over the threshold. She insisted we take the train into London today after what happened at the garden but now that we're here, I'm not sure if she can do it. We've been standing at this entrance for fifteen minutes now while she just stares inside at the fast-moving commuters. 'We don't need to take trains. We've got the van, and if you don't feel comfortable driving then I can ask Martin. I'm sure he'll say yes.'

'No. It'll be so much faster if we can get around the city on trains. Plus I need to do this at some point and I'd rather do it with you here.' She starts breathing heavily. 'Yesterday was tough.'

'Don't push yourself if you're not ready.'

'I'm ready,' she whispers, although I think she's talking to herself not me.

An alarm sounds overhead, alerting passengers to an incoming train. 'Okay, well, if you're sure, then that's our train,' I say.

Her eyes flick up to the screen. 'Oh. That was fast. Okay.'

She edges through the entrance and up to the barrier, scanning her Oyster card. An attendant quickly lets me through the extra-wide gate, but I struggle to keep up with Alice. She darts between exiting passengers and continues pushing forward to the platform. The train is just pulling in when we get there. It screeches to a halt, the sound throbbing my ears. She cups her ears with her palms and looks at me. I gesture to the opening doors but she doesn't move. People swerve around us like a river around a rock. I wheel myself to the yellow lines but I can't get over the lip of the train. 'Alice?'

She rushes to my handle and thrusts me on, jumping in behind me. The doors slam shut immediately after. She collapses onto the row of seats beside me, beads of sweat along her hairline. She pants heavily.

'Are you OK?'

'Yeah,' she gasps. 'I'd just forgotten how busy the trains get. The buses are so quiet.'

'It's London. It's always busy.'

She wipes the sweat with the back of her hand and leans into the seat. She closes her eyes. I can't tell if she's meditating or what, so I keep an eye out for our stop. More and more people push on at each station, struggling to get around my chair. I mutter apologies and shift forward then back, then forward again. Alice's eyes are still pressed shut, her jaw clenched tight. The stops get more frequent as we get further from the quiet Surrey countryside, and closer to the bustling city centre.

'Alice?' I whisper. 'We're almost at Waterloo.'

Her eyes pop open and lock onto the crowd that's quickly formed inside the train.

'Excuse me,' I mumble to people, gesturing to the exit door as we start to make our way off the train. Alice eases my chair off the edge back onto the platform. The doors close behind us.

Waterloo station is packed. Lunchtime work crowds battle passengers and tourists for ticket queues and food carts. The shops here are rammed, with long queues snaking outside Costa and the ticket office. Shopping bags, backpacks, suit-cases, briefcases, handbags, takeaway sandwiches, coffee cups. Everyone carries something. Babies crying, tourists squealing in excitement as they take selfies, people talk loudly on phones as they rush to the tube to continue their journeys. The speakers overhead struggle with the station noise, announcing continued security restrictions. Police officers in black uniform roam the station concourse, and hover near the entrances and exits.

A woman hurries up to one of the officers, bags in hand. 'Excuse me, are trains still stopping at Leicester Square?'

Leicester Square.

Their voices dull and fade, as a wave of nausea hits me. I glance up anxiously at Alice, wondering if she just heard that too. She stands in the concourse, completely ashen. Her mouth is agape and her shoulders start trembling. She def-initely heard that conversation too.

'Alice?'

She doesn't respond.

'Alice?' I touch her hand. She's cold. Her breathing is

getting heavier, louder. Soon she's gasping, like she's choking. Is she really choking? She clutches her chest and closes her eyes.

'Alice.' I grab her shoulders as she huddles into my chair, curling her knees up into her chest.

I glance over at the police officers, who stand with their backs to us. I remember seeing a guy who'd just run his first marathon. He'd sat with his head between his legs, a foil blanket around his shoulders while event medics calmed him down, rubbing his back. They encouraged him to have sugary drinks and snacks. They breathed slowly with him and counted from ten. I'd thought at the time he was having a heart attack, but my dad said his body was going through some kind of shock, perhaps from overexertion or inadequate hydration or nutrition. I'm assuming Alice is properly hydrated and fed, and hasn't recently run a marathon, so I presume she's OK in those areas. But I should try and calm her down, before the police sees us. 'Alice, take a deep breath. It's OK,' I whisper.

She grips my armrest on the chair, still gasping for breath.

'Breathe slowly. I'm going to count down from ten, OK?'

Her eyes are still closed, her face white. What if she passes out?

'10 . . . 9 . . . 8 . . .'

Her breath hitches.

'7 . . . 6 . . .'

Then it slows.

'5 . . . 4 . . .'

Her shoulders stop shaking.

'3 . . . 2 . . .'

Her grip on my chair loosens and her hands drop to her knees.

'1.'

She opens her eyes and glances up at me. Her eyes water and her cheeks warm red like her hair. My hand is still around her. I slowly drop it and return my hands to my lap. She looks around the concourse, glancing up at people as they pass us.

'No one saw,' I lie.

She nods then struggles back up to her feet. She smooths down her dress, which matches her grey tights. She takes a deep breath and stares down at the ground. 'Can we go back now?'

Alice

I sleep terribly that night. Distorted memories of the bombing colliding with images of sharp green grass, abandoned fields and rows of blood-red tulips. When I eventually peel my eyelids open and let the sun in, I see my dad dressed in casual wear standing in the doorway. He holds a steaming mug of coffee and a plate. 'Good morning,' he smiles. He pushes the door further open and comes closer. When he sits and slides the plate onto my bedside table, I see two croissants already smeared with butter.

'Where's Mom?' I mumble, still foggy from my nightmare.

'She's downstairs, but I wanted to sort breakfast for you this morning. I didn't know if you still like these for breakfast, so I made some oatmeal with brown sugar too. And also a big fruit bowl with yogurt.'

'They call it porridge here, Dad.' I reach for a croissant and slowly sit up to take a flaky bite. Pastry shards drop from my lips.

'I thought it might be nice if we spent time together today. Maybe you can show me more of the neighborhood?'

'I'd love to but I'm meeting Jack today.'

'Again? Where?'

'Mrs A's helped me organize something in the city for him.'

'The city? Alice, I don't know about this.'

'I'll be fine, Dad.' My mind wanders back to the train station. I don't know what set me off. It could have been the crowds, the noise, the police. All of it. Whatever is going on with me is happening more frequently. But I can't tell him that or I won't be allowed out again.

'Sure you're okay?'

'Definitely.'

He nods, and pats my leg on top of the quilt then eases himself off the bed, and heads for the door. 'Open or closed?'

'Closed, please.'

Jack's mom is standing beside the van when I walk up. 'Good morning, Alice.'

'Morning, Mrs Addington.'

She glances at the house then turns back to me. 'I just wanted to make sure everything is going okay with Jack. Does he seem . . . better?'

Better?

'Uh, he definitely seems more chatty?'

She smiles. 'I think these little trips will really help.'

'I hope so.'

'And you're doing well yourself?'

I swallow hard. 'Very well, thank you.'

'Good. I made some phone calls and today should be no problem at all. Sounds like a lovely day.'

'Thanks.'

'How did the other day go? Did you both manage to make your way round the train station okay?'

'Um . . .'

'Went great, Mum.' We turn and see Jack in the doorframe. He's wearing a pale blue collared shirt and navy chinos. He shimmies himself out the door and down the ramp. 'Crowds make it a bit difficult to get around with this chair, which is why we'll stick with the van. But Alice handled it all like a pro. Isn't that right?'

I nod, without looking at either of them. My cheeks warm and I hope I'm not going red. I seem to be lying a lot today.

'Well, Martin says he's happy to drive you into the city and help out when needed,' his mom smiles.

Martin coming with us actually makes me feel a little safer, assuming he's not just the Addingtons' pastry chef. Is he?

'So where to today, Captain America?' Jack asks me.

'It's a surprise,' I say, as Martin starts easing Jack's chair into the vehicle. Then he slides into the driver's side. He drives faster than me, swerving confidently between lanes. Occasionally he glances back to check we're okay. The van is silent, other than the churning of wheels on gravel, and the tapping of Jack's chair against the metal panel that mostly holds him in place when we turn a corner. I consider asking Martin to switch on the radio, but wonder if that would distract him from the road or from his observations – he is looking out for security threats, right? I hope this isn't just a jaunt into London with the family and car for him.

We pull in to a darkened car park and he eases the large

vehicle in a yellow marked space close to the elevator. When I look at Jack I notice he's also seeing the large DISABLED sign beside our parking space, but when he catches my eye I look away and feign disinterest.

When the elevator doors open, we're in and soon ascending to the top floor. The lift rattles and dull overhead lighting casts shadows across the ground. Martin is stoic behind him, his jaw tense and his shoulders pulled back. A soft ping lets us know we've arrived at our floor. When the doors slide open, a young brunette in a gray pencil skirt and white shirt greets us.

'Good morning. My name is Sara and I'll be assisting you on your tour of the Shard today.' She pulls out paperwork and we start signing our names, along with answers to survey questions such as, Why are you visiting us today? and What do you hope to gain from your visit? This is more taxing than a school exam. Martin fills out his then takes Jack's, without asking him if that's okay. This isn't what I had in mind. This was supposed to be for us, a fun way to spend our morning, a way to get away from all this formality and fear. Now we're standing here listening to Martin and Sara iron out security risks which includes going over the stair access and the privacy policy for the cameras.

'Um, Martin?'

He turns and looks at me, almost surprised, as if seeing me for the first time.

'This isn't exactly how I planned it,' I say. 'I know you're helping us today but is it okay if Jack and I just walk around for a bit and enjoy the sights?'

'Yes, I'll just be a minute—'

'Alone.'

Sara nods and glances up at Martin. She gets it.

'I'm not sure how Mrs Addington would feel about that,' he says, his eyes scrunching.

'You know her better than me, but I think she'd want her son to enjoy a bit of normality for a change. Please?'

He nods and slides his phone out of his back pocket. 'Call me if you need anything.'

'Number's already on speed dial,' I say, tapping my phone into the air. I take Jack's handles in my hands and gently guide him back into the lift. I punch the button for level 72 that's next to a small shiny silver plaque inscribed SKYDECK. The lift shudders slightly then ascends at a speed that almost knocks me off my feet. 'I think I just saw my life flash before my eyes.' After a few seconds we bounce in place and the doors slide open. 'Is there a slower lift for the return journey, by any chance?'

'Thanks for that, by the way,' Jack says.

'Getting rid of Martin? He's great and all, but we don't need a babysitter.'

He rolls his eyes and mutters, 'Agreed.' His wheels click over the threshold as we enter a wide, bare lobby with glass walls and tall doors that lead out to the Skydeck lounge.

The automatic doors slide open and immediately the view takes my breath away. 'Wow.' I pull out my camera again and take two perfect shots – one of the view itself and one of Jack watching it.

'Camera away. You can't experience this behind a lens.'

'This view must be nothing compared to what you've seen before.'

'You know, I've been all over the world, but I've never been here. I've never seen London like this. Can you push me up closer?'

I nudge Jack right up to the barrier until we can't go any further and breathe in the freshest air I've ever tasted in London. 'I couldn't get us both up a mountain, so this is the closest I could find to a summit.'

'It's perfect,' he smiles, gazing out, his eyes widening.

Sky-high buildings surround us on all sides and angles, but none of them reach close to the Shard. We tower above the whole city, every single person within it. We're standing on top of roofs, of businesses, of people. We're standing on top of anything and everything that could hurt us. No one can reach us here. The wind tangles in my hair, whipping it all around my face and neck. I grab what I can and stuff it back inside the bun on the crown of my head and return to the view before me. I close my eyes, the breeze tickling my lids, and feel the sheer sensation of height – and freedom – on my skin.

When I was younger, my parents took me hiking on the East Coast during a rare deployment break. I complained the entire way up – my legs were tired, my shoes were scraping my heels, I had a blister under my big toe, my back hurt. All I wanted was to return to our tiny rented apartment, read my books and order pizza. The outdoors didn't suit me, never has. But when we reached the summit even I was out of words. Standing at the highest peak of what I'd just climbed, looking down at the blanket of oranges, reds and yellows around us, I got it. I began to understand why people did things like that. All of a sudden my feet didn't hurt anymore. On that day, with my parents standing either side of me, I vowed to not let myself become buried in textbooks and after-school activities like Mandarin tutorials. I promised myself I'd stop and look up once in a while. We moved the next week to another part of the world. Strange, I haven't thought about that day again, until now.

When I finally open my eyes, I don't know how many minutes have passed but I become aware I haven't said anything to Jack in a while. I turn to him and see his eyes are closed too, so I drag a cushion from the lounge chair to his side and sit down. We stay here, not saying anything to each other, for the whole morning. Just staring at the city, undisturbed by its shadows, by its terrors. From here, in this very moment, London is the most beautiful place I've ever seen. And for the first time since the attacks, I'm not scared of it.

Jack

'So, Jack. What do you think?'

I slowly turn over the plastic model in my hands. My fingers graze the knees where sockets hold the prosthetic legs in place. It looks so easy like this, on a plastic doll. No pain, no risk. 'What if it isn't successful? Can more damage be done to me?'

'To your legs?' Dr McKenzie asks.

My mum told me she's the best Consultant in Prosthetics Medicine. She drove in from the Oxford Centre for Enablement (OCE) just for this meeting. I wonder what she charges an hour. I nod and suddenly feel a phantom pain in my left shin, like when I was younger and I used to get shin splints at the beginning of my training.

'Well, of course, as with anything, there's always a small risk. In this case, post-amputation complications can include neuroma formation, stump pain and phantom limb pain and related skin conditions. But based on your evaluation for suitability, I don't foresee that. I think there's a very good chance you'll be up on your feet with these in no time.'

My mum makes a choking sound beside me, and when I turn I see she's crying. I put my hand on her shoulder. My dad sits beside her, smiling and nodding at me. He's thinking it too – with these, I can run again, I can hike, I can find my way back to the old me, the old Jack. I'll take whatever risk comes with it, because these prostheses are worth it.

We complete whatever paperwork is needed from us at the meeting, sign forms, accept risks, take leaflets for further reading. My dad and I sit in the waiting room, as my mum negotiates with the receptionist the first available date for trialling the prostheses. My dad thumbs a *Men's Health* magazine. He stops at an article entitled, 'Strength Training for Distance Runners'. Before, I'd sit beside him, reading over his shoulder, analysing the tips, the nutritional advice. We'd reminisce about past runs we'd done together, events we entered together, places we saw together. We'd maybe take out our phones and start scrolling through photos. Laughing, sharing stories. But today we sit at opposite sides of the waiting room. It's a small space but today it feels like an amphitheatre. We may as well be in different countries.

'. . . that soon? That's fantastic,' my mum says, looking back at me, a huge smile on her face.

I feel it, the shift. This is it. Everything changes from here, and I've never been more ready.

I wheel myself over to my dad, who looks up slowly. Then I manoeuvre in at the side, and like we used to do, I start reading over his shoulder. And like before, he dips the maga-zine to let me see better.

Alice

'You really have to go already?'

I lean against the hallway cupboard door, watching my dad lace up his boots. The camouflage uniform stands out against the bright white walls of the house.

He stands, towering over me. 'Sorry, I've pushed back deployment as much as I can. But I have requested a much shorter stint this time so I won't be away for long.'

'Sure I can't come with you both to the airport?'

'No, I'm flying out of the military base today. Your mom will take me.' He walks over to the foot of the stairs. 'Although if she's not down in the next five minutes I might miss my flight,' he calls up, winking and smiling at me.

'That wouldn't be so bad,' I mutter.

He rests a hand on my shoulder and smiles softly. 'I'll be back soon.'

'I know.'

'But I always go with you to the airport.'

'It's fine, really. You stay here, get ready for your day with Jack. Your mom says you have to leave soon. Where is it today?'

'I thought I'd give him the all-American day out – arcade games and burgers.'

185

'That's my girl.'

'Yeah, I called ahead and there's a ramp to get in and some of the arcades boxes can be lowered for wheelchair accessibility.'

He nods approvingly. 'You're really doing a lot for him.'

'What will communication be like this time?'

'I'll be stationed a little further out so we won't be able to Skype as often as we have done but whenever I can check in I will.'

'Yeah, okay.' There's so much to say to him right now, so much I want to tell him, to ask him. But whatever I say will only frighten him, make him stay, and he can't keep jeopardizing his career for me. We need the money. We're barely keeping afloat with the expense of staying in London. No, I need to deal with this myself. It's the only way.

Before I can spoil it by saying anything more, Mom rushes down the stairs, car keys in hand. 'Sorry, sorry. I didn't know what to wear.' She slams her feet into sandals and hops around trying to clasp the strap with one hand.

'You're just going to the airport,' I laugh. Then I realize what she means. She stands at the bottom of the stairs, looking at Dad. She's dressed in a long floral dress with a pale yellow pashmina. The necklace he gave her last time he was home for their twentieth anniversary swings delicately from her slender neck. She's wearing makeup for the first time in a while – pale pink lips to match her dyed hair, rosy cheeks, a swish of mascara on her top lashes. She always dresses like this for him when he leaves. I never really understood it until now. She does it in case she never sees him

186

again, so that it's his last image of her. She doesn't see what I see, how he looks at her regardless of what clothes she has on or what chemicals she puts on her face. One day I hope someone looks at me that way.

'I'll get the car started and meet you out there,' she says, squeezing my dad's arm. She turns and waves her phone at me. 'Alice, text me when you'll be home later?'

'Will do.'

The door shuts behind her, a sad silence filling the hallway between us. What if this is the last time I'll ever see my dad? I rush into his arms again, my cheek against his chest like when I first greeted him at the airport. He gives my back a pat, as if to signal 'it's time' then bends down and heaves his bag over his shoulder. 'You'll let me know if you're not okay, right, Alice?'

I nod, biting my lip.

Then he kisses me on the forehead, and leaves.

Jack

Sweat starts dripping onto the grass. I lean forward a bit more. Almost there. Pressure builds in my hips and a dull ache quickly turns to throbbing pain. Just a little more. My fingertips stretch outwards, straining from my hand so much that it quivers. I clench my jaw and keep reaching.

I came out for a 'wheel' around the garden paths almost an hour ago but while trying to take a photo of a new family of geese on the pond for Instagram I'd dropped my phone on the bank. Now I can't reach the thing. I could call Martin or my mum for help, but I don't want to have to do that. I hate asking for help. I already feel helpless, but calling for help to pick up a phone seems pathetic. No, I'm almost there. I edge out the chair an inch more until my middle finger finally touches the corner of the phone.

Suddenly, I feel unstable and I pitch forward. I hit the ground, my right arm plunging into the pond. Water splashes up on my face. It startles the geese and they scatter, splashing up the water more. Now I'm sinking into the bank, going deeper into the water. Heat builds inside me as panic rises to the surface. What if I can't get out? What if I drown?

I flap my arms and dig my hands into the soft earth around

the pond, clawing my way up from the bank. Collapsing onto my back on the grass, I start screaming at the sky, throwing every swear word I have in my vocabulary. Words I've never said out loud. But I swear and scream then swear some more. Then I start thumping the ground with my fists, my left hand holding the phone.

All this for a phone. I'm so pathetic. I'm so weak. I can't do anything. I hate this. And I hate myself.

I close my eyes and try counting back from ten like I did with Alice that day in the train station.

10 . . . 9 . . . 8 . . . 8 . . . 8 . . .

I crush my phone screen in my hand, wanting to hear the glass crack, wanting it to dig deep into my skin, make me bleed. My phone vibrates in my palm. I open my eyes and suddenly become aware of how still the air is, how quiet it really is here.

When I look down, I see a message from Alice which consists of a *Howdy* followed by an array of emojis including two American flags, a burger, a milkshake, something that looks like a TV screen and a trophy. The tension starts to fade, my body relaxing into the ground, and I release a shaky laugh. Never thought I'd think this, but I'm actually happy to hear from her.

Alice

The sound of gunfire fills the street as the door swings open. I immediately freeze.

A red neon ARCADE sign hangs above our heads and the smell of chicken wings and burgers tell me this is okay, this is safe.

'You alright?' he asks.

It's just a video game.

It's not real gunfire.

It's clever graphics and a sound box.

Not real.

'Yeah. I was just making sure this is the right place.'

'What, there's more than one cheesy American arcade with greasy food and cheap flat beer?'

'In London, yes. You'd actually be surprised by how many.' I thrust his wheels over the metal ramp into the arcade and let the automatic door close quietly behind me. 'Welcome to the world of video games.'

'Wow,' he mumbles.

'What's first? Donkey Kong? Mario? Big Buck Hunter? Pac-Man?'

'I don't know. You choose. I've never played any of those.'

'You've never played the classics? You're so missing out!'
I wheel him over to Pac-Man because it's the first wheelchair-accessible one I see and start rifling in my money bag.

'No, never played the classics, or any video game actually.'

I let the bag of 50ps drop from my hand onto the top of
the monitor. 'What?'

'I've never played a video game,' he says again, holding
his hands up. 'Is that so bad?'

I pull a chair over and sit in front of him so we're facing
each other. 'You're a seventeen-year-old boy, how does that
happen?'

'Well, quite easily, actually. My mum absolutely hates
them. Banned them from the house before they even entered.'
He picks up the bag and pretends to do a bicep curl with
it. 'Why do you have this many 50ps?'

'I had to go to two banks to get that much change. You're
welcome, by the way.' I snatch the bag off him and drop two
coins into the coin slot. The familiar blue maze and yellow
Pac-Man pops up on the screen, followed by the yellow dots
and colored ghosts. 'So really – you haven't played one game,
even for five minutes?'

'Nope.'

'Weird. How did you waste away your youth?' I move
aside to let Jack have a turn. 'Follow the dots but avoid the
ghosts.' I stack more 50ps on the side table beside an empty
beer glass in case we need them. 'Well, while you and your
family were rubbing shoulders at galas with Prince Charles,
I was spending my adolescence the proper way.'

'Playing video games?'

'Gaming isn't just shoot-'em-up gunfire games like Call of Duty, or zombie survival role play. Some games are strategic and help develop your problem-solving and reasoning skills which in turn can be applied to many academic areas.'

'Ah, I knew we'd find a way back to your textbooks and your school grades,' he laughs. 'And here I was thinking – for a split-second, of course – that you were maybe, possibly, potentially, slightly cooler than me.'

He's doing pretty good for his first turn on Pac-Man. Of course, he's even good at this. 'Wow, cooler, eh? I'll take that compliment. It might be my only one from you.'

'Probably,' he smirks.

I suddenly feel as if all the air has been sucked out my lungs. That smirk, that same smirk, the last time I saw it was across the street at Leicester Square, right before – right before – before—

'Alice?'

I can't breathe. The air, it's not coming back. I'm hanging suspended in an airless, ventless space, unable to move forward, to break free.

'Alice?'

A high-pitched frequency, like an out-of-tune radio, screeches from somewhere behind me then erupts into gunfire again.

'Alice!'

When I open my eyes, I'm on the ground on my knees. And I'm rocking. My hands are over my ears and I'm curled up into a ball between Jack's chair and the arcade machine. I'm covered in sweat and my knees are sticky from the beer-stained floor. I put my hands down to steady myself and my fingertips graze something moist and yellow, like mustard. God, I hope it's mustard.

I slowly look to my left and thankfully don't see anyone watching me. Then I turn to my right and see a girl standing at the bar casually looking over. I turn back to the floor and pretend to have dropped something.

'What was that?' he says.

I eventually look up and see Jack staring at me. I don't know why I was hoping he hadn't noticed. Of course he noticed.

'Did you just have another panic attack?'

I open my mouth, not sure how the words are going to sound, and clear my throat. 'I thought I dropped something.'

'You had another panic attack.' It's not a question this time.

I nod gently and then start to pick myself up. I slide back into the chair, hand on the table beside me to keep my balance. Stickiness everywhere. This time it feels like stale beer or spilled fizzy juice.

'When are you going to talk to someone about this?'

'Like who?'

'Your GP? A counselor?'

'My dad found this group that meets up once a week at a Methodist church by Twickenham Stadium, not too far from my house,' I mutter.

'Great.'

My shoulders start to soften and relax. 'It's on Monday evenings. I can meet you there or if you want to pick me up then we can go together?'

Jack squints his eyes. 'Oh, you mean both of us go?'

'I thought when you said 'Great' that you wanted to go too, that we would go together.'

He starts shifting uncomfortably in his chair. 'I don't know, Alice. I don't think I would enjoy that.'

'Well, I don't think it's particularly enjoyable for anyone who attends. It's there to help us.'

'I don't think I need it, like you do.'

I gaze down at the floor, feeling my cheeks flush again. 'What I mean is—'

'Let's just forget about it for now. I came here to have fun with you. Fancy another game?'

'Let's skip the game.'

My shoulders drop. Did I just ruin the afternoon? 'Do you want to just go home?'

He shakes his head and looks off to the right towards the bar. 'No, let's get a drink instead.'

'Good idea. I probably need something sugary after that episode, like a Coke or Dr Pepper. Do you guys have Cherry Coke over here?'

'No, I mean a drink drink.'

'What? Like an alcoholic drink?'

'Yep. Please tell me you've had alcohol before?'

'No, I'm underage. And so are you.'

'By less than a year. Besides no one checks ID.'

'You're serious? You're going to try and get served alcohol here? Now?'

'We both are.' He pushes on the wheels and starts heaving himself towards the bar. The front of his wheels hit the foot stop as he reaches the counter. 'Excuse me, can I have a pint of IPA, please?'

I saunter slowly over to him, and stand sheepishly behind him like a child waiting to be reprimanded. The bartender grabs a glass from the sink and starts pulling the lever down, pouring golden ale from the beer tap into the glass. That was worryingly easier than I thought. I've never tried to get served before. America is really strict with underage drinking. My mom got ID'd once. More than once. She looks young, I guess.

'What do you want?' Jack asks, gesturing to the bartender.

Oh, it's my turn. What do people drink at this kind of place? Something cheap, casual, cool, like a beer I'm sure but whenever I've tried some of my dad's I've always been less than impressed. It's bitter and tastes like sand. I can't order wine, like my mom drinks, because I wouldn't know what to ask for – even if I did I seriously doubt a place like this has a wide range of wines to choose from. I could do hard liquor and a mixer? Maybe something fruity, like apples? I like apples. Or maybe a cocktail. I know a few names of cocktails from dinner menus.

'Can I have a Cosmo, please?' Those are my mom's favorites. That and margaritas. Damn, I should have asked for a margarita, that sounds way cooler.

Jack squints and looks up at me. 'A Cosmo?'

The bartender leans on the counter and stares at me. Beads of sweat prick my skin and I feel a trickle down my back. She's worse than my dad, and he's a trained drill sergeant equipped with years of experience of operating lie detecting tests.

'Do you have ID?' she eventually asks.

'No.' I start to turn away.

'You didn't ask me for ID,' Jack says.

'Okay, do you have ID too?'

'No, I don't. Not any need to carry around a driver's license anymore these days,' he gestures to his wheelchair. 'Not since I got my legs blown up in the London bombings a couple of months ago. Remember those? She was there too.' He waves a hand at me. 'We almost died.'

The bartender takes a step back and for a moment I wonder if she's going to cry, or maybe just call to her manager to throw us out. She glances over her shoulder then turns back and nods. Within the next three minutes Jack has a pint of beer in front of him on a small round table and I'm perched on a chair holding a wide-lipped glass filled with pink frothy juice. It even has an orange peel decoration. I poke at it for a moment, then unravel it from the glass edge and bring it up to my lips.

'Don't eat that,' Jack says leaning forward. 'It's a garnish.'

A garnish? Right. I knew that. I loop it back onto the glass and sit back still holding it up to my face like I'm posing for an Instagram picture.

He smiles as he raises his beer. 'Are you going to drink that?'

'Of course. It's not for show, you know.' Actually, I hadn't considered drinking it, or finishing it. I just ordered it to join Jack.

He leans forward, that same unnerving smirk that stabs at my insides and almost forces me back to that day. 'Cheers.'

196

'What are we cheersing to?'

He shrugs, 'I don't know. Cheers to being completely messed up?'

'I'll certainly cheers to that.' Our glasses meet and tap.

I hesitate for a moment, then let the liquid fill my mouth and trickle down my throat. It's sweet and fruity. And burns. Warmth pricks at my throat and fills my belly. It's a sugary mixture of oranges, cranberries and lemons. I can see why my mom drinks it.

'Here, it's my turn,' he says pulling my Polaroid camera across the table by its string. He cups it gently in his hands and nods to my drink.

I roll my eyes, then return to my Instagram-worthy pose – martini glass in hand, pouty duck face. I think I've nailed it. Those Instagram social media influencers have nothing on me.

He laughs and a slow whirl of the lens snaps and spits out a sticky image of a girl who doesn't look anything like me.

'Well, what do you think of the Cosmo?'

'Actually, it's pretty good.' I take another sip, which turns out to be more of a gulp.

'Slow down!' he laughs.

'Martin's coming back for us, right? I don't have to drive?'

'Yeah, but still, slow down. I can't return you to your parents in a state. They'll never let you out with me again.'

'You – a bad influence?' I take another sip, a smaller sip this time. 'What were you like? Before, I mean.'

He takes a swig of beer and clears his throat. 'I was . . . lucky.'

'Lucky, how?'

'Things were easy for me.'

'Sum up "Old Jack" in three words.'

'Three words, eh? Okay. Brave. Crazy . . . Free.'

'You don't feel any of these things anymore? Not brave or free?'

He puckers his lips, creases burying into his forehead. 'Your turn.'

'Well, I guess my three words are ones I'd still use now. Cautious. Organized. Committed.'

'Sounds like a person who has a lot of control in her life.'

'Not really, I mean, yes when it comes to certain things like academia or my extracurricular activities, but no when it comes to the bigger decisions in my life, like where we live, where I go to school. That's out of my control, entirely dictated by my dad's military career and deployment rota.'

'Sorry.'

'Don't be. I'm really lucky when it comes to my parents, they've been really supportive. Especially my dad, because he gets it, you know. How about your parents?'

'My mum tries, she does. My dad, he's another story. He comes from that English stiff-upper-lip background. I can't really talk about how I feel around him.'

'At least you have your friends?'

Jack shakes his head and takes another drink, the beer spilling down his chin. He clumsily wipes it away, an unfamiliar look of sadness or pain in his eyes. 'I don't like to talk about this kind of stuff with my friends.'

'Why not?'

'I suppose I don't want to burden them with it, or sound like I'm complaining all the time. I know I'm lucky, it could have been worse that day. But sometimes, waking up, remembering what happened . . . it just sucks and I want to say that, you know.'

'I know.'

He shrugs. 'At least the flowers and cards have pretty much stopped.'

'Finally,' I smile, taking another big sip of my drink, feeling warmer like my insides are melting.

'Yep, there are only so many sunflowers a person can stand after a while. And roses. Those things prick.'

'I hate roses, reminds me of Valentine's Day,' I say.

'Bad experience?'

'No.'

'There's a story here, I can tell.'

'Shut up and drink your beer.'

Jack

Rain beats down hard outside, hammering the windows in the living room. It drowns out the dance music pounding from the speakers by the TV system. Bodies are packed in, standing in corners, slumped on sofas, in the kitchen, the hallways. Everyone from school is here. Except Alice. I was going to ask her if she wanted to come with me tonight, but I don't think parties are her scene. Besides, I can't imagine her here with me and my friends. It's odd because we've been spending so much time together lately, but we're essentially strangers to each other. I didn't know her before this, and probably wouldn't have ever had a conversation with her otherwise. We have no mutual interests, no shared friend groups, absolutely nothing in common. Before that day, she'd have been cooped up in some library or hipster coffee shop sipping a ridiculously named frothy milky beverage with powdered sugar on top like a pumpkin and nutmeg spiced latte, writing poetry and reading Jane Austen. Before that day, I'd be here, at this party, with these people, drinking this beer. I'd have run at least 20km, maybe biked too. And I'd be standing in that corner, away from the music, laughing with Will, Euan and Alex, and probably with Lauren at my side. Alice and I are polar opposites, always will be. So, why would I rather be hanging out with her right now?

'Want another beer?' Will leans in, holding a bottle in his hand. It's slightly warm, but I take it anyway.

'So how you been?' It's strange, asking someone else how they are doing, how they feel. Actually, it feels pretty good to not be the one being asked for once.

'Yeah, good,' Will says, taking a swig from his bottle. 'Been busy.'

I know what busy means – running, cycling, hiking, camping, hanging out with friends. I used to be busy too. Now if I'm not with Alice, I'm spending my days at home wheeling myself around a house that feels smaller and smaller every day.

'It's good to see you, Jack.'

'Yeah, you too.'

Will leans against the doorway and starts playing with the label on his bottle. Why is it so awkward and formal between us now?

'Jack!' I turn and see Alex and Euan coming through the door, six packs under their arms. Behind them is Lauren and her friend Verity. I wave, immediately feeling stupid for doing so. A wave?

They gently clap me on the back, softer than usual, and huddle around me. 'How you doing?' asks Alex. Back to me again, I guess.

'Yeah, good.'

'Heard you're back in for surgery in a few weeks?'

'Just a minor op.'

They nod and gaze down to the floor. I suddenly become aware of how loud the music is around us, and how far everyone is standing away from me. I don't blame them. I'd act the same, I think. If the bomb had happened to one of them, I'd probably avoid them altogether. What could I possibly say to someone in a wheelchair to make them feel better? I'd just end up saying something stupid or feeling awkward around them. No one wants to spend time with someone who got their legs blown off.

'Oh hey, I'm actually going to be getting prostheses,' I blurt out, hoping to lighten the mood slightly.

'Pro—?' stammers Euan, gazing up like he's trying to pronounce the word in his head.

'Prostheses,' repeats Lauren, rolling her eyes. She looks at me and smiles. 'That's great, Jack.'

'What is that?' asks Euan.

'Basically, it's plastic legs. But it means I'll be out of this thing,' I say, slamming the arm rest on the chair.

'You mean you'll be up walking around again?'

'Yeah, hopefully.'

'And running? Will you be able to run again?' asks Euan.

'Don't be stupid.' Will smacks him on the arm.

'What? My cousin says you can run a marathon with pro – pro – um, plastic legs.'

Alex looks down at me, his eyes wide. 'Is that true, Jack? Will you be able to run the London Marathon in prostheses?'

'I don't know. Maybe . . . Really?' I gasp. My cheeks suddenly warm and a familiar sensation fills my belly, just like when I'm about to start a run. That early stage of an

202

adrenaline rush, like your body knows what's coming and it's already getting ready to move. I hadn't thought about it before. Is this true? Can I still run the marathon next year with my dad?

Alex claps my shoulder. 'Definitely look into it. That would be amazing. We could all run it together!'

'Fancy a beer outside?' asks Will.

'Nah, you all go on ahead. I'm getting picked up in a few minutes.' Truth is, I haven't texted my mum to come get me yet. But now I can't stop thinking about this marathon and all I want to do is go home and google it. I need to know if this is true. If it is, and I can, this changes everything.

Alice

'Close your eyes, Alice.'

I blink furiously, my body fighting the urge to comply.

'It's okay, go on.'

My eyelids drop and darkness fills my sight.

'Tell me what you feel, physically, I mean. What do you feel in this space?'

'I feel . . . cold.'

'Okay, good. Tell me more. Be specific. What is it exactly in this space that makes you cold?'

'I feel the fan blowing on my bare skin—'

'Good. Where is the fan?'

'It's in the corner of your office, behind your chair.'

'Okay. What else?'

'I feel the leather from the chair sticking to my bare legs even though I'm cold. I feel my hair tickling my back where some of it has fallen out from the ponytail.'

'What about sounds; what do you hear in this room?'

'The fan, your voice, the clock on the wall, the traffic outside—'

'Try to focus on the sounds inside this room, your immediate space, your "bubble," shall we say.'

'Okay. Well, now I hear the phone ringing from reception but I guess that's outside this room too.'

'What do you see?'

'Nothing. You made me close my eyes, remember?'

'Exactly. You can't see anything. But do you feel safe?'

'No. Is this exercise supposed to make me feel safe if I close my eyes? Should I be closing my eyes outside if I don't feel safe?'

'This is just an exercise to get you to draw inwards, to focus on the now, the immediate space, and what you're feeling in it. It's supposed to take you out of your thoughts, out of your memories.'

Nothing can take me out of my thoughts and out of my memories. But at this point, where nothing has worked and the prospect of returning to school in the fall seems out of the question, I'll try anything. Even this, whatever this is. CBT? Hypnosis? Meditation? All I know is my mom and dad are paying £60 an hour for a one-on-one session with a renowned PTSD therapist. And it costs me almost a fiver on the bus to get here.

'Let's focus on the breath now. Start to draw a breath in, taking it in through the belly. Now hold it in your mouth for 1 . . . 2 . . . 3 . . . and release. And again . . .'

My eyes flicker open. Dr Morton is staring right at me. I blink them closed again. I don't know why I thought she'd be writing something, or maybe checking her phone.

'Let's try again. Breathing in for 1 . . . 2 . . . 3 . . . 4 . . . hold for 1 . . . 2 . . . 3 . . . 4 . . . and release.'

We do that again a few more times, and after that I don't

remember doing it. I just remember the breath, her voice, the fan whirring, the audible shiver of the laptop as it charges at the wall (I saw it plugged in when I first sat down). I remember the coolness of the leather on my skin turning to warmth then heat as I fall deeper. Fall where, I don't know. Inside my mind, my thoughts, somewhere I'm not supposed to be going. But I go there.

It's quiet. The cement of the pavement is warm under the soles of my feet. It's summer here. My shoulders are bare and the cardigan lies by my toes. Leicester Square is deserted. It's just me. The roads around me are empty, the bus stop is free of passengers queuing. My watch suddenly feels heavy on my left wrist and I raise it up. It's 10:54 a.m. The big hand quivers, momentarily pushing back on the movement of time. I know what comes next because this is a nightmare I've lived more than once. I've been here, I've stood here. I know what happens when it strikes 10:55 a.m.

And just like that, it happens. People appear all around me, frozen mid-stride. Then a gust of gray blows through the crowd, burning them one by one. I feel the heat on my shoulders and on my cheeks. Ash burrows into the wool of my cardigan which still lies by my feet. Dust fills my nostrils. Screams fill my ears.

'Alice.'

I awake with a jolt, one foot slapping against the wooden flooring. I'm back in the office, the whirring of the fan, shiver of the laptop screen as it reboots. Dr Morton is kneeling beside me, her hand rests on my hands which are clasped on my lap.

'Alice, where did you go?'

'I don't know,' I lie.

She slides onto the sofa beside me and I unclasp my hands. They're soaked in sweat so I wipe them on my shorts. 'It's normal when you witness a traumatic event like you did to revisit the scene. Your mind will want to wander back to that day, not because it really wants to but because it's triggered or cued to do so by something that reminds you of that event. A certain song, or a sound, or—'

'Weather sometimes gets me too, not all the time. It rained that day,' I mumble.

'Yes, you can even be triggered by weather sometimes depending on how you're feeling at the time.' She shifts closer. 'My sessions will hopefully soften the occurrence of these flashbacks and eventually eliminate the triggers. Because if the flashbacks become too much of a regular occurrence your memory can get triggered by anything. It eventually doesn't need a visual or auditory cue to flip, it becomes neurologically embedded. That's what we want to avoid. Because once that happens, you can't control it. You become hostage to your memories of that one event.'

My hands are wet again, so I drag them down from the pockets to the edge of my shorts. Sweat, tears, I don't know which. All I know is that I'm losing what little control I had.

What happens when I've lost it all?

Jack

Alice pushes the remnants of a burger around her plate, stabbing an onion ring with her fork but not eating it. Her fiery red hair is tied up in a bun today. It's breezier than usual so she wears a yellow linen scarf and lets it hang over her khaki coat. We're sitting at a table outside of a restaurant that used to be Lauren's favourite. Inside, the shelves are filled with crystal glasses of various shapes and sizes, all mismatched and all with a backstory. There are champagne coupes from London speakeasies of the 1920s and a martini glass from the Ritz in Paris where Hemingway drank after freeing it from the Nazis. I thought Alice would love it here. But she looks like she just wants to go home. 'How did it go on Tuesday? You didn't say much about the therapy session in your texts?'

She sighs and drops her fork and knife to one side of the plate. 'It was OK, I guess.'

'Just OK? Tell me about it.'

She shifts in her chair and reaches for the last of her foamy frothy double-something caramel latte. 'Well, firstly the office was exactly how you'd imagine,' she scoffs. 'She's got this huge pot plant in the corner and a leather armchair that looks like it reclines, a box of tissues on the table—'

I laugh with her, even though I know her going isn't funny at all. None of this is amusing in the slightest.

'Then she made me do this breathing exercise like we were meditating and—'

'Jack!'

I turn and see a couple of guys from school that I haven't seen in months. I can feel a big smile spreading across my face. 'Hey!' I reach out and meet their hands, quickly slapping them. 'Alice, this is Trevor and Rob. They go to our school.'

She waves awkwardly at them.

'How you doing?' Rob asks me.

'I'm OK. Doing better.'

'Hey, I heard you'll be up out your chair soon?'

'Yeah, that's the plan,' I grin. 'I'll be getting my prosthetic legs soon so hopefully next time you see me I will be out the chair. For good.'

Trevor slaps me on the shoulder. 'That's amazing. So you think you'll be back at squash training by next year?'

'Next year? Try this year,' I say. 'And I'll be back to beating you both in no time!'

'Well, we'll leave you both to your lunch. It's so good to see you out and about. I think I just missed you at Sarah's party last weekend. I got there about ten minutes after you'd left. I was gutted,' smiles Rob.

'I didn't stay long. Sorry.'

'Let's definitely hang out soon? And let's make sure we connect at Will's party in a couple of weeks. You still owe me a beer,' he smiles. They glance briefly at Alice before they walk away but she's not looking up.

I turn back to Alice. 'Sorry, keep going with what you were saying about the therapy.'

She waves me off. 'Never mind. Anyway, there's not much to say about how it went. It was only the first session.'

'OK, well, keep me updated, yeah?'

'Will do,' she nods. She sips on her latte which is probably cold by now. 'You went to a party last weekend?'

'Yeah, just to catch up with the guys. It was a last-minute thing.'

She fidgets with the ring on her finger, not really looking at me.

'I would have invited you, but I thought you'd be busy since it was so last-minute.'

She looks up and smirks, 'Busy?'

'Well, I didn't think parties were your scene.'

'They're not,' she says, rolling her eyes.

'But you're welcome to come to the next one. It's at my friend Will's house.'

She makes a face, pulling her lips to the side as she seems to consider this. 'OK, maybe I will. Just to check it out.'

I hadn't expected her to say yes. I'd assumed she'd laugh me off, but I guess she does want to come. I should text Lauren, though, so she doesn't see me come in with another girl. I wouldn't want her to get the wrong idea, and think Alice is my girlfriend or anything. Saying that, I texted her last week just to say hi and haven't heard back. I'm hoping she does come to the party, then maybe we can chat, possibly reconnect. With all this talk of these new legs, and possibly getting back to running and everything I do best, including competing, I'm starting to feel a bit more like myself again. Getting out the house with Alice this summer, being back out in the city, I'm finally starting to feel like the old Jack. Maybe it's time to start putting my old life back together again.

Alice

We pull into the car park and turn off the engine. A deep breath escapes my mouth. Thankfully, it's not too busy today. I called ahead to ask about peak and off-peak times so we could avoid the crowds. I don't do well with crowds right now.

My head aches and my jaw is tight from another night of restless sleep and bouts of nightmares. But I awoke with a mission today. Regardless of how I'm feeling, of what's going on inside my head, I'm going to give Jack a good day. It's not fair to him. I started these little outings to cheer him up and get him out the house, and I can't stop trying now. He's beginning to move on with his life again. He's getting prostheses, he's hanging out with his friends again, he's even been posting photos on social media (yes, I check). I can't punish him for getting better just because I'm not. I might feel trapped, suffocated by these flashbacks but I can't drag him down with me. He's got a lot going on too. I can't expect him to listen to me talk about how miserable I am all day long.

No, today will be a great day for us both. Everything needs to be perfect, no matter what.

He screws up his face as he looks out the open door. 'Thorpe Park?'

'Yup.' I ease him down the ramp and out onto the tarred car park. I'm getting good at this. I'm pretty fast locking him down and even faster unclipping his wheels and getting him down the ramp. I don't even need Martin to help me anymore. He can just sit there – in the driver's seat, of course, after I got bumped from that position – texting on his phone to whoever. Probably to Mrs Addington, just to confirm her son is still alive and hasn't been accidentally wheeled into oncoming traffic by me. His chair doesn't even feel that heavy. Sure, it's not like pushing an empty shopping trolley around Tesco but it's not like a wheelbarrow of bricks either. Maybe I'm getting stronger. I definitely noticed some slight definition in my arms when I got dressed this morning.

He's looking at me, still with his face scrunched up. 'Thorpe Park? Really?'

'Yeah, why not?'

'What rides am I going to be able to go on? Or is the plan to wheel me to the barriers and have me watch other people have fun?'

I give Martin a small wave and start pushing Jack towards the entrance. 'Actually, I called ahead and you can go on the rides. Not all of them, sure, but most.'

'Most?'

'Well, some.'

I slide a print-out of the online tickets Mrs A slipped into my bag before leaving and get ready to hand them over. I unfold them and bend back the paper, hearing the crease crack. Whoa, did these tickets really cost £70 each? Where are we, Disneyworld Florida? I'm glad she didn't listen to me when I initially insisted on paying for them myself at the front gate today. I only brought £40 in cash with me. I thought £15 max for each ticket plus an extra tenner for two Cokes. I wouldn't have even had enough for one admission.

'Tickets, please.'

I hand them over to an assistant at the metal barriers and she gestures us through the wider entrance for prams, strollers, and well, wheelchairs – although I wonder how many of these she sees here on a daily basis. Maybe more than I think.

I push Jack over to the map and pull out the orange Post-it note from my fleece pocket. 'Okay, there's the Flying Fish—'

'That's a kids' ride—'

'Storm in a Teacup—'

'Kids' ride—'

'Mr Monkey's Banana Ride—'

'I don't even have to look at the map key to know that's definitely a kids' ride.'

'Okay, here's one. What's Nemesis Inferno?'

'Not a kids' ride. Let's do that one.' He drives forward on his wheels and starts heading in the direction of a rollercoaster that apparently twists and turns at speeds of over 50mph, and to me sounds like it ends in a burning inferno.

'I go into surgery on Monday,' he says casually.

'What? Why another one?' I'm finding it hard to swallow. Another surgery? They'll cut into him again? What more could the surgeons take from him – he's already lost his legs?

'Worried about me?' he smirks.

214

'No, of course not,' I say, turning my head away so he doesn't see my face.

'Well, don't be. I'll be fine.'

I can't turn back to him, not yet. I swallow hard, the lump stabbing my throat.

'Oh cool, there's a *Walking Dead* ride, can we try that one next?' he asks.

I fumble with the Post-it note, my fingers getting sticky in the July heat. 'Um, no sorry. That's one we can't do because of accessibility restrictions.'

He shrugs. 'Okay, we can do that one next time, when I have my new legs then.'

We pass large clusters of people: families, groups of friends, young couples who look about our age or maybe slightly older like university age. I pass girls in cute summer dresses, tight denim shorts, floaty skirts and strappy sandals that loop up their calves and look fit for a gladiator arena. I suddenly become aware of my black leggings that are too tight for me on the thighs and my baggy T-shirt emblazoned with *Star Wars* graphics with my fleece tied around my hips. The old Jack would never walk with me in a crowded public space like this. Thankfully we don't know anyone here.

'Jack?'

A tall, slender blonde in one of those floaty skirts and strappy sandals stands before us, her hand slotted into the hand of a boy who looks like Alex, Jack's friend. Jack's mouth is agape as he stares at them. Then he clears his throat, 'Hi, Lauren.' Jack glares at the guy next to her. 'Alex.'

'It's so good to see you,' she says dropping Alex's hand.

'You look good, Jack,' he says.

'How are you?' Lauren asks.

'Good.'

'Sorry, it's been so busy. I've not had a chance to text you back,' she smiles, nervously.

'Don't worry about it,' Jack says.

'It's just been so hectic,' she goes on. 'I've been doing a summer term at Edinburgh just to get a feel for the place and I've been working—'

Oh, she works, that's a surprise.

'—at Victoria's Secret in Mayfair.'

Of course she does.

'Again, don't worry about it,' Jack mutters, still staring at Alex.

An uncomfortable silence spreads between us like a spilled liquid.

'I was going to call you—' Alex stammers, holding his hand out.

But Jack thrusts his chair forward. Alex startles and steps into Lauren knocking her off-balance momentarily. 'Enjoy the rides,' Jack calls back to them as he propels forward down the path.

I stand there, fidgeting with the sleeves of my pullover, wondering how to politely leave the conversation after Jack's dramatic exit. 'Um.' I look between them both, wondering how to leave the conversation too, after Jack's dramatic exit. I point to Lauren's shoes. 'Um . . . cute sandals.' Then I brush past them and hurry towards Jack who's disappearing into a crowd of kids wearing *Walking Dead* masks.

I finally catch up to him at a snack shack. 'Thought you were about to take out like thirty kids back there.'

'I was. Thankfully they moved for me.'

'So that's Lauren?'

'That's Lauren.'

'And that's Alex?'

'That's Alex.' He slows down and shakes his head. 'Can't believe he's with her. And that he never told me about it. He didn't need to ask my permission, but he could have warned me at least.'

'Sorry.'

'Some friend,' he shrugs. 'Real friends don't date your ex.'

I gesture to a turn in the path up ahead to get us back on the route to Nemesis. 'Why is she an ex, if you don't mind me asking?'

He shrugs, 'We just drifted apart after the incident. But I thought with things starting to get back to normal – with the new legs coming, that we'd . . . I don't know, sounds silly now.'

He slows down, the chair eventually rolling to a stop.

'Sorry,' I mumble.

He shrugs again, pretending not to care. 'It's fine. Anyway, where is this ride? I think we're just going around this park in circles. And the last thing I want to do is bump into them again.'

'It's just over there,' I point. Maybe Thorpe Park wasn't a great idea. Who takes someone in a wheelchair to a roller-coaster theme park? Did I honestly think he'd be satisfied being carried into a giant teacup and spun around like a five-year-old while I took photos of him? Nemesis better be an amazing ride. 'Here we are.'

'I think the queue starts there.'

'Lucky your mom got us the super unlimited all access pass for a whopping £70.'

'Seventy pounds? That's pretty good actually, I thought it'd be more than that.'

'That's per person.'

'Yeah, I know.' He stops at the wheelchair barrier. 'Alice, are you sure I can go on this?'

I wave my Post-it note at him. 'Of course. I did my research.' The entrance springs opens and we follow a marked path that weaves around a couple of big pillars to a large platform. Riders spill out from metal gates and rush to sit in the rollercoaster carriages. A couple of kids argue over who gets to sit in the front row until their parents scold them and have them sit behind. I watch the attendants pull on the safety bar before signaling to the operator to start the ride. The carriage crawls at a slow pace, moving further away from the platform and closer to the edge of the track where it drops off and zips through the spirals.

An uneasiness washes over me. Why are we here again? Oh yeah, this was my suggestion. Breath catches in my throat, and my fingers start tingling. Stay calm, Alice. Don't freak out here. 'Ready?' I grit my teeth and try to force a smile. Jack shrugs, looking around like he too was expecting some kind of a burning pit of inferno to justify £70 a head. I wheel him past the large queue and right up to the carriage at the back. The back is the safest, right?

But when I get there I realize I don't know how to transfer him from the chair to the carriage. I hadn't really considered that before now. I thought there would be a special carriage for wheelchairs and – like the van – I'd push him on and lock down the wheels. But every carriage looks the same – and there is nowhere for feet. The carriages are simply seats, in rows of two, where the rider is suspended over the track with their legs dangling. How is Jack supposed to ride this? But I definitely asked about the accessible rides and was told this was one. Wasn't it? I wrote it down on my orange Post-it note; it must be right. Okay, here goes.

Jack looks up at me, small creases forming in his forehead. 'Um, Alice—'

'Don't worry, I got this.' The attendant is busy talking to a mom who's trying to pass her son off as meeting the 1.4m height restriction when he clearly doesn't, so I walk up to the main queue. 'Excuse me,' I ask two guys a lot taller than me (and who look like they frequent the gym), 'are you able to help me transfer my friend from his chair to one of these seats at the back?'

The guys look at each other. 'I'm not sure if he'll be allowed to ride this,' one says.

'Yeah, he can. I asked ahead.'

They nod and follow me back to Jack.

'Alice, no. I'm fine. I don't need help. Let's just leave,' Jack protests. But I don't listen. This is our fun day out, we just need to make it more, well, fun. And it will be. This ride will be amazing. I just read on the sign that there's fire. Well, volcanic special effects but that's what I'm talking about. There are water cannons too. Can't beat that.

Before Jack can speak again he's hoisted out of his seat, the bottom of his collared shirt slipping out from the waist of his jeans. His thigh stumps dangle in the air, as he's dragged through the air in one swift motion, and slid into the back carriage. He immediately slumps to the side.

'Excuse me.' I look up and see the attendant rush over, having just refused entry to the under-1.4m boy. 'Sorry, but he can't ride.'

The guys bend down and slide their hands under Jack's thighs again, heaving him up. 'No, he's fine there,' I say to them and turn back to the attendant who's now standing in front of me. 'No, he can ride. I called ahead and asked the person on the phone specifically what rides he'll be able to go on.'

'Well, I don't know what you were told but he can't go on this one.'

'Alice, can we leave?' Jack asks quietly, his limp body still suspended in the air by the two guys.

'Look, it says here on my note that he can go on Flying Fish, Storm in a Teacup, Nemesis—'

'He can't ride Nemesis. Look at the sign, it says a height restriction of 1.4m—'

'Well, he's taller than that, obviously, look at him. I mean, not now maybe, now that he's in the chair but when he wasn't in the chair he was much taller than 1.4m.'

'He has to have function in his lower body, which is also a criterion. Look.' He points to the lettering under the health and safety heading: Riders must have full functionality in at least three limbs, minimum of one functioning hand.

'Well, he has that. I mean, look – two arms, two hands, that's four.'

'No, it means minimum two arms and one leg or two legs and one arm.'

'A hand is a limb,' I argue.

'Alice, please,' pleads Jack from beside me. I didn't realize he was still lifted in the air. Those guys really are strong.

'Fine. Then why do you have a fast-track accessible entrance if you can't accommodate wheelchair-users on the ride?'

'That entrance is also for spectators. Your friend is welcome to watch you ride the Nemesis.'

'Why would he want to watch me ride it? He obviously wants to ride it himself.'

'Alice, just leave it!' he shouts, sounding so frustrated.

We all turn to Jack, still hanging in the air. Now the whole shirt is hanging outside the jeans, and somehow in the chaos, his phone has fallen out his pocket onto the ground. I gesture to the guys to return him to the chair as I bend down to grab the cracked iPhone from the ground. I hear Jack's startled cry before I hear the chair fall. When I look up I see the chair tipped onto its side and one of the guys trying to move it back to upright with his foot, while his friend balances Jack. I grab Jack's hips to steady him as the guy stumbles backwards. 'Careful!' I shout.

He regains his balance, his face going as beetroot red as

Jack's, and soon the chair is back on two wheels and he's safely returned to it. He doesn't wait for me, he turns the chair around and thrusts himself towards the exit. I weakly thank the guys, give the good old middle finger to the attendant, and hurry after Jack. I follow him down the exit route, back around the pillars, and out to the sunshine. The glare penetrates my eyes and I put one hand up to my face while the other fumbles for my sunglasses which are on the top of my head, pinning back my wavy hair. My mom always says this is why I need the arms refitted and tightened so often. She says I'm stretching them on my head. She's probably right.

When I catch up to Jack he's somehow veered off the paved path and has found himself on the recently watered gardens surrounding the water rides. I watch him push away at the dirt trapped under his wheels, fresh clumps of grass and mud scattered around him. He's stuck, just like in the community garden – why do I keep picking places with wet grass?

I slowly walk over, hands in pocket. 'Sorry,' I mutter.

He breathes heavily as he wrestles with his chair, panting with the effort. 'It's fine. It's not your fault.'

'I promise someone told me you could ride that—'

'Alice, it's okay.' He stops wrestling the wheels and leans back. 'It'll all be different when I get the prostheses. This won't happen again.'

'What? Getting stuck?'

'Getting turned away from things because they're not wheelchair-accessible.' He looks away. 'It's just not fair.' Sweat beads on his forehead and his chest heaves in and out heavily. I don't know what to say, how to make him feel better about the Alex-and-Lauren situation, so I sit down beside his left wheel. The grass feels wet beneath me and scratches at the small patch of skin below the bottom of my leggings. We both stare at the big rollercoaster that carries screaming kids up a ridiculously high level, only to drop them into a pit of water. Looks stupid now, really. I can't believe I momentarily wanted to be one of those kids in tiny plastic carts being hauled over an edge to plummet down, just for the fun of it.

'I hate rollercoasters,' I finally say.

'Me too.'

A young boy on my right catches my eye and I watch him run with a pink ice cream over to his mom. The double-scoop cone is piled high, and is already dripping on one side, running down his arm. He stops momentarily to lick his arm, tilting his hand a little too much. The top scoop slides off and drops to the ground at his feet. He stares at it for a second, then screams engulf the air around us, drowning out the shrieks from the big, stupid rollercoasters Jack's not allowed to ride on. I scoff, feeling a large smile stretch tight across my face.

Jack looks at me, smiling. 'Are you laughing at that kid dropping his ice cream?'

I shrug and start plucking daisies from the ground. 'Do you blame me?' My cheeks relax as the smile fades from my face.

'For laughing at the kid?'

223

'No, I mean for what happened that day.'

'Alice, I can't talk about it—'

But I don't let him cut me off, not this time. 'We've never talked about my letter to you. I've never asked you anything about that day. But we did collide, and argued for a few minutes at least. That would have been enough time for you to have run further, to have got further away from Leicester Square.'

The streets, the rain, Jack, the books as they tumbled to the ground. I close my eyes and feel the heat—

'Alice!'

I slowly open my eyes and suddenly become aware of my heavy breathing and the twisted, groaning sounds I'm making. Jack's hand is on my shoulder, and he's squeezing. He's counting again, softly whispering numbers as my breathing slows and begins to regulate again. I swallow hard and wipe the sweat from my forehead.

'Better?' he asks, still squeezing my shoulder.

I nod, desperately trying to simmer down the emotions building inside me. I want to ask him again because he didn't answer my question. But the words don't come out. They're stuck inside me, just like Jack's wheels in the grass. So I say no more about it. I look up at the sky-high rollercoasters and drop towers filling the park's skyline, hearing screams of excitement, screams of – I don't know. Those aren't the same screams I still hear in my head at night, that's all I know.

'You okay?' he asks me.

I suddenly imagine Jack, tall, standing over me with his prostheses, his broad shoulders above my head. That's where he belongs. Not below me, but above me, above all this. I don't want to say anything, but I'm scared. I'm terrified once he has his legs fitted that he'll go back to who he was before all this. Because I can't go back to who I was. I'm not the same person and new legs can't help me. I don't recognize anything about myself when I look in the mirror.

'Yeah,' I smile weakly. 'Let's get you back, eh?' I stand up and reach for his chair's handles. First, I ease the front wheels off the grass, balancing the weight at the back, then slowly drag him onto the paved walkway.

'Thanks for today, really,' he says, looking up at me.

'I'm sorry it got ruined because of that stupid ride.'

'If it makes you feel better, I bet there was no "burning inferno".'

'Yeah, it would have been one single candle and a dumb sound effect,' I mutter. 'Let's go get ice creams instead.'

Fall Backwards

PART 3

Autumn's cries can be heard through summer,
Red, orange, yellow and brown,
Stain the leaves and dry the tips,
They crust,
They crumble,
They fall,
Like the bricks on the building and the glass windows,
They break, and float down towards the ground,
They land around our feet,
Like the dead, the leaves turn to dust,
Like my nightmares, they burn to ash,
We close our eyes and fall back,
And hope someone's there to catch us.

Alice Winters

Jack

I awake slowly, harsh light piercing my eyes as I force them open. For a moment I don't know where I am. Then flashes of the bombing come rushing back, filling my head until it pounds and throbs. I see a girl standing at the other side of the road staring at me. I see Alice. She's mouthing something to me, but I can't make out exactly what she's saying. She's angry, she's waving her hands. I walk closer to the edge of the pavement to hear her better. A loud explosion erupts in my ears. Smoke and fire pull me into a thick cloud and I can no longer see Alice.

'Jack?'

My fingers grasp and find soft blanket as bile rushes to my throat. Hands are on my shoulders, pulling me up to a sitting position, then leaning over the side of the bed. When I'm finished vomiting, the same hands return me to the pillows.

'Is this normal, doctor?'

I recognise my mum's voice and suddenly remember where I am. I'm in the hospital. Again. But why am I back in the hospital?

'Yes, Mrs Addington. It's very common to get nauseous

when coming out of surgery. It's just the anaesthesia wearing off. He'll probably feel nauseous for a couple of days after but then he should be fine.'

Gentle hands touch my forehead, stroking my hair back. 'Jack, it's Mum. How are you feeling?'

I try to talk but no words come out. I'm being pulled up again, this time a cold cup is placed to my lips. When I try to drink, half of it spills down my chin. They're rubbing my mouth now, like I'm an infant feeding for the first time. I guess this is something I should get used to. Hospitals seem to be a part of my life now.

My whole body aches as I stifle a cough so I let it out. It scratches my throat and tears at my trachea. My lips sting like they're cracked and bleeding. I get this a lot when skiing or mountaineering in colder climates . . . I mean, I used to get this. But maybe I will again – yes, I remember now. I'm here in the hospital for hopefully my last surgery . . .

I grasp at the bed covers again and try to pull myself up. 'It's OK, relax. You're in the hospital, honey.'

I nod and rest my head back on the pillows. 'How did it go?' I mutter. My head is pounding.

'It went really well, the doctor said. They removed a lot of scar tissue from around your thighs which was causing you the nerve pain.' She squeezes my arm. 'Oh Jack, it couldn't have gone any better.'

A deep sigh escapes my throat and I squeeze my eyes shut. Finally. I'm starting to see some light at the end of this long, dark tunnel.

'How long will I be in here for this time?'

'Just a few days then some rest at home.'

'Then physio?' I ask.

'Then you can start physio,' she says. When I open my eyes I see Mum brushing tears off her cheeks.

'Mum, it's OK. I'm fine. I'm not in any pain. I'm on some pretty hardcore pain relief,' I smile.

She smiles back but it's not real. 'I know. It's just seeing you back here in this place . . . it just reminds me of before.'

'I know, me too.'

'Of course,' she says as she rests her hand on my shoulder. 'Sorry, I shouldn't be talking about myself here. This must be harder for you.'

A knock on the door startles both of us and when I turn I see Alice in the doorway, a ridiculously large bouquet of flowers in hand and a stupid balloon floating above her head that says GET WELL SOON. She's wearing thick yellow woven tights and a skirt; she's probably not even aware it's bunched up on one side. Her red curly hair is tucked into a navy scarf. She waves awkwardly from the door. 'Hey, you.'

'Hey,' I say, gesturing for her to come inside.

'I can come back later if that's better?'

'No, Alice. You stay,' says my mum. 'I'll pop downstairs and grab a coffee.' She turns to me. 'Your dad will be back this afternoon.'

'He was here?' I ask.

'He was here all night. For the surgery too. I had to force him to go home to get some sleep. I didn't know you were going to wake an hour later. Now I feel bad for sending him away.'

231

Alice and my mum exchange polite air kisses, with me wondering if Alice has seen that on a movie or something. She waves goodbye one last time then drops her bag heavily on the floor. The balloon escapes her hand and floats up to the ceiling, bouncing off the lights. 'So.'

'So.'

'And we're back here again.'

'I should just get a room named after me.'

'I wouldn't be surprised if your whole family has the hospital named after you,' she says, falling into the armchair beside the bed. She drops the flowers on the floor by her feet. 'Sorry, more flowers. The hospital gift shop is very limited in its range. Balloons, flowers, chocolates. And I didn't trust myself to not eat the chocolates in the hallway so flowers it is. Anyway, I heard the surgery went well?'

'Yeah, it went OK.'

'Did they say when you can start physio?'

'Probably by next month.'

'Great.'

'Didn't fancy starting back at school this term?' I know she'll hate this question.

'Nah,' she shrugs, pretending to be more nonchalant about school than she actually is. 'My mom and dad have finally decided that home-schooling's better for me. I've always learned more through my own research and home studies. School is just a formality.'

'Spoken like a true home-schooler,' I smile. 'How do you feel about not going back at all this year? It's your last year. You'll never get this high school experience back.'

She plays with a hole in her tights, pulling at the fabric. 'It's not like I'd be going to prom or anything. I'm sure I'll have a better time learning at home. What about you?'

'I'm actually excited to get back to school, get back to my old routine. And I've missed my friends.' I wince as soon as I say it. 'I mean, you're my friend, of course, but I just meant my old friends.' I run my fingers through my hair nervously. 'So what subjects will you be focusing on this year at home?'

'Well, I've already created my own schedule and managed to fit in daily Math, Physics, Chemistry, French—'

'Ah, Française. Ma langue préférée. Comment ça se passe pour toi?'

She stares at me, blinking fast. 'Um . . . I haven't started French yet. I'm not really a languages person so I don't know how that's going to go. I tried Mandarin once but my tutor conveniently quit. Besides, I can barely understand English cues let alone ones from a different language.'

'Then why are you studying it?'

'Because apparently it's a desirable skill for universities here.'

'Oh, you think you'll stay in London?'

'I wasn't sure, but I think I'd like to now,' she smiles.

The door opens and Will and Euan now stand awkwardly in the doorway waving, also holding bouquets of flowers. 'Hey, man,' says Euan.

'Hey, I'm Will,' he says, holding his hand out to Alice to shake.

'Yeah, we've met before,' she mumbles, taking the hand anyway.

'Right,' he says, nodding. 'Annie, right?'

'Nope, it's Alice.' She scrunches up her mouth and half smiles at me. 'I'll leave you all to it.'

'Good luck tonight,' I call to her.

Alice

It's exactly eight steps from the pavement to the front door, plus two more steps to the sign-in board inside and four more down to the room where the support group is being held. That's a lot of stairs. The door is wedged open by what looks like the Bible. I'm apparently early so I scribble 'Alice W.' on the sign-in board and take a flyer.

Coping with Survivor's Remorse?
You are not alone. Survivor's remorse – otherwise known in the medical field as survivor syndrome – is a psychological condition associated with the feelings of surviving a traumatic event when others did not.

I stop reading past the sixth line and fold the flyer, tucking it inside my jacket pocket, my fingers trembling with nerves. The meeting room is more of a small function hall with chairs arranged in a circle all facing inwards. Next to the entrance is a long folding table with an array of soft drinks and paper plates filled with cookies and muffins. I shakily slosh some apple juice into a plastic cup and cradle it in the crook of my elbow as I balance a couple of cookies. I make my way to 'the circle' and choose the chair nearest the door, for quick and efficient exiting if need be.

Next in after me is a tall boy, dressed in skinny jeans and a gray hoodie. He heads straight for the snack table. He turns and heads towards me. 'Oatmeal and raisin,' he simply says before folding into the chair next me.

'What?'

He points to the napkin of cookies in my lap. 'Oatmeal and raisin.'

'Oh, I thought the raisins were chocolate chips,' I mutter.

'Beginner mistake. They never spring for the chocolate chip here.' He's wearing a name badge, stuck to his shirt pocket. WYATT. 'Why not chocolate chip?' he continues. 'Or better yet, let's splash out and offer triple chocolate.'

Two more people come in. A blonde woman who's very overdressed – unless she's going out to a bar right after this, which in London she might be – and an older gentleman in a white shirt and evening chinos, dressed like he genuinely thought he was getting a church service tonight and not this.

'You're not wearing a name badge,' Wyatt whispers to me.

'What?'

He gestures to the table in the corner that has a cup full of markers and pens, and a roll of sticky white labels.

'Oh, thanks.' I fumble at the table, taking an embarrassingly long time to write the five letters of ALICE in various colors and styles. It's all about first impressions. Then I carefully attach the sticker to my chest, being mindful not to pat the ink that's still wet.

The door shuts loudly and I spin around, marker still in hand.

'Hey, everyone, sorry I didn't get here earlier. The tube was rammed tonight.' A short, stocky guy rushes in, a notepad under his arm. A thick beard covers half his face. He notices me and a big smile spreads across his face. 'Oh, a newbie tonight, nice. Welcome. I'm Ian.' He waves at me from across 'the circle.'

The Circle. Sounds like we're all partaking in a cult ritual tonight. Maybe we are.

'Come, join us.'

I return to my place, the oatmeal and raisin cookies still sitting on a napkin under my chair.

'Nice design choice,' Wyatt winks, pointing to my name badge.

Ian clears his throat and talks directly to me. Everyone else must be a regular here. 'All of us here suffer from PTSD in one form or other, whether it be physical or emotional, myself included. Trauma is trauma, no matter how or where you feel it. I began these meet ups over three years ago with an emphasis on psychological and emotional safety, and recovery. I'm not a doctor or a psychologist so if your GP is recommending you see one, please do that.' He waves to the door I just came through. 'You're not late – come in, Sara.'

Another girl joins the circle, totaling six. More than I expected here tonight.

'So, here we are. Together. Supporting each other.'

I don't know why but I suddenly feel guilty, like I'm

cheating on Jack or something by coming here without him. We just spent so much time together over the summer, and what happened to us was very much our shared tragedy – but now I'll be sharing it with others, with strangers. And my story is so fused with Jack's that it'll be hard to share mine without sharing his. I wish he were here beside me but tonight I'm here alone. And after Jack gets his new legs, and returns to his old life which is all he talks about, then I might find myself alone more often. I'm happy Jack's getting the prostheses, I am. It's just hard seeing him move forward while I just feel stuck, trapped, reliving that morning at Leicester Square over and over in my mind.

Damn, I forgot to bring tissues with me tonight, and I already feel wetness pooling in the corner of my eyes.

'Alice, do you want to share anything about yourself with the group?'

I look up and realize everyone is staring at me.

'Um . . . no I'm okay,' I stammer.

'It's okay,' Ian says. 'It's a safe place here.'

Nowhere is safe.

An engine roars to life outside the hall window and I suddenly spring up on my feet. Warmth swirls in my belly, and I start to feel short of breath.

'Alice?'

They're all still staring at me.

The engine gets louder. It's so loud it's hurting my ears. Does no one else hear it? Why are they not covering their ears like me?

I can't hear Ian, but I see he's up out of his chair walking

238

towards me. I stumble back and grab my bag from under the chair. It knocks the cookies off the napkin onto the dusty floor. Then I hurry to the door. I hear my name called as I rush down the hall and up the stairs back to the main lobby.

When I get to the car park, I don't hear my name anymore. It's raining again. I take a deep breath and gulp the night air wildly. My chest still throbs and hurts, like I'm having a heart attack. I stumble through the parked cars and sit down on the edge of the pavement that faces out to the cemetery. I'm still wearing the name badge. The raindrops hit the letters and they start dripping, sliding off the label until it muddies the name so much that I can't see an 'A' anymore. Soon I'm wearing a label that looks like it's been tie-dyed with an array of rainbow colors.

I slide my phone out of my coat pocket, bringing the flyer with it. It falls to the ground beside my boots, landing in a puddle. I stare at it, floating, wet. Now I see books in the puddle, an umbrella, a cup on its side with coffee spilling out into the rain. I see Jack, running past me. I feel him, running into me. My chest hurts again. I frantically type out a message to Jack, the words all jumbled and hurried. He calls right away. As his voice calms my breathing, my eyes flicker to the flyer still floating in the puddle, absorbing all the water, then sinking to the bottom beyond reach.

Jack

'Right, Jack, just a little more.'

My hands grip the metal bars, sweat starting to make them slide. I tighten my fingers around the bars. I've lifted more weight than this hiking. I had to shoulder Euan's weight once when he went over his ankle climbing the Cuillin Munros on the Isle of Skye. This is just my own weight and I'm a lot lighter than Euan. This should be easy for me. But it's not.

'Can you go a little further?'

I nod, not wanting to look weak by saying no but this is burning my shoulders. I try to take a deep breath in and start to inch further down the bars to where the blue mat meets the shiny tiled surface. Breath gets trapped in my airways as I clench my jaw and start to struggle. My arms buckle first, folding at the elbows. Patrick, my physiotherapist, thrusts his hands out and catches me.

'Good work, Jack. That's the furthest I've seen you go. You're getting stronger.'

I know he's probably right, but none of this feels any easier now than compared to my first few sessions and I don't feel like I'm making progress at all. But I've lost a lot of muscle mass since March, progress is going to be slow building it back up. I need to be kinder to myself. I'm still in a great position for the legs to be fitted. Besides, it just feels so good to be back in a gym, strength-training. I'm feeling more and more like my old self.

Noises from the rear corner pull my attention as Patrick helps me transfer my weight back to the wheelchair. I sink into it, a sigh escaping my throat. Sweat drips down my back. I glance over and see another amputee in the back. He's older than me, broader in the shoulders. He steadies himself on the bars for a brief second then glides down them seemingly without any effort. He turns at the end, momentarily shifting his weight to one arm to do so, and comes back. His amputations seem above the knee like mine, but from his clothes and the silver chain I see swinging from his neck I'd say he lost his legs in war not the bombings here in London.

It's just the two of us here in the training room today so it seems bigger than usual. There are long silver bars like you'd find in a gymnastics class, equipment machines, a couple of treadmills and rowers, and a line of stationary bikes mounted at various inclines. Last week there were about five of us plus the physiotherapists and I could barely hear Patrick. I glance back again, that veteran guy is the only one I've seen here with a double amputation like me. I wonder how long he's been coming here? Is he waiting for prosthetics too?

'Doing OK otherwise?' Patrick balances his coffee cup in one hand and his calendar in the other.

'Yeah, I'm fine.' My chest heaves in and out as I try to regulate my breathing. My body feels so foreign to me now. I don't recognise any sensation. Everything I sense physically is new and unfamiliar, and sometimes scares me. I feel pain where I shouldn't. Last night I felt like I had an itchy foot. I know there's nothing there but it still itched, and when I couldn't relieve the itching it just got worse. The doctor said these are just 'phantom pains' and normal for amputees, but sometimes they're so strong that they keep me awake at night. I wonder if I'll still continue to get them once the artificial limbs are fitted?

'We're getting close. Only two weeks away until the prostheses come in, right?'

'Hopefully the socket mould fits this time.'

'Are you still keeping up with the skin desensitisation programme?'

'Every night. I've been massaging my thighs and rubbing them with a warm damp face cloth.'

'Good. How about the compression bandages I gave you? They'll really help prevent a build-up of fluid around the area where they'll attach the socket.'

'I'm wearing them right now.'

'Great. You're doing everything you should be doing.'

'How long after do you think I'll be able to walk unassisted?'

'Well, typically the rehabilitation treatment for prostheses is extensive and long. We need to strengthen the muscles in your core, back and arms, improve your stamina and endurance overall, so you're able to cope better with the demands

242

of wearing not one but two artificial limbs. You're essentially learning how to walk all over again.'

'And running? When can I run?'

'You're eager to get back at it,' he smiles.

'Of course. I want to do everything I did before.' That's why I'm doing this, to get back to the old Jack. The only Jack I know, and the only Jack my dad knows. 'So I'll be able to run normally again?'

'Not "normally", your stride will be different to accommodate for the artificial limbs but yeah, after a lot of treatment and training, and if you continue to keep doing what you're doing to ensure a successful prosthesis attachment then I can't see why not.'

I turn round and see the veteran back in his chair. For a second we make eye contact, each looking at one another's injuries. He's relaxed in his chair, like it's simply an extension of his body. He wheels it with ease and turns smoothly with one hand. He looks strong, effortless. He makes jokes with his physio and swings back in his chair, momentarily balancing on just the back wheels. I feel so clunky and awkward in mine compared to him. Although I'll be out of it soon.

'That's Charlie. He's here all the time. He doesn't stop training. Why don't you go over and say hi?' says Patrick kneeling down to me.

'No, it's fine.'

'You sure? I know he doesn't look it, but he is actually friendly.'

'Maybe next time.' I start to push myself towards the door. 'Same time tomorrow?'

'You're not scheduled in until Friday.'

'You free tomorrow, though?'

'Well, yeah, I could see you between half one and half two, but don't you want to take it easy, rest for a day or so?'

'I'm not going to get out this chair by taking it easy.' I start pushing harder, feeling an uncomfortable strain in my shoulders. I'll have to ice them tonight to prevent inflammation like last time. 'See you at half one tomorrow,' I call back.

Alice

When I open my eyes, I see a white-rimmed corkboard lying on the floor, and my mom. She's on top, holding me. She's saying my name, over and over again. I hear my breathing, heavy and erratic, and I feel sweat down my back. My hands are shaking. I blink hard and gaze around the room. I'm at home, in my bedroom. Beside my mom are a stack of books she got for me scattered wildly across the floor like they've been knocked over: *Understanding PTSD: The Journey to Finding Peace, Overcoming Your Fears, Controlling the Mind*, and my favorite title, *From Surviving to Thriving*. I haven't looked at any of them.

My breathing slows and my body calms, the fatigue instantly setting in. 'What happened?'

My mom holds me tight. 'Ssh. It was just another panic attack. It's okay. You're safe.' She strokes my hair. 'You're safe,' she says again.

I wriggle out of her grasp and sit back against the corkboard that fell, still panting, chest still heaving. I sound like I've run a marathon. I feel like it too. Why does this keep happening to me? Why is it getting worse?

'Please, Alice, see a doctor with me.'

'Mom, I'm fine,' I stammer. I tried therapy, I tried the support group Dad recommended, none of that worked. What else is there?

'Alice, you're not. Maybe we should call the therapist and get you back there. Or we can look into checking you in to a private PTSD clinic, or—'

'Mom, stop.' My head is throbbing.

She stands up and starts pacing slowly. 'I'll call the GP again. Maybe there's medication that will help?'

Medication? I need drugs now? 'Mom, I don't need to see a doctor or a therapist, or go to a stupid church peer group or read any of the self-help books you've been getting me from the library that are totally useless, or pop pills. I don't need any of that!'

'Then what, Alice? What do you need? Please tell me, because your dad and I don't know how to help you. We don't know what to do anymore.' She slides down the door and drops to her knees beside me. She cries, wiping tears away with the back of her hand.

I scoot over and put my arms around her. She grips me tightly. When I finally let go, she's stopped crying. She tucks a loose strand of hair behind my ear like she used to when I was younger, and brushes the tears off my cheeks. I wrap around her again for another hug, resting my head on her shoulder. I gaze at the corkboard that I knocked over during the panic attack. It lies on its side, filled with flathead pins securing photos of the summer just past. The photos I took of Jack, the ticket stubs from Thorpe Park, a dried sprig of rosemary from the community herb patch. This is as close

246

as I've come to decorating a bedroom. I always keep the walls bare, the wardrobe minimal, the drawers untouched because I never know how long I'll be staying. Makes the move to the next place quicker and easier.

A knock from the front door downstairs startles me and my mom grips me tighter to soothe me. Then she lets go. 'Back in a minute.' I hear voices in the hallway, one I recognize immediately. I throw on an oversized hoodie emblazoned with my dad's alma mater, Norwich University in Vermont, and go downstairs to meet Jack. He smiles at me from the bottom of the stairs, his thick blond hair combed neatly to the side. He wears a gray jumper with a blue collar from his shirt sticking out, and cradles a cup holder in his lap.

'I'll leave you guys to catch up,' my mom smiles, her eyes still red and puffy. 'Jack, it was lovely to finally meet you.'

'Pleasure is all mine, Mrs Winters.' He nods politely as she leaves us.

'Very charming,' I scoff as I thud down the bottom step. 'I didn't expect to see you here?'

'You canceled our cinema trip today. I wanted to check in, make sure you're okay.'

'Sorry. I thought I'd be able to do it, but I started to panic about being in a tight space with people sitting so close, wondering what would happen if . . . if . . .' My breathing starts shortening again.

'It's okay,' Jack says quietly. 'I understand.' He gestures to the backyard. 'Want to get some air?' We don't have a ramp from the back door down to the grass so I sit beside him

247

on the small patio, curled up on a cushion from the sofa. He hands me the cardboard holder from his lap, which holds three paper cups and a small cluster of sugar packets and stirrers.

'What's this?'

'Figured I'd return the favor from the hospital and bring you coffee, but I didn't know what you'd feel like so I got a selection. This is a pumpkin spice latte, this is honeycomb, and that's a cappuccino,' he points. 'There was a hot chocolate but your mum stole that one. She looked like she needed it.'

I smile, reaching for a latte. 'Thank you. My mom loves hot cocoa. And you Brits make a good one here.'

'Thank you,' Jack nods, like he personally made it and didn't just buy it from the Starbucks on King Street.

I cradle the cup in my hands and gaze out at the garden, wondering if Jack has ever seen one this small in size. The air is crisp and dry, and if I breathe hard enough I can just about see my breath. We only have one tree in the garden and the branches are already stripped clean, the red and brown leaves strewn on the ground around the roots. The swing creaks eerily in the breeze.

'I'm sorry I've been so busy,' he says, also watching the swing creak back and forth. 'I've been training every day at the clinic, in the gym at home in the evenings or the pool.'

'It's fine, really. You've got so much going on, and you get fitted with your prostheses soon.'

'Thursday.'

'You don't need to be driving all the way out here to check up on me.'

'First, it's only a half-hour up the M3 and second, this isn't an inconvenience to me, Alice. If you need anything, even just to talk or go for a walk, I'm here. Just because I've been busy and spending time with Will and Euan, doesn't mean I'm too busy for you.'

I gaze down at my feet, at my woolly gray socks on the cold patio stone, and sigh deeply. I feel guilty he's come all the way out here, for me. He's got so much to be happy about right now, he's finally getting his life back. He's so much happier than when I first met him at the hospital. All I'm doing is bringing him down.

'Have you been back to the church group?' he asks.

'No, not yet.'

'Why not?'

'Because I ran out the first time. I suppose I'm just a little embarrassed,' I shrug, picking at the edge of the plastic lid.

'You've got nothing to be embarrassed about. Look, I'll go with you next time if it means you'll go.'

'Really? You'd do that?'

He nods.

'Thanks,' I smile, taking another sip. He doesn't have to say anything when he's there, but just having him next to me will help a lot.

'Come on,' he mutters, turning himself around in the chair. He's already so much smoother navigating that than what he used to be. I can't help but smile. 'Get dressed. We've got an adopted herb patch to tend to.'

Jack

'How does it feel, Jack?'

I glance at the prosthetist, Dr McKenzie, then over at my mum who eagerly sits on the edge of her chair. I don't know what to say. I don't know what I was expecting, but it's not this. This feels – strange. Extending from my thighs all the way down are two very artificial-looking legs. They're smooth to the touch, cool beneath my finger pads, and the texture is weird. And the colour, what colour is that? It's the default colour of the emoji faces on my phone, a rich yellow that's neither tan nor beige. I hate using emojis, Lauren used about five per text, but if I used one I always changed the colour to a more realistic-looking shade. But I can't alter the colour on these, they're permanently set to default.

Oh God, I have emoji legs.

'Jack?' asks my mum.

What do they want me to say – I love them? Oh yes, they're perfect, they look just my own legs, I'll never be able to tell the difference. And the durability is outstanding. These legs can definitely get me to the top of a Munro or to the finish line of a marathon.

'I know what you're thinking,' Dr McKenzie says as she moves closer to me.

I doubt she knows what thoughts are going through my mind right now.

'They're not your legs. I know. They can't ever replace your legs.'

OK, maybe she does know.

'But these will hopefully do a lot for you in terms of enhancing your way of life. In an ideal world, we wouldn't be sitting here at all. You'd be out there, doing what you love to do. But we're not in an ideal world, so this right here is the best option for getting you more physical movement and freedom.'

Freedom. She's right. These strange-looking, bright yellow emoji legs are an opportunity to get back to all the physical activities that I love, and just because they look weird right now, doesn't mean I won't get used to them. I will. And besides, once I put trousers on no one will be able to see them anyway. I'll be standing tall again and no one will have to crouch or bend down to speak to me like I'm a child. I'll be tall again, right? These aren't the artificial legs of a short person? Girls hate short guys.

'Do you want to try standing on them?'

I nod hesitantly. I've been waiting for this day for a long time, ever since we first discussed prostheses. Here we go. I look over at my mum who takes a loud, sharp inhale and slowly shimmy off the clinic bed, scooting one inch at a time. I take Dr McKenzie's hand when she offers it and start to shift forward.

My mum stands beside me and smiles. 'It's OK, we'll catch you.'

I take a long deep breath, squeeze my eyes closed and let go.

The first thing I feel is pain. Overwhelming pain through my thighs to my hips as the weight of my whole body rests on two pieces of hard plastic. Then I feel nauseous as my body sways and rocks. I grip Mum's shoulders and the specialist's to steady myself. I lift my left leg and let the weight shift to the right, and try to take a step. My torso lurches forward, pushing my hips back and I slide back down onto the bed. My mum catches me before I can fall back. Another burst of sharp pain shoots up my thigh as I try to stand again so I sit back down and take a sharp breath in. It hurts so much.

'It's going to be uncomfortable and probably painful at first so don't be discouraged. That's why we encourage a desensitising programme to build tolerance and so that your limbs get used to the impact of the movement. But it doesn't last long, and soon you'll be moving in them pain-free. Remember how awkward you felt in the wheelchair when your first got it?'

I nod, that time in my life at the hospital feels like so long ago already. I hated that chair at first. Hated being in it, hated feeling like I couldn't leave it. But then I got used to it and getting around in it became more natural, like these will. I just need to train harder and persevere. I can do that.

'You mentioned you wanted to recommence your physical activities?' asks the specialist.

'Yes, I want to get back to running. And climbing, hiking, skiing—'

'Jack—' My mum can't stand to hear this again. She tells me my life now is different, not worse, just different. She doesn't understand. She probably never will. Who could possibly walk in the shoes of an amputee who recently lost both legs? Don't excuse the pun. It was intentional.

'So, it's possible now? With these?' I ask Dr McKenzie.

'I did get you endurance prostheses for high-functioning physical activities like every day walking. In terms of running, we'll see how you get on with these and with your new physiotherapy training programme and if all goes well, we can discuss other options for getting you back to your optimum fitness, such as looking at the Össur running blades.'

'Great!' I exhale. 'Can you order them now?'

'Running blades are very expensive; they cost around $15,000-$18,000 per limb. And they tend to work best with below-the-knee amputations but your injuries meant an above-the-knee double amputation so for that reason it's better for us to start with these – along with an aggressive training plan to learn how to move smoothly and efficiently before thinking about speed and pace. You also need to learn how to compensate for the loss of muscle, bone and knee joint in both legs. Let's start there for now, yeah?'

'But we can have this conversation again soon, right? Once I've had success with these?' I ask.

'Of course.'

I bite my lip in elation, gazing down at the new prostheses. I'll be back up running in no time.

Alice

Alice, I'm so sorry but I won't make the therapy group tonight. Patrick's had a cancellation for an evening session at the training clinic and I couldn't say no.

I roll my eyes and shove my phone in my pocket. I've been standing in the car park in the dark for ten minutes and now I have to go in there alone and face everyone. I sigh and gaze back at the church building, the bright lights from inside illuminating the cars around me. I sigh and shove my phone in my pocket. I think I'll just miss it tonight too. I was dreading going in, even with Jack beside me. Maybe I'm just not ready for this. I'm not ready to talk about it, or face it. I'll walk slow, maybe get a slice from Pizza Bella or a coffee and walk along the river, take the long way home. That way I can pretend to my mom that I went tonight. She and my dad are so worried about me. I don't want to worry them more.

'Alice?' I look up and see Ian at the steps.

'Oh, hi.'

'You coming in?'

'Um . . . sure.' I follow behind him, cursing myself for not thinking fast enough. I should have said no, or said I was waiting for someone then just left. Now there's no backing out.

He turns and smiles at me. 'It's nice to see you here again.'

'Hope I stay longer this time,' I laugh nervously.

He smiles with me, but I can tell it's a sympathetic one. He opens the door to the hall for me and I step inside, immediately seeing the circle of chairs. Wyatt is here already. He waves to me from the circle. I hesitantly wave back. Ian starts unpacking an array of snacks from a bag onto the folding plastic table by the door. A carton of orange squash, a battered box of oatmeal and raisin cookies and what looks like over-ripe bananas in a plastic bowl. They really could do with some funding.

'Snack?'

'No, thanks. I just ate,' I quickly reply. I take a seat and slide my bag under my seat wondering if I should excuse myself to the bathroom just so I can run away discreetly before this starts.

'Nice to see you back, Alice,' says a woman from behind me, who I think is Sara from last time. She takes a seat opposite me in the circle and smiles. I'm surprised how many of them remember me. I'm not particularly memorable, or so I thought. The rest of the group shuffle in through the door, pick through the snack table and sit down.

'Shall we start?' asks Ian. 'First, welcome back Alice.'

'Sorry about last time, just running out like that,' I mutter, feeling my cheeks warm.

'No need to apologize for anything here. Your reaction was perfectly normal. Everyone here has walked out at some point.'

Again, they all smile and nod.

'What's important is that you came back.'

Not really – I just couldn't escape the car park in time.

'I don't want to put you on the spot, but do you want to introduce yourself again to the group?'

I stand, pushing the chair back and clear my throat.

'You don't need to stand unless you want to.'

'Oh.' I plop back down in my chair. 'My name is Alice. I go to high school in the city. I'm from the US but we've moved around a lot throughout my life.' What else do I say? 'I like reading, poetry, and . . . animals.' They're still staring at me. 'And my favorite food is pepperoni pizza.'

'Hi, Alice,' they say, strangely in perfect unison.

I wave awkwardly from my seat.

'Thank you, Alice, for that.'

'You're welcome,' I mutter.

'Let me tell you why I'm here, and then if you feel comfortable, you can tell us why you're here,' Ian says. 'I joined the army when I left school, was deployed soon after that, and by nineteen had my first assignment in the Middle East. The things I witnessed there were very difficult for me to understand and when my unit lost some men, I had to return home. I was experiencing what I'd later find out was something called survivor's remorse. I was plagued with guilt at having survived what many other people hadn't. And since my injuries weren't physical, that made it harder for my family and friends to understand.'

'How did you overcome it?' I ask.

'There's no quick fix, I'm afraid. It took years of therapy,

256

peer support groups like this, and talking about it. Talking about it is the first step.'

Years? At best I was hoping for six to twelve months, but I could be feeling like this for years?

'I was . . . um . . . at Leicester Square back in the spring,' I slowly say.

Wyatt leans forward in his chair as the rest nod.

'I didn't sustain any physical injuries, not like some, but I guess what I'm feeling could be survivor's remorse. I don't know. It feels more like fear to me.'

'Fear of what, Alice?' asks someone.

'Having it happen again, maybe?'

'Have you been back to Leicester Square since?' asks Ian.

'No, why would I?' I scoff. Did he not just hear me mention the word 'fear'?

'I know it would be really difficult, but sometimes returning to the scene can help release trapped feelings.'

My chest immediately feels tight, and my breathing gets a little faster. 'I don't think that would be a good idea,' I shake my head. There's no way I'm going back there. No way.

'It might help you overcome your fear.'

'Maybe. Or it might trigger an even bigger panic attack,' I gasp.

'You won't know until you try. It's a strategy that's worked for some people.'

'It worked for me,' Sara says quietly, her eyes on me.

'I'll think about it,' I mutter, then sit back in my chair, hoping he gets the cue that I'm done talking about it for the night.

He nods then looks round the group. He's got it. 'Does anyone else want to share anything this evening?'

Wyatt eagerly raises his hand, practically jumping out of the seat. I lean back and listen to him ramble on about a bumblebee he saw dying outside in his garden, and feel an ache in my chest again. I rub it and hear Wyatt move onto a more general discussion on the fragility of life. When he finally finishes talking, we do a seated meditation of some sort, like my mom does on her yoga mat in the mornings, where we concentrate on our breathing.

At the end I stay a few extra minutes, thanking people for listening, or more so apologizing for occupying half the meeting. Everyone is really nice, really welcoming. I actually didn't absolutely hate it tonight. I think I would come back here, even without Jack. But I wish he was here. Even if he doesn't need it like I do. I think about Jack in the gym training with his new legs, getting stronger, getting braver. I'm so happy for him, happy he's so focused and motivated now. Happy. So if I'm so happy for him, why do I feel suddenly jealous? I wish my life was moving forward like his. But I'm still here, reliving that morning. Over and over and over. The repetition of it all is tedious, and tormenting.

Jack

The reception at the physio clinic is covered in fake spider webs and orange tinsel. Two cheap plastic pumpkins sit by the entrance beside a table with a jar full of sweets and a HELP YOURSELF sign. One of the pumpkins still has a round £1.99 sticker on it. These are the worst Halloween decorations I've seen.

'Jack.'

'Patrick.' I push myself forward in my chair towards the door he holds open. My new legs hide under my black joggers and the strange flat bottoms I'm supposed to call feet are shoved tightly into an old pair of trainers. I wheel myself through an entryway of more fake webbing and into the gym. There's a woman at a table in the far corner working with a therapist on lacing a shoe. I can see the shaking in her hands from here. Near the door is the same guy as last time, Charlie, I think his name is. He's at the pull-up machine, his truncated thighs perched on the edge of a rubber platform as he pulls himself up to the top bar. I count beyond ten by the time I stop staring and wheel myself over to Patrick's training station.

'Let's take a look at these then,' he says squatting down.

He shimmies my trouser leg up over my fake knee joint, held together by what looks like flimsy silver screws and plates. 'Fantastic. These are the new models, meant to withstand more impact. Nice.'

'I'll be switching to running blades as soon as I can.'

'Those are tough to train on. Fantastic once you get there.'

'Can I enter the London Marathon with running blades?'

'You'd have to ask the events team but I think there's an exception that says you can.'

'I'll contact them. I've already got my place in the next marathon.'

'You're talking about running next year's marathon, the one in April?'

'Yeah, why?'

'Jack,' Patrick stands and leans against a weight machine, 'that's less than six months away.'

'I know, I've trained for events or climbs in less time than that.'

'But you're working with artificial limbs now. That's completely different.'

'Where's your optimism, Patrick?' I say, wheeling myself over to the weight machine.

'Jack, as your physiotherapist, I need to warn you that training for an event like that using new artificial limbs sometimes takes a couple of years of training and—'

'Patrick, I'll be fine. I already feel great in these prostheses! Should I start with chest press reps?'

We continue the rest of the session mostly in silence except for the occasional counting of reps and instruction to move onto the next stage of the training programme. When it comes to the walking bars, he helps me to my feet and grips me from behind. 'Ready?' he asks.

My hands tighten around the bars as I shift from one foot to the other.

'Try easing off the bars for the walk back, putting more of your weight onto the prosthetics.'

Dull pain throbs at my thighs when I do so and as it builds I have to bite my lip to stop myself from screaming out.

'Doing OK?'

I nod and force a smile. If I let on how painful it is, he might ease off the training intensity and I can't do that. I need to get ready for the marathon as soon as. I can't afford to take it easy.

'Why don't we end it there? We'll start to shift our focus from upper-body training to lower-body training more over the next few weeks – start to add more of your body weight to these limbs and work on balance. How are you feeling in them?'

'Great. Fantastic.' I have sweat pouring down my back and hairline. I'm so sore. And all I want to do right now is remove these legs and throw them into the Thames. Great and fantastic is far from what I'm feeling. 'Same time tomorrow?'

'Why don't we take a rest day, see how your thighs are tomorrow and pick it up again on Friday?'

'I'll be fine for tomorrow, really,' I argue. 'I'll let you know if it gets too much.' That's another lie. I wouldn't let him know, I wouldn't admit that. Not even to myself. But training takes consistency and that's the only way I'll see faster progress. I still feel guilty for not going to the support group with Alice on Monday night but this training is so important right now. These prostheses are still so new to me, and I'm still feeling a lot of discomfort. A lot. Once I'm past this, I can ease off the training and be there more for Alice.

'OK, can you be here for two?'

'I can do that,' I nod. As I'm wheeling myself towards the exit, I pass Charlie the veteran guy. We lock eyes for a second then he looks away.

'Hey,' I say as I get closer to him.

'Hey.' He goes back to rubbing the towel over the back of his neck. I want to say something else but I don't know what. The only thing that connects us at all is our mutual loss of two very missed limbs. I stay for a moment too long, switching between a statement about the weather or a question about his time here, then I start for the exit again.

'Looks good,' he eventually says, gesturing to my legs.

'Yeah, they're new.'

'Right. How do they feel?'

'OK, I think, but I don't really know how they're supposed to feel.'

He pulls a thick navy hoodie out of his duffel on the floor and slams it over his head quickly.

'Have you thought about getting prostheses?' I ask.

'Yeah, I'm on the waitlist. Takes months through the NHS. Maybe even years, who knows?'

I resist showing the expression building. Of course, he's on the waitlist and I didn't have to wait because I have private healthcare through my family. I feel guilty. He's more deserving of these artificial legs than I am. He's earned them, whereas I was simply in the wrong place at the wrong time. He put himself intentionally in danger to save others and had he known he would end up in a wheelchair his whole life he'd probably still make the same decision again. Who knows how long he could be on that waitlist? And I'm sure at $15,000-$18,000 per prosthetic, per run blade, they are completely out the question for him. I've travelled all over the world and seen different levels of poverty, sure, but being here, face to face with a true war hero, I've never felt more ashamed of my wealth than I do now. I wish I could take these off now and hand them to him, say, 'Here, you take these. I don't deserve them.'

But instead I say, 'Good luck' to him like an insensitive idiot.

He nods and gets back to packing his bag.

'If you don't mind me asking, how did your injuries happen?' I finally prompt.

'Car accident.'

'Really?'

'Yeah, I was home on leave, had just served two terms back-to-back in South Sudan with Op Trenton, I was crossing the street and got hit. Drunk driver.'

'Oh, sorry.' I wasn't expecting that. I'd assumed it was a war injury overseas, not one inflicted by another person here in his home country. That seems worse for some reason.

'You? Car accident as well?'

'Actually no, Leicester Square bombings.' I wave at my

wheelchair. 'I was standing close to the blast zone, apparently.'

He stops packing and sits back in his chair. 'Shit.'

I nod, everything I feel pretty much summed up by what Charlie said.

'Well, look, if anyone knows how you feel it's me so if you ever want to chat then I can give you my number?'

I pull my phone out my pocket and start keying in the numbers as he rattles them off. As I slide my phone back into my pocket, I notice Charlie's hand is extended. I slide mine into his and we shake. His grip is firm and steady, whereas mine feels limp and unsure. I leave it at that and push myself through the door. When I get to reception I hear an older guy making a complaint to the front desk about how his walking cane just got stuck in a low-hanging fake spider web and almost tripped him.

Alice

'Are you sure you want to be here tonight?' he yells over music that's so loud it might crack the walls.

'Does the music have to be that loud?' I ask, jaw clenching. 'I mean, you can't really hear the words at this volume. Sorta defeats the purpose of playing music at all, right?'

Jack laughs like I'm joking. He's wearing his prostheses tonight, covered up by a pair of gray chinos and shoes, like actual shoes. He's out the chair but he uses a walking cane in each hand for balance when he moves. 'I've already asked them to turn it down. This isn't that loud, Alice.'

Is he kidding? I could float a coffee mug in here with these reverberations. I place my hands over my ears. My whole body heats from the inside. That tingling, it's back. My fingertips and toes only start to tingle like this when a panic attack is coming on. I've started writing down the physical sensations in a journal so I can learn to spot them early on. Ian told me to do that, and it's actually helping. A lot of what he's been saying makes sense to me now.

Uh, the tingling. It's getting worse.

It's too loud.

Too loud.

Too—

'Can we go outside? Please!' I scream.

Jack nods and slowly maneuvers through the living room, past a group of people who seem to know him. Actually, everyone here seems to know him, and they all greet him with a boyish slap on the back of some sort. This is probably what it's like at school for him too. No wonder he misses it. To me, Harrogate is just another school. Just another hallway, just another cafeteria, just another classroom, and just another set of cliques. The only thing that stands out compared to the dozens of other schools I've been enrolled at is the library. Harrogate has an incredible library. But I guess now that I'm being home-schooled, Harrogate is no longer my school.

'Is this any better?' he asks.

We're now outside, in a garden that looks more like the grounds at Versailles. Actually, I take that back, Jack's garden looks like Versailles. This is perhaps slightly smaller but still large enough to warrant a mouth agape expression for at least five minutes. 'This is the garden?'

'Jack! Over here!'

We turn and see Will and Euan with a couple of girls sitting over by the gazebo. They wave and then make incomprehensible hand signals in the air.

Jack laughs and starts to move awkwardly down the stone path towards them. He doesn't look particularly stable or comfortable in his prostheses but he says they're great, so he must be doing well with them. 'Mind if we go over and sit with them?'

266

I nod hesitantly. I was just hoping it would be Jack and me tonight. With his hectic training schedule it's been over two weeks since I've seen him. Every time I try to arrange something he's got a physio appointment or a remedial massage or a session booked with a PT at the gym or with the swim instructor or he's seeing his friends. He's always busy. And I never am. As much as I didn't want to come tonight, I wanted to see Jack, but we've been here for fifteen minutes and all I have to show for it is possible ear damage from the music volume. And now we're going to sit with a group of people I don't really know and make small talk.

'Hey!' Jack says greeting everyone when we get over there. I'm less enthusiastic and simply wave silently. He sits down and immediately starts a conversation with Will and Euan that I'm not a part of. The two girls start conversing about something they saw on Instagram, and I sit there awkwardly gazing around the extremely large garden wondering why I bothered to come at all.

Jack laughs loudly with his friends, then reaches for the champagne bottle out the ice bucket on the table. The fizz bubbles and cracks as it rises all the way to the rim. Then he drinks it like it's a glass of water. He holds up the bottle to me.

'No, thanks.'

'You don't drink?' asks one of the girls. She's perched on one of the armchairs, legs crossed at the ankles. She's wearing a pair of tight jeans with a tucked-in silk blouse, and a pair of tan stilettos that I wouldn't be able to walk one step in. Her black leather handbag with gold trim – or is it a satchel?

– sits on the table by the champagne, probably too expensive to be cast to the ground like mine is.

'Not really.'

'She had a Cosmo in a bar once and almost threw up after,' grins Jack.

They all laugh. Why would he share that story?

'You guys are spending a lot of time together. You a couple now?' asks Euan, with a smug little grin on his face.

Jack laughs even harder now. 'No, no.' He dramatically shakes his head, like the word no – twice – wasn't enough. I didn't realize it was so far-fetched for us to be considered a couple. It's not that I have feelings in that way for him. I'm just not that offended by Euan's question like he apparently is.

'Oh, see you hurt her feelings,' Euan says, pointing at me.

I feel my cheeks warm, and my belly flip a little. I just want to go home. Jack makes an expression that I can't read, and downs the last of his champagne. Then he reaches for another.

'Should you be drinking like this on your meds?'

Now his face is as beetroot red as mine. I don't mean to embarrass him or nag him, but I should say something. He had a beer inside too. What if I didn't say anything and the alcohol caused some horrible side effects with the medication?

'I'm fine,' he mutters.

'I just think you should slow down.' I bite my lip.

'You sure you're not a couple? You're certainly bossing him around like you are,' Euan quips. Everyone laughs, except me. And except Jack.

He leans in. 'Why don't I ask my mum to take you home?'

I think that was an attempt at a whisper but after a beer and two glasses of champagne, it definitely wasn't a whisper. I gaze up and see his friends awkwardly looking at each other. No matter where you are in the world, high schools are all the same. 'Fine. Do whatever you want,' I mumble, as I pick up my cheap bag from the ground and swing it over my shoulder.

Jack staggers quickly after me. 'Alice, wait. I can't keep up,' he pants.

I stop at the fire pit and turn around.

'I'm sorry. But I can see you're uncomfortable being here and you're not having a good time. I wasn't trying to be rude or exclude you from the group.'

'Sorry, I wasn't trying to boss you around. You're almost an adult. I'm just really tired and drained from the last few weeks. Let's forget it,' I mutter.

'Forgotten,' Jack says, gently smiling at me. He gestures back to the table, back to his friends. 'Come over for a bit?'

'No, I'll just get the bus home but thanks. I'm quite tired.'

'I know I've been busy but let's hang out next week, okay?'

'I'd like that,' I smile. 'How about Monday?'

'Monday I'm at the clinic in the morning, then I have tutoring in the afternoon.'

'Tuesday?'

'I'm in London on Tuesday morning meeting with the headteacher about my return back, then I have tutoring at school, then I'm having dinner with the squash team. Wednesday I'm back at the clinic, then in the pool for an afternoon session, Thursday and Friday is tutoring and training, then I'm away at the weekend with my mum and dad to the Lake District.'

'Hmm,' I sigh. He really is busy. 'How about the following week?'

'That Monday I'm free?'

'Great, let's do that. That's the week of Thanksgiving so I'll plan something for us.'

'I know things have been hectic and we haven't hung out as much as before, but we're okay, right?'

'Yeah, we're good,' I say, leaving Jack to go back to the party, back to his old friends and his old life.

Jack

'Slow down,' Alice calls after me as I speed down the promenade at Brighton Beach in my wheelchair. I awoke today with my thighs throbbing and burning again, so even though I'm wearing the prostheses, I'm happy to spend some time back in the chair. It's practically empty here apart from a couple of dog-walkers. The November chill keeps away the beachgoers and tourists. Not me, though. I've never liked the beach in the peak of summer. Too busy, too crowded, too uneventful. What's exciting about sunbathing all day long? I prefer beaches when it's like this. Deserted, with a crisp autumn breeze coming in off the ocean. The cold's never bothered me. I welcome it. Alice, on the other hand, is covered head to toe in as many layers of thick fabric she could probably find in her whole wardrobe. She waddles behind me, panting heavily under the numerous bundles of wool. She's carrying a large picnic basket that swings wildly off her hip, clattering whatever is inside.

'Warm enough?' I call back.

'I don't think I wore enough socks. My toes are like icicles.'

'What was that?' I joke.

'Slow down and you'll be able to hear me!'

271

I rest my hand on the edge of the wheel plate and lean back in the chair, letting it slow itself.

'I said my toes are like icicles,' she says, finally catching up.

'Do you want my socks? It's not like they're serving a purpose. Plastic toes, remember?' I kick off my shoes and lean over to slide the socks off. She smiles awkwardly and takes them, veering off to a bench to put them on.

'Do you want to see how well my chair does on the sand?' I say, pointing to a dip in the edge of the path that leads down.

'Not really.'

'Come on.' She rushes to grab my handles as I start to lower myself onto the sand. The front wheels sink in immediately.

'Why aren't you walking today?'

'What can I say, I missed the chair,' I laugh, not wanting to worry her. Also, she might tell my mum if she knows that I'm having a lot of pain and then my mum will make an appointment with Dr McKenzie again. 'When you said we were coming here, I figured the chair was easier.'

She nods and kneels down beside me. She opens the basket and starts unpacking small plastic containers of I-don't-know-what. She closes the basket and places the containers on top like a table. 'So, I have made you a feast today. And by a feast, I mean a traditional Thanksgiving Day meal. And by I, I mean my mom has done all the cooking, of course.'

'Of course. So what do we have here? Am I scared to ask?'

'In this one is sliced turkey.' She stops and glances up at me.

'I know what turkey is.'

'In this one is a green bean casserole, here's some candied yams and this is my mom's famous corn bread.'

'You might have to explain those.'

'Green bean casserole is basically green beans in a creamy sauce with crispy fried onions on top. This is sliced yams with maple syrup and brown sugar—'

'Is that dessert?'

'—and corn bread is, well, corn bread. I don't know how to describe that. It's just good and is always served at the table on Thanksgiving Day as a side.'

'Happy Thanksgiving, then.'

'It's not till Thursday, but I know you have training then so I didn't know if I'd see you. So, have you ever had a proper Thanksgiving meal cooked by Americans before?'

'Actually no, this is a first so thank you.'

'You're very welcome. Turkey?'

'Sure.'

She pulls out two paper plates emblazoned with the American flag and matching napkins. She looks around.

'Forgot something?'

'Silverware. Oops.'

'Don't worry, I can eat with my hands.'

'What? A member of the Addington family eating with anything other than pure gold silverware? Wait, can you get gold silverware or is that a contradiction?' She gingerly fingers a little of everything onto my plate and passes it to me. It's cold and looks a little mushy now, but she seems to have gone to a lot of trouble so I finish the whole plate before she's even got through a quarter of hers.

'Do you like it?' she asks, her eyes lighting up.

It tasted about as good as it looked. And the sweet yams? I don't understand why anyone would serve sweet with savoury. Even the corn bread was sweet. It was more like a muffin. I don't think we'll be celebrating Thanksgiving Day in the Addington household anytime soon. 'Loved it, thank you.'

She plays with the rest of her plate, pushing a yam away with her thumb to get to a small mountain of fried onions. 'Shame you couldn't make it again last week to the meet-up at the church?'

'Yeah, sorry, I've been in the gym and pool at home in the evenings. How's it going anyway?'

'It's actually going well. I like the people there, and it's really casual. We basically sit around in a circle and chat. There's even cookies.'

'Do you have to talk?'

'There's no pressure at all to talk. It's only if you want to.'

'Have you talked yet?'

'I've shared a little about that day. But not as much as some of the other people there.'

'Maybe next time.'

'There's one tonight,' she smirks.

'Um . . .'

'Try one meet-up, that's all, and if you hate it I won't mention it again.'

'I can't manage tonight, but soon.'

She nods and thankfully changes the subject. 'Can't believe it's only four and a half weeks until Christmas. Where has the year gone?'

'Feels like it was only last week you were dragging me to a garden in the middle of nowhere to plant rosemary,' I laugh, thinking back to that time, when my days were unoccupied and I'd look forward to those outings with Alice. 'If it wasn't for you, I'd probably have spent the whole summer cooped up in the house.'

'Do you think our rosemary survived?'

'No, that's definitely dead,' I laugh. The waves overlap and a gulping sound fills the air around us. I wonder what the water would feel like on my bare skin. I want so badly to stand and walk into the water, feel it rise to my thighs and up to my waist; the cold sharpness of the ocean prick at my skin and flood my whole body. 'Do you want to go for a swim?'

She stares at me, eyes wide. 'Are you crazy?'

'No, I was actually being serious,' I smile. 'Come on.'

'It'll be freezing!'

'That's the point. Live a little,' I tease.

'We could get colds or worse, pneumonia.'

'Quick dip and out. I'll time you,' I grin.

She rolls her eyes, and mutters something inaudible. Then she starts taking off her shoes. I laugh and join her, bending down to remove the prostheses. But as I unclip them from the socket, a searing pain takes control. I wince and squeeze my eyes shut.

'Are you OK?' she asks.

It burns. I can barely swallow the pain is that bad. 'I'm fine,' I stammer. 'Just got a funny sensation, don't worry, it happens all the time. It's normal.' I bite my lip cursing at revealing so much to Alice. 'Maybe we should skip the swim for now though.'

'Oh, thank God,' she sighs, dropping back down into the sand.

Alice

I'm standing at the library steps on a particularly dry crisp morning. A light dusting of snow sits by my feet after last night's flurry. I have a hardbound copy of *War and Peace* in my hand, similar to a book I carried on the day. I didn't exactly stop to pick up my belongings in the midst of a terrorist attack so that book is now gone, along with the others, but I wanted to keep the details as close to the day as possible. Ian said it would help. So, here I am. What now?

I'm panting, breathless, my chest is heaving. My fingertips tingle like before but this time the sensation that churns and churns inside me is dread, not panic. I made it this far, I got here. I battled my way through the commuters and the tourists to do so, risking another panic attack, in public and on my own - for this moment. I can't turn back now. I can't give up. Or I might never be here again. I look around. The streets bustle with people, some don't even glance up, others take out their phones and snap photos. We're all in London for different reasons, but we're all here together. And I need to stop staring at everyone like they're an enemy.

My feet slowly ascend towards the main entrance. It's quieter in here than last time but then it was a Saturday. I

277

certainly wasn't riding the tube on a Saturday at peak time. I walk past the librarian's desk; same woman, even looks like the same clothes she has on. I stretch my fingers out and graze the books on either side of me as I walk down the Classics aisle to where I always sit. The armchairs are empty, thankfully. I drop my bag on the ground and still clutching the book, I sit in the chair. The leather feels foreign on my back and under my thighs. I take off my winter gloves and close my eyes, remembering when I was last here. The noises, the smell, the feel of the leather under my palms. It's like it was yesterday, not eight months ago.

A bang startles me and I drop my book. It hits the ground and makes a similar sound. When I look up, I see a woman standing in the aisle, book by her feet. She mouths 'Sorry' to me then bends to pick it up. I slide my gloves back on and stand to face the window, which looks out onto St James's Square. I see runners, cyclists, walkers. And for a second, a split second, I think I see Jack. Running. Rain falling around him. Dodging other runners and walkers, he takes up so much space for one person. But when I blink and look again, it's stopped raining and he's gone.

I know what's next.

And I don't want to do it.

I bury my face into my gloves and let the tears come.

Please, no. I can't. Not today. This is enough.

I lean back and take a loud deep breath in. I have to do this.

I stand up, taking my book with me, and walk out of the library. The librarian smiles at me as I leave. I hurry down the stairs then start the route, searching for the bench I never made it to that day. A man in a suit bumps me but I keep pushing on. Pushing through the crowds, the chaos. And then the crowds part, and there it is. Leicester Square.

I stand frozen, facing it. Safety barriers encircle areas and buildings still to be replaced, repaired, rebuilt. There's still so much to be done here. I'm not the only one needing time to heal, to move on. Leicester Square suddenly isn't as terrifying as it was. Because like me, it's a victim too. Like me, it still lies in pieces; concrete shards of memories of that day. I walk around the Shakespeare fountain, touching the marble with my bare hands again. The air is crisp and bitter on my exposed fingers, but I still feel so warm inside. No, not warm. Burning. I'm burning inside. A young couple stand up from one of the benches opposite the fountain and walk away hand in hand. I take their spot, resting my book on the bench beside me. I unwrap my scarf from around my neck and slide the hat off my head. I tilt my head back and feel the December air nipping at my nose and ears.

I made it. I'm here.

And I'm still alive.

Jack

I hear her voice before I see her face.

When I finally turn around I see she's shouting to me from across the road. She's calling my name. She knows me. The soft city wind strikes her hair and lifts it away from her bare shoulders. She carries two books, neatly tucked under her left arm squeezed tight to her ribcage. They're tattered hardcovers, the bindings frayed. I can't make out the titles from here, but she carries them protectively like they're important, like they mean something to her. She's standing awkwardly, toes facing inwards, on the edge of the pavement by the pedestrian crossing. It's flashing green but she's not crossing. She's not alone. Crowds of people gather around her. They all look in the same direction. They all face me. She calls my name again. I turn back at the pavements ahead, my legs throbbing from the run. I still have so many more miles to cover. I have so much further to go.

I hear my name again. When I look back at her, she's alone now. She's still standing at the edge of the road, she's still not crossing, but her books are scattered around her on the ground by her feet. They're covered in a murky brown liquid which spills out from a dropped coffee cup by her heels. The books are wet. They're ruined. My phone beeps and the screen lights up. When I glance down I see the familiar Strava statistics – the graphs, the pace analyses, the run segments. Then I feel it. The flip in my belly, the shiver up my spine. The two words that enter my mind and tattoo themselves on my skull. Two simple words – *Run, Jack*. I pause, a moment too long. I don't run, I wait. And then I feel the heat. It burns.

When I jolt awake, I come to and realise I'm in bed at home. I'm here, I'm safe. My chest is covered in sweat which dampens the top bedsheet. My pillow is wet from my neck. I take a deep breath and reach my hand out to touch the wall. It's really home. Then my hand pulls in and rests on my pounding heart. I concentrate on my breathing in an effort to calm the beating. I release my hand and run my fingertips across the covers, over my thighs, but I don't feel the leg I'm stroking. I grip the window ledge beside me and pull myself up. I quickly whip away the covers, letting them fall to the bedroom floor. My legs, where are they? My hand rushes to my face and muffles a scream before it escapes fully. My legs are gone. Where my legs should be are two swollen, dark red stumps that end at my thighs. My knees, my calves, my ankles, my feet, the blisters that always eat away at the skin on my toes from running – they're all gone.

Then I remember. The dream I just had was real. That nightmare really happened. And I can't stop the screaming. It flows from my belly, out my mouth and spills into the bedroom. It floods the house, stains the walls. They fade when I come to and realise I'm at home in bed. I pant wildly

281

and try to forget the nightmare that just consumed me. And when I can't forget, I text Alice and she calls me. And we talk until the images fade from my eyes and the screams fade from my ears. We talk until I'm laughing again.

Alice

I open the window, the crisp air hitting me in the face. It's freezing, but sunny today. The sun beats warmly on my cheeks. I close my eyes and feel it soak through my skin.

'Alice, it's like the North Pole in here! Close the window,' my mom calls to me, struggling to get a big cardboard box through the door. She wrestles with the doorframe, cursing under her breath, her rose-hued hair flying over her face. Last month she dyed her ends a frosty blue. She suits the pink better.

'Sorry, it's just such a beautiful day,' I smile. I close the window, securing the latch and help her carry the box over to the kitchen table.

'What is this?'

'Well, since it looks like we'll be spending Christmas here I thought it would be nice if we decorated a little.'

'Really? We never decorate.'

'We're never able to,' she corrects me. 'But one of the neighbors said they were getting rid of a lot of old decorations from their attic so asked if we wanted them.'

I open my mouth to make a quip about old people and rusty old Christmas ornaments, but then close it. Whatever we put up in the house is meaningless, because Christmas is about family. I wrap my arms around her instead. 'Mom, whatever you do will look amazing. Now let's see what's in this box.'

She bites her lip and feigns anticipation, slowly opening the lid. 'We have . . . one ceramic Santa for the doorstep—'

'It's London, so it may not be there in the morning but I like your optimism,' I smile, taking the Santa from her. It's heavier than I thought so I quickly put it down.

'Three boxes of baubles for the tree—'

'We don't have a tree.'

'Some garland, tinsel, and these I'm really excited about.' She pulls out four large metal candy canes. 'Stocking holders! See the hook?'

I nod and peer over at them. 'Finally, we can hang our stockings over the fireplace again.' When we started moving around more regularly and with minimal notice, we knew we wouldn't be able to take all our things so we chose only what we absolutely needed, like some clothing, and absolutely treasured, like my *War and Peace* hardcover that I found in a second-hand shop down a cobbled alley in Boston's west end, next to Mike's Pastry Shop on Hanover. For my mom, it was photos, her wedding rings, a necklace my dad gave her for an anniversary and our Christmas stockings that my Nana knitted for us just after I was born. Every year, no matter where we are, we put them out. Because we've not decorated before, the stockings are usually laid out on a coffee table or the kitchen counter. We couldn't do gifts really because of money and also because we couldn't accumulate too many things that we'd then need to pack for the next transfer. But we always had stockings. My mom would fill my dad's, my dad would choose things for my mom's that I'd buy if he was away, and they would do mine together. On Christmas morning, we opened them. Chocolates, hand cream, a novelty toothbrush, nail polish (I'm partial to just a clear coat – practical and boring, I know), and small things like that.

She walks over to the white mantel and gingerly hangs three candy cane holders on the edge. 'There,' she beams.

'Looks great.'

'I know it's not a real fireplace with actual fire, but it glows . . . if you turn the switch on at the wall,' she shrugs sheepishly. 'Hey, it even flickers. We can have a twinkling fireplace for Christmas!'

I laugh and watch her unpack the ornaments out the box, inspecting them for cracks and scratches. She slowly puts them down and looks at me, intently. 'You're different this week.'

'How so?'

'You just are. You seem . . . happier.'

A wide smile pushes into the corners of my face, and I nod gently. 'I'm starting to feel a bit more like myself, I suppose. My old self anyway.'

'The PTSD group is helping?'

'A lot, actually. Ian – the guy who runs it – had me do an exercise last week and it was hard, but really helpful.'

She delicately cups my face with both hands, and tries to tuck my wild hair back but I can feel it slip out over my ears. She looks at me in a way that reminds me how lucky I am to have parents like mine. People who support me and will always be there for me, no matter how low I might find myself.

I pull her in for an embrace.

When I release I see she's crying, again. I laugh and slide off the table, getting her a sheet of kitchen roll to wipe her face. 'So, let's talk about a tree.'

Jack

I'm up early today and exhausted, having not slept much this week. My body craved more rest today and when my alarm went off at 6:45 a.m. I was tempted to roll over and turn it off. Even now I'm up and dressed, I could still go back to bed and sleep for hours.

My thighs are aching. I couldn't face massaging them with the gel before I put the prostheses on. The swelling and dark red sores made it almost unbearable to put them on. Hopefully an extra-strong coffee, a couple of pain meds and a google of last year's marathon images will motivate me to get into the gym. I've been on the treadmill every morning before physio to increase movement. I'm dreading it today, though. Even the walk to the kitchen is gruelling. My hands clutch the walls as I take each excruciating step. When I reach the kitchen, the waft of espresso and warm croissants fills my nostrils. But I've somehow lost my appetite walking here.

'Good morning,' my mum smiles. She sits at the table under the lamp reading the newspaper from yesterday. The night still sits outside the window. Sunrise won't be for another hour or so, now the days are shorter and the nights longer.

'Coffee?'

'Yes, please,' I say, collapsing into a chair. Normally I'd make my own breakfast, but I can't face getting up and walking around the kitchen.

'Croissant? Toast? I can make you some eggs since it's a busy day of training again?'

'I'll stick with coffee for now,' I mutter.

'You OK?' She brushes my hair off my temple. 'You look tired today.'

'I just didn't sleep well.' I cradle the hot mug in my hands.

'Why don't you take today off, Jack? Go back to bed for a bit, rest up. You've been working yourself too hard. Putting strain on your body isn't going to help you in the long term. It'll just slow your progress with the prostheses.'

I know she's right, but I can't stop. I need to keep going. A day off might turn into two days off, or three, and every day is critical right now. I can't skip a training day. There's only four months until the marathon. My run blades arrive the first week in January and it'll be non-stop strength and speed training from then on. I've already made a lot of progress. I'm not using the crutches anymore and I don't need a walking stick. I'm completely supporting my own weight now, and I'm starting to do some light jogs on the treadmill too. I'm taking paracetamol every four hours for the pain. Surely that should have subsided by now? Is it normal for it still to be this sore and uncomfortable?

A click of the toaster brings two perfectly browned slices up to the surface. In the corner of the kitchen, Mum fusses with the butter on a ceramic dish and pours a large glass of fresh orange juice. She walks back over with a breakfast tray, filled with small pots of honey, jam and marmalade. 'At least bring a tray into the gym with you, if you get hungry. You can pick on toast in between reps.'

'Thanks, Mum.' I rise and carry the tray down the hall, it wobbles as I wince with each step but it doesn't drop. When I get to the training room beside the pool, I quickly slide the tray onto a bench and take a deep breath. Then I pop two extra-strength pain meds in my mouth and wash it down with a couple of big gulps of juice.

Searing pain burns my flesh with each step I take on the treadmill. My fingers hover above the 'Incline' button, shaking involuntarily. I feel nauseous. The pain, it's too much. Sweat drips down my face, tickling my neck and shoulders. Then everything starts to get fuzzy in front of me. The heat pounds my skin and my heartbeat gets faster, louder. I can barely reach the emergency button pull-string on the wall before my prosthetic legs start to buckle under me. I grab for the string and fall with it. It tugs and a high-pitched alarm floods the room, spilling out into the hallway. I start screaming out in agony. My mum is through the door and at my side in no time. She fumbles at her phone while cradling my head in her lap. I succumb to the pain finally, closing my eyes and letting the darkness take me.

Alice

Here we are again, back in the hospital. Me in the armchair, Jack in the bed. Always Jack in the bed. He's been in there for too long. It's just not fair. And that poster is back. Does every bedroom in this hospital have that same stupid poster? They're going to keep Jack in for a few more days to monitor the infection, but it's bad. They had to take off the prostheses. I don't think he'll get them back.

'Can I get you anything?' I ask. 'Water? Coffee?'

He shakes his head. 'No thanks.'

'Are you in pain?'

He swallows hard and stares up at the poster. 'No, it's not too bad,' he says, his jaw clenched.

'It's okay to say if it does hurt. Nothing wrong with that.'

Outside the room, footsteps fill the hall, a food cart whirls through the room bringing lunches to patients. It's strange to think of Jack as a patient again. 'How long were your thighs like that?'

He shrugs.

'Were you in pain for long? Why didn't you say anything?'

Jack turns to me, his cheeks flushed. His bottom lip

trembles and for the first time in a while I feel my eyes stinging with tears.

'If there's anything I can do, please tell me.'

'Alice, thank you for coming here. But I just need to be alone right now. Is it okay if you leave?'

I nod slowly, and start fumbling for my coat and gloves. I glance over at the bag of magazines and sweets on his bedside table feeling silly for bringing them again. I want to help, I want to do something but there's nothing I can do to make him feel better right now. 'Call or text me if you want to talk?'

He nods and turns back to the poster.

'I'm sorry, Jack. I'm so sorry.'

'Me too,' he whispers.

Jack

Snow falls furiously outside my window as darkness descends upon my garden and driveway, swallowing everything in its path – the ceramic pots holding crisp, browned shrubs, the beech tree draped in tiny white lights, the path leading up to the front door, our house, me. A cold chill sits in the corner of my bedroom, occasionally pricking my skin. Cold never used to bother me but now I feel it everywhere I go. Cold shivers snake up my spine and sharply tickle my arms. I pull the hoodie down past my wrists and fist my hands inside the sleeves, searching for warmth. But there is no warmth to be found. Only more darkness.

Soft music trickles up the stairs from the living room, spilling in under my door. 'O Holy Night'. My mum's favourite. Familiar smells of bronzed turkey, sage stuffing and rosemary-seasoned roast potatoes from the tray outside my bedroom fill my nose, tempting me out. It's Christmas Day but I don't feel like celebrating. Nothing feels magical or special about this day. It's just another piercing reminder of time lost, of lost other things, my youth included. My fingertips graze over my thighs, massaging away the throbbing ache I still feel. The skin is still so tender and swollen to the touch. I can barely feel my fingers on my thighs with all the swelling. Beyond the stumps, where prosthetic legs once were, is nothing now.

It's been almost ten days since they were removed. Permanently. Dr McKenzie said it was something called verrucous hyperplasia of the amputated stumps – severe infection at the socket point of the prosthetic limbs meaning they had to be taken off indefinitely. She told my mum that problems like that are more common with lower-limb prostheses, especially when the amputation is above, not below, the knee. There was nothing she or anyone else could do. No one asked me how I felt. They just said, 'Sorry, Jack,' and then took my legs – again. My legs have been taken from me twice now. No one can ever possibly understand how that feels, and what that means for my future. Dr McKenzie suggested a cosmetic limb, one that looks like a real limb but doesn't function as one. It's for show only, I can't stand or bear any weight on it. I said no. I don't want to look like I have legs – I *want* legs.

I could have lived with the pain from the infection, maybe. I could have found a way to get past it, stronger pain relief perhaps. Anything to get me to April's marathon, to get me to that finish line. I know my time would haven't have been anywhere close to what it would have been, but the point is I would have still been able to participate with my dad. I would have still felt part of something, good at something. I would have had a purpose. I would have felt like me again. Now I just feel like a bombing victim.

I squeeze my eyes closed as they hurt. But I can't block

it out. Raindrops on concrete. Leather-bound books in puddles. Fiery red hair in a fog of ash and debris. An umbrella spinning on its head. Going around and around and around. And the heat. Insatiable, searing, blistering heat.

I'll never be able to escape it now.

Alice

I stand at the foot of the stairs at the Royal Botanic Gardens, looking for Jack, searching for the van. I'm bundled up in the thickest coat I could find in a box in the house, two pairs of gloves, a hat and two scarves. The winter here is brutal. The bitter cold found here is similar to New England, but I've still not got used to it. I pull a scarf up over my mouth, warming my breath, and glance again at the tickets in my hand. Our entry time for the Winter Lights festival was at 3 p.m. and Jack is already twenty minutes late which is unusual for him. I call him again. No answer. So I wait, but by 3:45 I realize he's not coming. I would go home, give up, climb back into my PJs and watch TV with my mom but this is so out of character for Jack that I need to go see him.

The bus ride from Kew Gardens to Richmond is quiet, but the South Western railway line is starting to fill with commuters. I sit, huddled in a corner of the train, with my eyes closed. Beyond the darkness I hear shuffling of footsteps, phone conversations, exchanges between strangers and friends. Beneath the gloves, my hands sweat and tingle. I count my breaths slowly, 10 . . . 9 . . . 8 . . . it regulates finally and I'm back to breathing normally. Although I still have them, the panic attacks are less frequent than they once were and they don't last as long. When my mind pulls me back to that morning, I concentrate on breathing and battle to bring myself back to the here and now. We practice this in the support group each week, and my mom guides me through a similar meditative practice in yoga. Yes, I do yoga now. I'm one of those people that wear yoga pants around the house and sit cross-legged on a mat 'ohm'-ing and chanting loud enough for the neighbors to hear. I never thought I'd say that. I also say 'Namaste' now. I'm not joking.

Outside the train, snow flurries and falls, lightly pattering the windows. When the conductor announces my stop, I gently flick my eyes open and with my gaze fixed on the exit I shimmy past people and let the cold air wash over me when I step out. I take a deep breath and quietly congratulate myself for another successful train ride.

The country lane to Jack's glistens with ice. The sun sets on my left, the afternoon sky already melting and twisting into night. I'm buzzed in at the gate by his dad and greeted at the front door by his mom. Her face is soft and she smiles, but the dark circles under her eyes tell me that it's been a tough couple of weeks.

'How is he?' I ask, as I take off my wet coat and shake the snowdrops off.

'He's not doing well,' his mom says quietly. 'He's not left his room much. He takes his meals in there too now. We've tried to give him space but now we're afraid that we've given him too much.'

I reach a hand out and lightly touch her arm. 'I'm sure you couldn't have done anything else. He's not been responding to my messages much recently and he never takes my calls. I thought when he said he'd come today that he was feeling a bit brighter, but when he didn't show I wanted to check on him. Hope it's okay I stopped by like this?'

'Of course,' she says.

I walk through the lobby, through the kitchen to the back of the house, past the gym until I come to his closed door where he's hung a DO NOT DISTURB notice on the front like he's in a hotel. Except I'm not the housekeeper, and I don't take KEEP OUT signs seriously. I knock lightly. 'Jack, it's Alice. Can I come in?' I wait a moment and hear shuffling from inside. At least he's still alive in there. The familiar sound of wheels comes closer and the door opens. Jack sits beyond the doorway in a pair of navy joggers and a gray school hoodie. He's unshaven and his hair looks matted on one side. I'm slightly taken aback by his appearance but I try not to let on. 'There you are,' I smile.

He wheels himself back and lets me in. I take a seat at the desk. Dark spills into the room, creeping into the corners. 'Do you mind?' I ask, as I reach for the lamp switch. He shrugs so I turn it on, brightening the room and him. He looks even worse in the light. I gaze around at the books on the surfaces, the postcards propped up by textbooks, the laptop on the desk. His room doesn't look too different to mine. His event medals are hung up by an exposed nail in the wall, and his travel books sit in a corner along with a sports jersey and what I assume is a squash racket.

297

'How are you?' I ask.

'I'm okay.'

I bite my lip. 'I waited for you today at the Royal Botanic Gardens.'

His face drops, and he sighs. 'That was today?'

'That was today,' I nod.

He runs a hand through his hair and leans back. 'I'm so sorry. I completely forgot.'

'It's fine. Don't worry. I just wanted to check on you anyway. I've not heard from you much?'

He gazes down. 'I've just been . . . busy, I suppose. I'm not ignoring you on purpose.'

'I know,' I smile. 'I'm just worried about you, I guess. You don't seem yourself.'

'Like I said, I'm okay.'

'Have you seen Will and Euan?' Not that I care too much about those guys, but if he's still seeing them then at least I know he hasn't completely shut himself off from the world. Just from me.

'No. I haven't talked to them. They text, but I'm not great with getting back to people's messages these days.'

So it's everyone he's shutting out, not just me. Silence fills the room as I sit awkwardly on the edge of the chair. This feels like the first time we met at the hospital, when I didn't know him. But I do now. I've gotten to know the real Jack, I think. The adventurous Jack that wants to go swimming in the ocean in late November, the thoughtful Jack that stopped by my house with coffee and dragged me out the house to water rosemary in a garden when I felt at my lowest,

298

the kind Jack who texted me every day in the summer to ask me how I was. I don't recognize this Jack in front of me. This defeated person who looks like he wants nothing more than to lock his door and never see anyone again.

'Let's go for a walk,' I suggest. 'We'll grab some flashlights and take a stroll in the snow. I bet it's beautiful at night here with the houses all lit up.'

'You go. I don't feel like it today.'

'Come on, you'll enjoy some fresh air.'

'No, thank you, Alice. Really, I just want to stay here.'

I nod and sit back down. I'm not sure what else to do. I was much easier to be coaxed out for a walk than him. 'Do you want me to book the Royal Botanic Gardens again for this week? I heard the light show is cool.'

'No, it's okay. I'm quite busy this week.'

That's definitely a lie.

'Do you want to order pizza and watch a movie tonight? I can call my mom and say I'll be home a little later?'

He shakes his head again. 'Actually, I don't mean to be rude but I'm really tired. Do you mind if I rest for a bit?'

'Oh, yeah, no problem,' I stammer, feeling a little defeated myself. 'I'll give you a call tomorrow.' I gaze back at him, one last time before I close the door. He sits slumped in his chair by the window, looking out at the gardens darkening outside. And when he glances back at me he wears no expression on his face, nothing I can read or understand anyway. He's just – blank.

Jack

'Sorry to just stop by like this,' Will says as he and Euan settle onto the sofa in the living room. 'But we've not heard from you in a while and we were just worried.'

First Alice, then them. I just need some space from people, is that too much to ask? But I smile and lie, 'I'm glad you stopped by.' I'm still in the same joggers and hoodie as when I saw Alice yesterday. No point getting dressed these days. I don't feel like going out or entertaining much. Although people don't seem to be getting the message.

Euan pokes at a shortbread finger on the plate my mum laid out on the Harris Tweed ottoman, along with crackers, dips, cheese skewers and olives. 'How was your Christmas?'

'Yeah, it was all right, thanks,' I mutter, even though I spent the entire day in my bedroom in the dark. 'Yours? Were you in France this year again?'

'No, we didn't go this Christmas since we'll be there shortly for the ski trip anyway.'

Silence inches into the room as Will glances at Euan, his face clenched.

'Oh, right. The ski trip.'

Will clears his throat. 'Yeah, we debated whether to still

go. I mean, of course, it's not going to be the same without you this year.'

'It's fine,' I mutter. 'Is Alex going?'

The room falls quiet again. 'Yeah,' Will says. 'He wanted to come today to see you too but he said you've not been responding to his messages? You know, he's really sorry about Lauren.'

I nod, but don't say anything else. I get the feeling whatever I say will just go back to Alex, and I don't play those games. When I'm ready to talk to him, I will. But the Alex drama is the least of my concerns just now.

'Maybe come next year for skiing? You could come and just chill out?' Euan suggests.

Chill out? Is that all I can do now, just sit in my wheelchair and *chill out*? 'Yeah, maybe next year,' I say. 'Where are you guys going anyway?'

'Um . . . well, we decided to still go to Courchevel like you'd suggested.'

'Oh.' I found that place. Out of all the options, I chose that specific location for our first ski trip without our parents. It would be the first of many. No matter where we were at university, in the world, what stage we were at in our lives, we agreed to always come together for an annual ski trip. I'm missing the most important one, our first one just us, and might miss the rest too.

'I know we talked about us all going there together, but we didn't think you'd mind if we still went ahead with it this year?' asks Euan.

'No, of course not. You should still go. It would make me

feel worse if you didn't,' I say, gazing down at the floor beneath my wheels. I don't want the guys to see the disappointment in my face.

'Well,' starts Will nervously, 'I'm glad you said that, because we've decided to still run the London Marathon in April too—'

Now this hurts. It stings. All these things were once within my reach, now they slip away and they're only plans made by others.

'—but we're going to do it for a charity. Raise as much money as we can for a good cause,' Will smiles.

'What charity?' I ask.

'The Jack Addington Foundation.'

'The what?'

'We've set up a foundation on your behalf. We want to run the marathon this spring in your honour.'

'Oh.' It's all I can say right now. Wow, I'm officially a charity. I'm not dead or dying, so why is there a foundation named after me? And they're running a marathon – *my* marathon, the one I fought for, the one I endured weeks of prosthesis pain – for a charity they've named after me. That's the only way I'll be a part of this – a face for a T-shirt that dozens of people will wear crossing a finish line that I'll never be able to step across ever again. I know they're just trying to do something nice, but why does it feel like such a cruel reminder of just how much I've lost?

'You OK?' Will asks.

I slowly shake my head, still in a haze. 'I'm just tired. I'm on some strong pain meds too.'

'Well, we'll leave you to get some rest,' he says, getting up. 'We missed you at the Christmas Half Marathon. A lot.'

'How did everyone do?' I quietly ask, not really wanting to know.

'I got a PB,' Euan grins. Will glares at him.

'I'll check it out on Strava.' I gesture weakly to my phone. Thanks. Another reminder of another race I couldn't enter.

They nod and start for the door again. 'See you when we get back, yeah?' Will bends down and gives my shoulder a friendly slap. 'We'll hang out properly.'

'Take some good photos of the ski trip,' I mutter softly, turning back towards the window. It's the closest I get to the outdoors now. The only breeze I feel is the one that slips in through an open window or a gap in the doorway. The only earth I can touch is the soil in my mum's plant pots. If I want to feel the rain on my face, I need help unlocking the top lock on the front door to access the ramp down to the driveway. I need help with most things these days. I'm just so tired all the time, so drained.

I hear the living-room door close behind me and the room falls silent again. Just me and this chair. My eyes flicker to the phone on my lap and I can't help but unlock the screen. I just want to see what I'm missing, just one more time then I won't look again. I open up the Strava app and the first thing I see is a partial run by me. I'm confused at first because it's my profile, my run. But I haven't used this app in a while. Then I realise what run this is, what day this is. The date, the time, the GPS map of my Saturday morning route, and where it ends – Leicester Square. I had been tracking my run the day of the bombing. This is the last thing I saw before it happened. My Strava screen. I had been looking at my phone when I felt the heat on my back. When I felt my body on fire. When I felt my legs torn from my body.

Oh God, I can't breathe. I start gasping for air desperately.

'Jack?' Mum is standing at the doorway. 'Did your friends leave already?'

I swallow hard and throw my phone on the floor.

'What is it?' She rushes over to me.

'Nothing, it's fine,' I stammer.

'Tell me, Jack. Please, just talk to me. I want to know how you're feeling.'

'Mum, not now.'

'If you won't talk to me, then please talk to someone.'

'I don't want to meet with a therapist, I told you this already.'

My eyes flicker back to the phone on the floor, to the screen frozen from that day, a never-ending reminder of that horrific, savage day.

'Why don't you go with Alice to the support group then?'

'No.'

'It might be helpful.'

'I said, no.'

'You might meet some other people your age with similar injuries.'

'It's not an injury, Mum!' I explode, feeling anger bubble up from every inch of my body. 'This is my life now! I've lost my legs! I've lost the prostheses! I've lost everything!' I push myself away from the window, away from her, and thrust myself down the hall, through the kitchen and down to the home gym where I slam the door closed. I won't be going in there anymore and I don't want to be reminded of what I no longer need. I won't be running in the marathon. I'll never run with my dad again, with my friends. I don't need any of those machines in there.

When I get to my room I just start throwing things. I close my eyes and hear the thrashing and breaking of everything I once treasured – my event medals, my squash trophy from school, photo frames of me and my dad climbing our first Munro. Everything is pointless now, all these things I once collected. In my hand I hold a rock from the Cuillin Munros. It digs into my palm, opening the skin. Blood trickles from my fist down my wrist and onto the floor. In my mind I can still hear her. I can hear Alice yelling at me on the street that day. I can feel my body slowing down to hear her, bending down to help her. I can feel my body on fire because of her.

A scream erupts from my throat and I throw the rock as hard as I can at the window. The glass cracks and pieces flake off and fall by my wheels. A cold wind trickles slowly into the room and tickles the papers on my desk. I can hear my mum screaming my name as she rushes down the hall. The rock lies on the floor beside a couple of jagged slivers of glass. I feel my mum tugging at the handles of my chair, pulling me away. I gaze down at the rock. I can't even break a window properly.

Winter Darkness

PART 4

The bleakness of winter casts a shadow,
Never quite escaping its depths we succumb to the dark,
Endless nights and lost time,
A vast sheet of white unfolds across the valleys,
A landscape of snow and ice,
Blanketing what spring birthed,
What once was awakened now sleeps,
All that remains is the gravestones of the dead,
And the fading footsteps of the forgotten.

Alice Winters

Alice

'. . . and I still wonder if I hadn't been driving the car, if it hadn't been raining, if I'd just been driving slightly slower, that he'd still be here today.' Sara drops down onto her chair, and wipes tears from her face. Ian leans in and hands her the box of tissues that regularly circulates throughout the meetings. We're almost out again. We nod and thank Sara for sharing. I gaze around the room, around the circle which gets bigger every month. Now there's nine of us here, including Ian. All for different reasons but ultimately all for the same purpose.

Jack should be here. I asked him again to come tonight. I do every week. Again, he didn't respond. He hardly ever responds now. I tried going over there again yesterday but his mom said he was sleeping, but I don't think that was true. Jack probably asked her to say that. He's not seeing anyone just now. He just sits in his room, staring out the window. Everything I've tried hasn't worked. I'm failing at helping him.

'Does anyone else want to share tonight?' Ian suddenly looks up, at something behind me. 'Oh, hello, come on in. You're welcome here anytime.'

I turn around in my chair to see who's a half-hour late to

the session. It's Jack. He hovers in the doorway. Ian and I wave at the same time, although Ian looks like he's marshaling a plane down on the runway.

'Come on. Join us,' he says.

Jack locks eyes with me and nods in acknowledgment. I push back and gesture to him to come beside me. He wheels himself towards the circle, his gaze down on the ground. When he pulls up to me, I feel a huge smile stretching on my face. I'm so glad he came. If this group can't help him, I don't know what can.

'Welcome,' says Ian. He addresses us, 'Let's go round and introduce ourselves and then our new member can tell us his name. I'm Ian.'

'Wyatt.'

'Clare.'

'Alistair.'

'Dan.'

'Louise.'

'Jane.'

'Sara.'

I clear my throat, 'Um, Alice,' and wave stupidly like he doesn't know me.

'I'm Jack.'

'Nice to meet you, Jack,' the group mumbles.

'Jack, no pressure to talk. Unless you want to share tonight?' asks Ian.

He shakes his head, no.

'Okay. Well, just know when you do want to share, we're here to listen.'

'Thanks,' he mutters.

Wyatt raises his hand. 'I'll share again?'

We all nod wearily. Wyatt shares about twice a week – and they're long shares. All I want right now is to pause the group so I can speak to Jack, find out what's going on and why he hasn't been responding to my messages and calls. Now I have to wait another hour, and another Wyatt share.

Wyatt leans forward in his chair, clapping his hands. 'I had a dream last night . . .'

And here we go.

Twenty-five minutes later, I find myself stifling a yawn.

Jack is just staring at the floor in front of him, eyes wide. I was hoping he wouldn't have to be subjected to a 'Wyatt Dream Analysis' on his first time here.

'Thank you for that, Wyatt.' Ian takes a large gulp from his travel coffee thermos. 'So, does anyone have anything else to share?'

Wyatt raises his hand again.

'Alice, you said at the start that you'd like to share. How about it? Only if you want to, of course.'

'Oh, right. Okay.' I did say that, I think. Great. I edge forward in my seat, still clutching a notepad and pen. This is harder with Jack here somehow. I would prefer to make this evening about him, about how we can help him, not be sharing my thoughts. But maybe if Jack sees me open up, he'll do the same. So, here I go. 'When I first started coming here, I was really in a dark place. I didn't feel like I could talk to anyone about it because my injuries weren't physical so I didn't think I had the right to complain or talk about myself, or what I was feeling.'

I choke a little, the words are tough to get out.

'It's okay. Take your time,' Ian says.

'I used to have bad nightmares. Still do sometimes but they're not as regular as they once were. These nightmares, I'd see them during the day. I'd look at an object and visualize it exploding, blowing up, crushing under the weight of a thick dense cloud of debris and ash. It could be the TV, a chair, but if I was outside it'd be worse because the things I visualized – a car, a building, a person – those are things I did really see explode that morning of the bombing. So I stopped going outside. I stayed in my room where it's safe, sometimes in bed, other times on the floor or huddled in the corner between my desk and wardrobe. Then I met someone who was going through the same thing as me, who knew exactly how I felt. And he helped me—' I look at Jack but his gaze is fixed down towards the ground '—and I started coming here, and learning strategies to cope when panic attacks surface, which they still do and maybe always will. But what's important now is that I feel better. I feel more in control than I ever have before. I feel happier, stronger. I feel—'

Is Jack leaving?

He wheels towards the door, not glancing back. Did I say something to upset him?

'Um, excuse me,' I mutter to the group, grabbing my bag off the floor and swinging my coat over my arm. I hurry after him as he makes his way towards the access elevator. 'Jack!'

He slows down, his back still to me.

'Are you leaving? Or do you just really need the bathroom?'

He sighs and turns to face me. His face is red, his eyes puffy and watering.

'I'm so sorry. Did I say something that upset you?' I stammer.

He shakes his head and takes a deep breath, trying to find the words. 'I . . . I'm sorry. I didn't mean to walk out while you were talking. I just couldn't sit there any longer.'

'Was it something I said?'

'No. I'm glad you're doing better. I'm glad you're feeling happier and stronger.' He sighs and looks away. 'I'm sorry, Alice. I shouldn't have come tonight. I've ruined it for you.'

'No, you haven't at all. I'm glad you came. Please come back in. Just give it to the end of the session and then see how you feel.'

He shakes his head. 'I just want to go home.' His hands are trembling. His shoulders shake softly. I take a step towards him but he just pulls back. Then he turns and leaves, and all I do is watch.

Jack

My fingers hover above the laptop. I know I shouldn't but I just want to look for a moment. I want to be reminded of a year that feels like a lifetime ago. So I open it up, type in my password (the last Munro I climbed + 01) and wait for the screen to light up. I'm immediately hit with my whole life in digital format. Folders of schoolwork, scanned-in awards, PDFs of trail maps from old hikes with my dad, and photos. Hundreds and hundreds of photos, mostly of travel, some with Lauren and others with our old chocolate Labrador Harley.

I click on last year's 'Race Events' and start scrolling through. From the junior triathlon in February to New York in November and ending at the Victoria Park Christmas Half Marathon in December, I count twenty-two events in total. That's almost two a month. I drag that folder aside and start scrolling through last year's ski trip. Here's me skiing backwards with Alex, just for fun. Here's one I took of myself standing at the top of a black run. I sent that one to Lauren, told her I missed her and wished she was there with us. I don't know if I meant it at the time. I liked her, a lot, but all I cared about was myself back then. All I wanted to do was travel, race, ski, climb. I didn't care with who. Sometimes I preferred doing that stuff alone, no one to worry about or to hold me back. I was always the fastest, the strongest, the most experienced in every group. Now I'd hold everyone else back. Now I'm the weakest.

I didn't know how good I had it back then. I took everything for granted. I was selfish and self-absorbed. And now it's all gone. I don't even remember stopping to enjoy it for what it was. Savouring the moment at the top of a mountain I'd just climbed, closing my eyes and feeling the cold breeze slap my cheeks as I flew down a ski run, revelling in the applause when crossing a finish line. All the while I did those things I was thinking of my next race, my next destination of travel, my next big achievement in life. I collected memories and accomplishments, but did I ever truly experience them?

Now I'll never get the chance again.

I've lost it.

I've lost everything. Of course I want to see Alice, but I just don't know how to articulate how I'm feeling. I don't want to see her better. I know that sounds selfish and I hate that I'm thinking it, but I am. I'm envious that she's moved past this and I can't. I feel like I'm stuck, and it's rotting away inside me. And I don't want her to see me like this either, like how I was on Monday night. Broken. I'm scared if she keeps pushing me to open up, to share, that I'll end up saying what I really feel. That deep, deep down, I do blame her for that day in Leicester Square. And that I'm scared I'll always blame her. I don't want to hate her and I don't want to resent her for getting better. Everything in my head is just so confusing and hurts me so much. I just feel on the edge all the time. And I'm scared I'll fall.

Alice

My palms are clammy. I'm dragging them down my winter coat every few minutes but I can't stop them sweating. Did Martin turn up the heat in the van?

Jack didn't text me but he responded to mine at least. He agreed to meet me, to go on a car ride somewhere but he doesn't know where we're going. I didn't tell him because I was scared he wouldn't come. I feel guilty tricking him into this, but honestly I don't know what else to do. I can't reach him. He's so far gone from me, from his parents, from his friends, from who he was before. He's a shell of the Jack I met. He's just been slowly slipping away since the prostheses were removed. But I hope I can bring him back by bringing him here – the Jack from the summer, the one who smiled, who laughed, who joked.

I gaze out the window, at the passing traffic, the increasing numbers of commuters and tourists, and know we're almost there. I glance back at him. He's not noticed where we are yet. He's just looking at his phone, staring at old photos of himself on Facebook and Instagram. He's obsessed with who he was before, and who he thinks he'll never be again. He's still that Jack. I just need to show him that. He needs closure, like I needed. The van pulls to a stop in a yellow-marked disabled parking space opposite Leicester Square. Martin flicks the hazard lights on and glances nervously at me. I turn around and face Jack who's finally looked up. His face whitens as he takes in his surroundings. 'Why are we here?'

I slide out the passenger seat and shut the door behind me, then I slide open his. The winter air hits him as he sits there, mouth agape. I have my back to Leicester Square, to what remains damaged months later. 'I know it'll be difficult. But when I finally came back here, it helped me,' I say.

'Alice, no—'

'Just come out for a few minutes and see. Please. We're already here.'

'No, I can't.'

'Please, for me. Please.' He takes a shaky breath and bends down to unclip his wheels. I catch him at the edge, lower the ramp and help him down slowly. When his wheels touch the pavement, he stops. He's trembling.

'Just come into the square,' I plead.

He follows me as I lead us both past the Shakespeare fountain, onto the street where we collided. He gets slower the closer we get. I think I have the spot now. We gaze down at the empty pavement, but I see scattered books, an umbrella and a spilled coffee cup. I see Jack running. I see him at the other side of the street looking back at me. I see a cloud of smoke and a surge of fire. I don't see him anymore.

When I look down at him in the chair, wondering what he sees, he's crying.

I reach my hand out and touch his shoulder but he shirks

318

me away. He rubs his eyes roughly with the back of his hand and glares at me. 'Why would you bring me here?'

'I thought it would help,' I stammer, the corners of my eyes watering.

'Does it look like it's helping?' He's so angry. I've never seen him this angry before.

'It helped me.'

'I'm not you!' His voice bellows around us, and a few passers-by stop to stare. 'Look at me! I'm in a wheelchair! All this is doing is reminding me of that, of everything I lost that day!'

'When I came here, it brought everything back too – the rain, the walk here from the library, us bumping into each other, the explosions . . . but then I felt better afterwards. It was like closure.' I open my arms wide like I'm embracing the street, the square, everything around us, everything that happened to us. Being back here just strengthens my resolve to keep moving forward, to put the past in the past and not let it control me. Why doesn't he feel the same? I don't understand why this didn't work for him.

'I want to go home,' he whispers, jaw clenched.

'Maybe if we walk around for a bit, you'll start to feel something,' I suggest.

'I feel something, trust me. Now I just want to go home.'

'Jack, just stay a little longer—'

'I want to go home!'

His voice carries through the air, through the crowds. People stop to watch, to listen to us. Jack looks around, his cheeks reddening. Then he thrusts himself towards me. I step back and let him go, watching him go back to the van, back to where's safe.

It didn't work.

I made everything worse.

Jack

I didn't sleep at all last night. After I came back from Leicester Square, I shut myself away for the rest of the day and the night. Being back there with her, back to that same street, it was just too much. I don't know how she managed it but I couldn't bear it, to be back there. I get what she's trying to do. I know I'm not really living now. I'm just orbiting the life I once had. And I know I can't do this forever, but I don't know how to stop thinking about my old life, thinking about that day. Losing the prostheses has destroyed me. I'll never get my old self back.

A loud knock brings me back to the room, away from my thoughts.

'Can I come in?' asks my dad from behind the closed door.

I mumble acknowledgement and push myself up. He slowly enters and sits by the desk. He's still in his work clothes, but his tie hangs loose around the collar.

'How was your work trip?' I mutter, not entirely understanding where the time has gone.

'Fine,' he nods. 'Your mum says you've not been out the bedroom since I left?'

'That's not true. I went to the kitchen once,' I shrug.

'Have you been outside? Have you seen your friends?'

'Don't really fancy the company right now. Prefer my own.' My head is suddenly throbbing, my temples aching. I just want to be alone again.

His face softens and he leans forward in the chair, closer to me. 'Jack, I also want to say something about the London Marathon—'

'Dad, you don't have to—'

'No, I want to just let you know that—'

'Dad, please, I can't talk about it,' I say, my voice louder than I intended. I'm not angry, I just can't bear more sympathetic words about the marathon from anyone, and my dad of all people, the one I was going to run it with, run it for. 'I'm sorry,' I mutter. 'I just have a headache and I'm not feeling great.'

'OK,' he says quietly. 'We can talk when you're feeling a bit better. I've taken the next few days off so let me know if you need anything?'

I nod weakly, and turn away. As the door closes, and the darkness of the air consumes me again, I realise I have no idea what day it is, what time it is, and when I last went outside.

Another knock startles me again. Why won't people just leave me alone?

'I'm sleeping,' I call out.

The door creaks open and Alice pokes her head around. 'Sorry, can I please come in? Just for a moment. You can pretend to be sleeping after that?' I nod and she sits in the same spot my dad was just in. 'Sorry to just show up again. I texted you after yesterday but you never responded.' She suddenly squints and tilts her head slightly. 'What happened to your window?'

'I threw a rock at it.'

'Hmm.' She looks pained as she thinks about what to say next, then shrugs. 'Anyway, I'm sorry again about bringing you back to Leicester Square. I should have asked you first.'

'I know you thought you were helping, but I can't go back there. Not yet.'

'I understand. When you're ready, I'll come with you. Or if you want to go alone, then I'll just be here to talk when you get back,' she smiles.

I bite my lip and take a deep breath. I can't break, not now.

'Is there anything I can do, Jack, to help you?'

I shake my head.

'I don't know what else to do,' she says quietly.

'I'm just drained,' I whisper, rubbing my forehead. 'I just need to rest.' I seem to be saying that a lot these days. Truth is, I sleep most of the day. How can I still feel so tired all the time?

She nods and stands, reading my cue. She walks over to the door then turns back. 'I know you just want to be alone right now. But I'm not giving up on you.'

Alice

I stare up at the poster of a man climbing a mountain on my ceiling. Shoes still on from a walk in the snow, jacket unbuttoned but wrapped around me, scarf on the floor. I'd wanted to know what it was like to just stare at this poster all day long like Jack had to, so I'd found a copy online and pasted it up on my own ceiling.

I hate it.

I tap my toes, boots banging together. I just don't know what to do about Jack but I know I need to do something, soon. He's slipping further away and I've never seen him like this before. I wish I knew how to help him. The peer support group wasn't successful. Revisiting Leicester Square just made him more upset. My texts, emails and phone calls have all failed to reach him. Everything I say isn't working. His mom is at a loss too. Patrick, his physio has been calling, and someone called Charlie too, but he won't take their calls either. I don't know what else to do. I don't know what he needs right now.

Ugh, I need to take this poster down.

I sit up and swing my legs over the bed. The corkboard of photos still sits on the floor, propped against the wall, reminding me of the summer we shared together. Of the outings, the sun, the rain, the laughs, the teasing, the tears, the panic attacks, the night terrors. Those photos remind me of a year that was both happy and heart-wrenching. My mom didn't understand why I pinned the photos up, why I'd want to be reminded of what was a difficult and painful summer for me. But it was also a time of healing, of learning. And a time when Alice Winters met Jack Addington. Sure, it's sad to look at sometimes but it's also calming, in a weird way. It reminds me of a summer that broke me then built me back up. I wish I could remind Jack there's still so much to do, to achieve, to experience. There's still so much to live for.

Suddenly, I sit up straight, the hairs on my skin pricking. Maybe there is something else I can try. One last thing. I slide my phone off my bedside table and start typing a text to Mrs A. I'm going to need her help. And my mom's. I open the bedroom door and call down the stairs. 'Mom!'

Her head appears at the bottom of the stairs. Her pink hair has now been dyed back to a more normal color. 'Everything okay?'

'Can you help me make something?'

'Of course. What do you need?'

'Can you look out the scissors, tape, glue, and anything you can find like ribbon, colored paper, borders, stickers?'

'What are you making?'

'A gift for Jack,' I smile.

325

Jack

It's strange the things you think of when you're all alone in a small space with hours and hours to just let your mind wander. The things your mind conjures are even stranger when you drift in and out of sleep, never fully knowing if you're awake or dreaming. Beautiful fragments of the past collide with sharp images of the present. The mind can be cruel. It can guide you through the most beautiful memories, then rip them away or mould them into nightmares. The cold ground of a mountain, the crisp air of a summit, the soft cushion of Lauren's lips when we first kissed, dissolve into darkness before re-emerging as something entirely different. Something I don't want to be thinking about, like that moment I first came to in the hospital, the feeling of nothingness after my thighs, the absence of ground under my feet. Then my mind cruelly brings me back to the soft touch of my mum's fingertips as they stroked my forehead as a child, the strong embrace of my dad's arms as he pulls me in for a hug at the end of a race, the slapping on my back from friends as we pose at the top of a mountain. And suddenly, I'm back to the bright yellow of Alice's umbrella the day of the bombing, the heat of the debris cloud as it engulfed me, the patter of rain on my face as I lay on the concrete drifting in and out of consciousness. My mind plays with sounds too, tormenting me all the same. The first song I remember hearing, the first playlist I created for a run, my parents' voices, the shouts and claps of race supporters, the sound of waves crashing against the bottom of a cliff, all eventually turn into the screams of agony, the beeping of hospital machines, the ticking of a clock in an operating theatre.

I close my eyes, squeezing them as tight as I can and try to imagine something else, anything else. Then I hear Alice, the muffled murmurings of an American accent coming down the hallway as she talks to my mum. The voice gets louder, filling the whole house, seeping in under my closed door which has a sign up to say I'm not feeling well and not to wake me until dinner. Then it gets softer, fading slowly away before it disappears forever. I don't know whether it was in my head, another fragment of a dream, or if Alice really was here. A soft knock on my door confirms it.

'I'm sleeping.'

I hear a sigh from behind the door, and feel a twinge of guilt in my belly. 'Alice dropped something off for you, I'll just leave it outside your door.'

Footsteps fade as she moves away. I take a deep breath and slowly open the door, afraid Alice is still out there and I'll have to fake my way through a polite conversation when all I want to do is sleep. Sleep and dream. The hallway is empty, dark. On the floor is a large square book of some kind. I bring it onto my lap and close the door again. It's wrapped in grey tissue paper with silver stars which rustles when I tear it off and let it fall to the ground by my wheels. It's a scrapbook or a photo album. I open the first page. There's a photo of me leaving the hospital on the day I was discharged. I didn't even know she'd taken a photo. My friends are pushing me towards the new van my mum had just bought. It's my face I can't stop looking at. On my face aren't tears of disappointment or a visible fear of an unknown future. On my face is a smile. I'm smiling. Across the van is a WELCOME HOME sign and I seem happy to be getting released from the hospital. On the page next to the photo are messages from the doctors and nurses who took care of me. The next page are photos of me at home – in the garden, by the duck pond, at the kitchen table. My mum must have given Alice these. Next to them are messages from my mum, my dad and even from my neighbours. My dad, he's proud of me, he says. There's a folded-up piece of paper inside. When I unfold it I see a cutout of a wheelchair but one that looks different to mine. The wheels are thinner and the frame looks lighter, with an option to hold on to dropped handle-bars like on a race bike. The cutout is paperclipped to a printout of an advanced entry to next year's London Marathon. I don't understand at first then I read the section he's highlighted in yellow:

The Virgin Money London Marathon is run under British Athletics, World Para Athletics and IAAF rules which clearly state that the marathon is an athletics event and only a recognised racing wheelchair is permitted.

Then I understand, he's telling me I can still enter and finish the marathon, not on artificial legs like I'd hoped, but with a racing wheelchair. With a racing wheelchair I can still do this. I can still achieve my goal of completing the marathon with him. That's what he was trying to tell me yesterday. And I didn't let him speak.

Photos of our summer last year dot the next few pages – of our trips to the community garden, to Thorpe Park, to the arcade, to the top of the Shard, to a silent disco in Hyde Park, our Thanksgiving Day picnic on the beach. There's that photo I took of Alice with her Cosmo cocktail at the arcade bar. Around it is a brief message from her. Thirteen words, that's all she wrote. That's all she needed to write. I skim her words with my fingertips:

> We're still here. We owe it to these people to keep on living.

The final pages aren't photos of me, or of her, but faces of all those who died the day of the bombing: Zaffir Ashok, an NHS nurse; James Maitland, a University of Cambridge graduate; Sarah Jones, a mother of two; David Chang, a local businessman. Tourists, families, friends, couples, even an off-duty Met police officer. Twenty-two people died that day and forty-eight were critically injured. Then there are photos and media images of other survivors like Alice. Like me. Yes, I am a survivor, and I need to keep on living.

I look out the window again – through what's left – at the sun setting beyond the hills. London seems so far away from here even though it's only forty-five minutes. Slivers of deep purple, misty grey and feathery white start to unfold over the hills and snake towards my house. Peppered into the deep purple hues of the sunset are spots of dark pink and red. It's the most beautiful sunset I've ever seen. And it's not one from the top of a mountain or from the edge of a forest trail after a run. It's from my own window. It's nature at its most raw and vulnerable, from my own house. My fingers graze the top of the scrapbook again, the images and words inside becoming ingrained into my mind. I can still feel Alice on the pages. I can still feel her strength. And as if it's ink spilling onto me from the pages, I let her strength penetrate my skin and sink into my flesh, onto the limbs remaining and the ones lost.

I close my eyes and see her standing at the other side of the road, the pedestrian crossing flashing bursts of green. Her toes slightly over the edge of the pavement, she stands facing me. Her fire-red hair lifting in the breeze. Her mouth opens and she's calling my name. The heat at my back gets warmer, stronger. But it doesn't take me this time. It builds around me, destroying everything else in its path then it turns to a small heap of grey ash at my feet. My feet are still on the ground, the concrete earth beneath my running shoes. The palm of my hands are clean. The debris is gone from my knees. My running shorts are still intact. And Alice, Alice is still there. She's still standing on the other side of the road. And her hand is stretched out towards me. I step out onto the empty road and I walk towards her.

I bite down on my lip and when I open my eyes finally,

I don't see the reflection of a gaunt, broken person in the mirror. I don't see the awards or photos of a time long ago on the walls. I don't see my running shoes on the floor that I reclaimed from the back of a cupboard. Or my reflective cycling jacket hanging on the wardrobe handle. I just see the sunset. I shuffle forward and open the window wide. Crisp winter air floods the room. My mouth opens wide and I gulp the air around me like it's the first time I'm taking a breath. Warmth pricks the corners of my eyes as I stare into the sunset. I take another deep breath, letting it fill every inch of my body, every moment of my memories. My hand rests on my chest feeling the thump and pound of every heartbeat.

Alice

I pull on another pair of gloves, the biting chill of February nipping at my fingers. It would be 18 to 20 degrees back in San Diego at this time of the year but here temperatures barely break 7 degrees on most days. Spring certainly feels like a long way away. It's been over a month since I gave Jack the scrapbook – and since he finally emerged from his bedroom from the thick haze of depression that had taken him from me. And exactly two hours and twenty-two minutes since we arrived here at the run track at school. I've been watching him and his dad race laps in his new chair for the past two hours while I sit on the astroturf in the middle with my poetry journal, a pen and a coffee that's cooling fast. I occasionally break from my writing and latte to take photos and scream cheers of encouragement. He's fast, and if he trains like this for the rest of the year there will be no stopping him at the marathon. He's already signed up for a half marathon in the fall and another by Christmas. He'll be a pro with this new racing wheelchair by the time next April comes around.

Sweat pours from him as he wheels past me in a flurry. I feel the ground tremble as he whizzes past. At this rate I'll have to invest in a motion lens for the camera to capture him. He flies through the finish line as the sound of his dad clapping reverberates around the track. I join in, clapping my palms loudly. Jack wheels over to me, chest heaving with effort.

'I just got my best time,' he pants.

'Nice! Congrats.' I toss my journal down and lean back on my hands, the cold ground piercing through my gloves. 'I'm going to have to stop coming here. People will start to think I'm some sort of groupie or something. Next thing I know I'll be wearing a T-shirt with your face on it.'

'It'll be an improvement on your current outfit,' he grins.

'Hey, if I have to sit out here in this cold I'm wearing three pairs of pants.'

'We say trousers here. Pants are something else,' he grins.

'It's freezing, I don't care what you Brits call them. Speaking of, my toes are going to fall off if I stay any longer. Mind if I head home?'

'No, you go on. You look cold. Besides, I have the therapist right after this anyway.'

'How is that going?' I ask, wiggling my toes to keep the circulation going.

'It's going well. I'm not one for talking about myself but it's a little easier to do in private I suppose.'

'Well, when you feel ready, we'd love to have you back at the support group on Mondays.'

'Well, when you feel ready, I'd love to read that journal of yours one day,' he grins.

'Absolutely not,' I shake my head.

333

'Come on. I'd love to read your poems.'

I sigh deeply, my warm breath filling the cold air around me. 'Fine.'

'Really?'

'Yeah, why not. But be warned, I'm no Robert Frost.'

'Who?'

'Just a warning, I wrote a little about last year and how I was feeling at the time,' I say quietly.

'I'd like to read those,' he smiles. His dad calls him back over. 'Hey, thanks for coming today.'

'That's what I'm here for,' I quip, jumping up. I swing my bag over my shoulder.

'Got your dress for Saturday?'

'What's happening on Saturday again?' I tease.

He rolls his eyes and wheels himself back to the start line.

'You're racing again?' I exclaim.

'Again,' he shouts back.

Jack

She stands at the doorway, the edge of her heels spilling onto the steps of the driveway. She tugs awkwardly at the neckline, pulling it up. She hears my chair come towards her and turns unsteadily. She holds her hands out as she totters on her heels then takes a deep breath. She's wearing a long emerald green dress and her red curly hair is pulled back off her face. She even has make-up on, I think. She laughs when she sees me. 'Don't we look a pair?'

I tug at the collar of my tux that feels tight and restrictive around my neck after months in nothing but pyjamas, hoodies and joggers, or 'sweatpants' as Alice calls them. I'm getting used to her jargon, and she to mine. I understand now that when she refers to her 'pants' she thankfully isn't talking about her underwear, and she now correctly uses the term 'knackered' instead of 'knickered'. When she told me she was so 'knickered' after our walk, I thought she was again referring to her underwear.

She glances up at the sound of laughter and the clinking of glasses from inside the house. Our parents have just met for the first time, and so far it's going really well. In fact, Alice's mum has really hit it off with mine. They may even become friends after this. It'll be nice for my mum to have a new friend, someone to spend time with outside of the house. Like me, she's spent most of the last year inside this building, surrounded by brick, antiques and a son who couldn't face the world. And from the sounds of it, Mrs Winters could do with a friend too. Who knew, first Alice and me, now our mothers?

Alice fiddles with the strap on her dress.

'You look fine.'

'Gee, thanks. I look "fine"? Is that a compliment?' she mumbles, still fiddling with her neckline.

'I mean you look nice – pretty.'

Her cheeks suddenly go red. 'Thanks,' she mutters. Then she shakes her head and shakes off my compliment. 'I'm totally bringing my sweatpants to change into after the dinner though. It's a seven-course meal – no dress is that forgiving.'

I smile and look past her, out onto the front garden. Raindrops hit the grass and overflow the bird baths. Droplets spatter on the stone and tickle our feet. We shift back, huddling under the archway of the front door.

'Can't believe it's raining tonight,' she says.

'Don't you have a brolly?'

'A what?' she asks.

'An umbrella,' I smile. There's one I need to work on.

'Yeah, but it's bright blue with yellow stars on it. It'll totally clash with my dress.'

'Look at you, turning into quite the fashionista,' I grin.

'Well,' she says in a very theatrical English accent, 'I am going to a fancy schmancy charity ball at the V&A Museum.

I have to look the part.' She starts parading around the lobby, and immediately stumbles over her heels.

'Do you have other shoes?' I grimace.

She pops her feet out of them, and kicks them away. 'Yeah, I have some sneakers in my bag. Do you think people will notice? It's a long dress?'

'Nah, you'll be fine.'

We turn and see Alice's dad in the hallway, dressed in military uniform. Alice has his smile. 'You guys ready to go?'

'Let's do this,' Alice nods.

We take the van, Martin driving, also dressed in a tuxedo. He had the day off today but he insisted on coming to support the cause which was kind. We ride most of the fifty minutes into the city in silence, occasionally exchanging glances. She sits beside my chair, playing with the bracelet on her wrist. The sun sets through the window next to me. It's bright tonight and stretches wide across the subtle hilltops of Surrey. Soon the sunset-soaked countryside fades into city buildings, dimly lit streetlamps, and bustling London streets.

The V&A Museum is lit in a pink hue with white fairy lights trickling down the walls. A harpist plays on the stone steps by the entrance to all incoming guests.

'I think it's really great what you've done with the Jack Addington Foundation,' Alice says, climbing out the van in her bright white trainers.

'Yeah, I hope the money we've raised so far and what we raise tonight will help out a lot of people like me to get

337

prostheses and other kinds of private medical care that's otherwise unaffordable. With some left over for the kinds of PTSD support groups like yours.'

'It was nice of you to invite the group tonight. And it's good of you to use the money that way.'

I shrug, 'It was that or a really cool trip to Las Vegas with the guys.'

'Shut up,' she says, rolling her eyes. She pulls her wrap up over her shoulders and fixes her hair, smoothing it over her ears. She takes a deep breath. 'You ready?'

'Are you?'

'I give it thirty minutes before I spill something on this dress.'

'I give it ten.'

She breathes hard next to me. 'Hopefully, I don't freak out inside,' she says shakily, referring to her panic attacks.

'Well, if you do then that's fine. Your parents will be there.' I lightly touch her on the arm. 'And I'll be there.'

We stand across the street from the V&A, raindrops falling all around us, hitting the pavement, washing over the ground by our feet. Alice unclips her umbrella and opens it up to the sky. Then she holds it over me, and shelters us both from the rain.

Acknowledgements

Firstly, a big thanks to the brilliant team at Peters Fraser + Dunlop, particularly to my agent Silvia Molteni, and to my lovely HQ family of six years at HarperCollins, including my editor Sarah Goodey. Both have worked tirelessly to make *After the Rain* what it is – a story about friendship and strength. Thank you to everyone on the design team who created such a beautiful cover, and to the publicity department for their fantastic marketing efforts.

I'd also like to thank my wonderful family and support network. Writing in lockdown and with a newborn baby wasn't easy, so thank you to everyone who helped us with childcare, especially my parents Sheila and Danny.

And finally, a big thanks to you, the reader. By reading this book you've helped me realise my writing dreams, so thank you!

Dear Charlie

Can a brother's love forgive the ultimate crime?

Brother, victim, murderer. Did anyone really know him?

At sixteen, Sam is supposed to be thinking about girls, homework and his upcoming application to music college, not picking up the pieces after the school shooting that his brother Charlie committed.

Yet as Sam desperately tries to hang on to the memories he has of his brother, the media storm surrounding their family threatens to destroy everything. And Sam has to question all he thought he knew about life and death, right and wrong.

Blackbird

Olivia disappeared the night the blackbirds died . . .

Perfect for fans of *One of Us is Lying* and
A Good Girl's Guide to Murder.

It was New Year's Eve, the night that dead blackbirds
descended, hours before Alex McCarthy's sister Olivia
vanished from a party.

Committed to finding out what happened to her sister, in their
isolated Orkney village, Alex knows that dishevelled – sometimes intoxicated – Detective Inspector Birkens is her best shot.

Yet as they uncover the secrets behind Olivia's last night,
Alex starts to discover things she may have been better
off not knowing . . .

We Are Not Okay

Four girls. Four voices. All unheard.

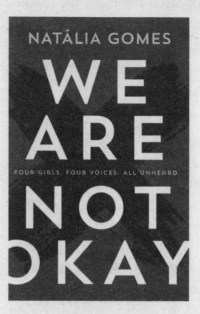

If only they could have spoken out.

Lucy thinks she's better than the other girls. Maybe if she's pointing fingers at everyone else, no one will see the secret she's hiding.

Ulana comes from a conservative Muslim family where reputation is everything. One rumour – true or false – can destroy futures.

Trina likes to party. She's kissed a lot of boys. She's even shown her red bra to one. But she didn't consent to that night at Lucy's party. So why doesn't anyone believe her?

Sophia loved her boyfriend. She did anything for him, even send him photos of herself. So why is she the one being pointed at in the hallways, laughed at, spat at when it was him who betrayed her trust?